W9-BRO-901

Dreaming Water

Also by Gail Tsukiyama

Women of the Silk
The Samurai's Garden
Night of Many Dreams
The Language of Threads

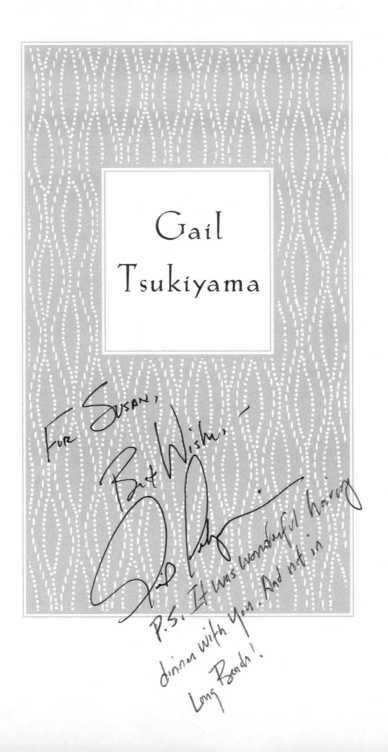

Gail Tsukiyama

For Susan,
Best Wishes, —

P.S. It was wonderful having
dinner with you. And not in
Long Beach!

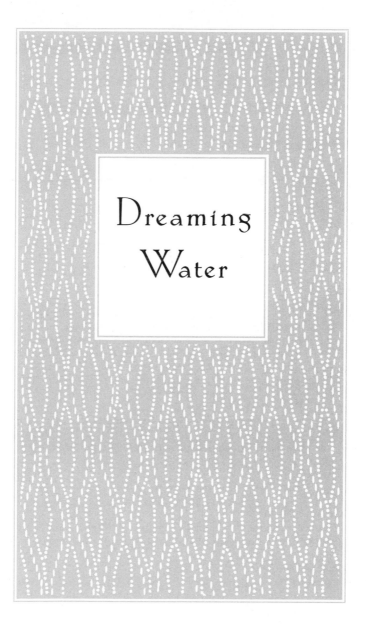

Dreaming Water

St. Martin's Press ✹ NEW YORK

DREAMING WATER. Copyright © 2002 by Gail Tsukiyama. All rights reserved. Printed in the United States of America. No part of this book may be used or reproduced in any manner whatsoever without written permission except in the case of brief quotations embodied in critical articles or reviews. For information, address St. Martin's Press, 175 Fifth Avenue, New York, N.Y. 10010.

www.stmartins.com

Book design by Gretchen Achilles

Library of Congress Cataloging-in-Publication Data

Tsukiyama, Gail.
    Dreaming water / Gail Tsukiyama.—1st ed.
        p. cm.
    ISBN 0-312-20607-0
        1. Werner's syndrome—Patients—Fiction.   2. Mothers and daughters—
Fiction.   3. Female friendship—Fiction.   4. California—Fiction.   I. Title.

PS3570.S84 D74 2002
813'.54—dc21   2001058896

10 9 8 7 6 5 4 3 2

For Sandra McCormack

ACKNOWLEDGMENTS

For their support and care, my ongoing gratitude to my family, my agent, Linda Allen, Christine Watkins, Sally Richardson, Joan Higgins, Merrill Bergenfeld, and to my editor, Linda McFall. I want to thank Dr. Junko Oshima from the University of Washington, who graciously answered my questions. Any mistakes are entirely my own. And thank you always and again, Catherine de Cuir, Cynthia Dorfman, Blair Moser, and Abby Pollak.

Yesterday is history.
Tomorrow is mystery.
Today is a gift.

ELEANOR ROOSEVELT

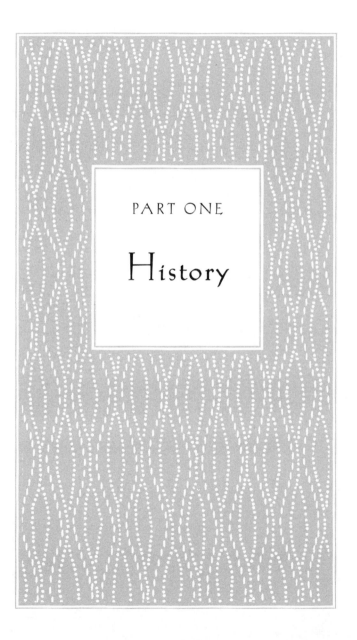

PART ONE

History

CATE

A Heart of Stone

As a child I was afraid of the dark. Whenever I heard some strange noise in the night or imagined a shadow to be something it wasn't, the rapid beating of my heart startled my whole body. Then came a swift intake of breath held so long and so stubbornly I thought it would be my last, my head filled with the quick litany of *HailMaryfullofgracetheLordiswiththeeandpleasebewithme*. Only under the covers of my bed did I feel protected from the outside world. Now that I'm a sixty-two-year-old woman, my fears have become more defined than those nebulous creatures that creaked and sighed in the night. Now I know that daylight holds the real monsters, and that prayers aren't always answered.

These thoughts flicker through my mind as I lie in bed and wait for my daughter, Hana, to call from her room. Glancing at the clock, I see that it's just seven-thirty. The rich morning light of early spring streams through a gap in the curtains. I hear a chorus of birds as I pull back the curtain to see a glorious day, the hills behind the house aglow. It's been a cold, wet winter and I welcome the thought of a sunny California morning, one of those clear, crisp days that holds such a stunning light you can almost reach out and touch the sky. It's a small hope but the kind I dare to allow myself nowadays—simple, obtainable things like a strong, hot cup of coffee, a movie that ends happily, the beautiful hair-raising crescendo of a Puccini aria.

Half an hour from now, around eight, Hana's thin voice will cry out to me, "Mother! You up?" Sometimes I'm afraid I won't be awake to hear her call or, even worse, that there will be no call. So I've developed this habit of listening all the time, my head cocked slightly to one side like that RCA dog, in a perpetual state of waiting.

Twenty-five years ago, Hana's slow growth combined with her increasing fatigue brought us to the University of California San Francisco Medical Center. Until then I thought she was simply a late bloomer who would catch up with other kids her age over a summer spurt. After her checkup, Hana's doctor called us into his office. He was medium height and had thick, dark eyebrows that made him look stern and serious. There was nothing wrong that he could detect during her checkup, but he wanted to run some tests to check her pituitary and thyroid glands for other probable causes affecting Hana's growth. "Just to be safe," he said, in a direct, careful manner. Then he mentioned a patient he'd also seen with Werner's syndrome, which he explained was an aging disease, characterized by short stature. He clicked his pen and looked up from the file on his desk, his gaze moving from Max to me. "We'll also need to get both your family histories," he said, his voice softening. "Right now, Hana's still too young to be diagnosed with

Werner's, but it's best to be aware of all the possibilities."

It was the first time I'd ever heard of Werner's syndrome, and all I could think of was how could any of this be happening to my child? And why on earth would anyone want his name attached to a disease? "Who is this Werner?" I asked. I remember my husband, Max, sat beside me, stunned. Thirteen-year-old Hana sat outside in the pale green waiting room, healthy in every way so far, except that she was still the size of a nine-year-old. Even now I can feel the shock of the doctor's words slowly numbing my entire body, as if that meeting were happening all over again.

In the early seventies, Werner's syndrome was largely unknown even to doctors. It wasn't so extensively documented as it is now, though its scientific explanation might as well be in a foreign language. All I've ever needed to understand is this—Hana carries a gene that is producing an abnormal enzyme that moves throughout her body like a guided missile, gradually damaging good cells and causing her to age prematurely, two to three times faster than normal. And though overt signs of aging wouldn't appear until her early twenties, we were suddenly shocked into the realization that her life had taken an unexpected turn.

But, unlike me, Hana isn't afraid of anything. She strikes out at each day with such joy, as if waking up alive every morning is the biggest surprise of all. For her, fear is not an option. She takes life as it comes, and if the years come faster than they should, she grabs at them, too.

I close my eyes, just to rest, then awake with a sudden jerk, startled out of a dream of Max that sadly slips away. The clock reads almost nine-thirty. I've fallen back to sleep and don't know if Hana has called. The house is completely quiet, except for the thumping of my heart as I hurry downstairs to her room. Please, I think to myself, let Hana be all right. Please don't let her have wet her bed again. But she's lying perfectly still in her adjustable bed, the kind that rises and lowers at the push of a button, her feet elevated, gazing up at the ceiling. The small room, next to Max's study, has a closed, slightly medicinal smell to it.

"Two hundred forty-two, two hundred forty-three . . . I've been counting stars," she says between breaths, her upward gaze unwavering.

I look up at the gold stars Max hand-painted on the ceiling when we moved Hana downstairs five years ago. I'd caught him standing on an old paint-splattered ladder in the middle of the room, and asked him what he was doing.

He looked down, pushed up his glasses, and said matter-of-factly, "I'm painting stars, Cate."

"But why?"

"For Hana." He smiled, then looked back up and continued painting.

Hana was the child we used to wish for on so many stars dotting the nighttime skies over Falcon Beach. The way their light illuminated the dark ocean made us believe that wish might come true. I couldn't help feeling selfish then, for I knew my wishes had already come true. When I met Max Murayama, suddenly all the fears that I'd harbored became something else, something to fight against. Max was worth fighting for. And so was our love, and our marriage back in 1959. An Italian American woman and a Japanese American man, we were the first interracial couple ever to live in the small Northern California town of Daring.

Falcon Beach, a forty-five-minute drive from Daring down the winding coastline, was our refuge, where we sat in Max's beloved Thunderbird and watched the sunset. We'd usually leave right after he taught his last history class of the week at Brandon College on Friday afternoons. But it wasn't until twilight, when the beach was in shadows and nearly deserted, that we'd carefully make our way down the path to the long stretch of rocky sand. Max loved the ocean. "My ancestors must have been fishermen," he said, staring mesmerized at the endless, darkening sea. "It feels like home here."

I laughed, knowing that his ancestors were anything but seafarers. Max's parents and grandparents had been horticulturists, growing and selling carnations and chrysanthemums in Southern California. Their feet were firmly planted on the ground, though Max's heart and mind rose and fell with the ocean.

We walked freely down the beach hand in hand, touching each other in the comfortable, intimate way of married couples. Under the veil of darkness, surrounded by the cool, salty air and with Max's arm firmly around my waist, I felt all the ease and security I'd prayed to feel in the daylight. In our new hometown of Daring, for the first year of our marriage, we strolled down streets lined with struggling lawns and Victorian and bungalow-style houses. I remember the sweet, pine-scented air and the towering redwood trees, which stood dark against the pale horizon. Like a couple of strangers, we walked two feet apart, offering a quick smile and nod to everyone we passed. Pretty soon I became known as the nice young woman with the *foreign* husband. And Max was labeled a variety of nationalities from Chinese to Indian by our well-meaning but ignorant neighbors. They were still suspicious of his being Japanese, and of the war he'd been too young to have anything to do with.

Then three years later came Hana, the beautiful child who was a fine blend of the two of us, filling the gap between us when we walked down the street, holding us both by the hand and tying us all together. She'd been the miracle after my two miscarriages.

They were a boy and a girl, it grieved me to think, because even though Max would never admit it, I know he might have liked a son to carry on his family name.

"Sometimes you're more Japanese than I am," he teased.

It's true; sometimes I am more Japanese than Max was, or at least just as much so. I hold things in, the good and bad memories that still soothe and sting after so many years. I've stored them away, in those small compartments in the back of my mind like in one of those Japanese secret boxes. But lately, the past seems to be unlocked and creeping slowly forward.

Even three years gone, Max still seems to be alive in every room of the house, as if he's hovering over us, making sure we're safe—the brightest star of all.

Hana suddenly stops counting and smiles my way. She looks like a small and fragile bird in her big bed, wisps of thin, gray hair spread across her pillow. "All's well," she says happily, a ring of triumph in her squeaky voice. "I thought you might want to sleep in for a change."

I'm relieved beyond words to know that she hasn't wet her bed again. It's been just over a week since the first accident, and each morning since, I've entered her room filled with anxiety and a knot of panic at the base of my throat at the thought of her body losing control again. The nightstand next to her bed is littered with books, her glasses, her beloved recorder, rubbing alcohol, a bottle of aspirin for headaches, antacids, a family photo in a silver frame.

"I certainly did that." I smile. "Ready to get up?"

She nods and holds out her thin, pale, almost translucent arms to wrap around my neck so I can help her up. Hana's ankles have swollen again, and the arterial ulcers have worsened, making it hard for her to get about by herself. Every day I change the bandages and check for any sign of melanoma, dark spots on her feet and legs that may be cancerous and are so common among Werner's patients. As I pull her up, the lightness of her body surprises me once more, wrapping against mine in a perfect fit, just like the little girl I used to carry sleeping from the car. But now it's a different story. Now she clings to me not as a child but as a thirty-eight-year-old woman who is dying of old age. We are growing old together, Hana and I, even though lately it seems as if she's leaving me behind.

I can easily admit that while I'm past the age of caring what people think about me, I do care how Hana feels when people stop and stare, or shake their heads when they don't think we're watching. "How are you feeling, dear?" and "You're looking well" are the most common comments from all the neighbors, who are increasingly awkward and uncomfortable around us. I suppose I can't blame them. In the past ten years, Hana has aged at an astonishing rate. She has the appearance of an eighty-year-old woman, although her mind remains young and vital. Lately, it's been hard to get her to leave the house, except for our daily walks at a nearby park, and even that can be a struggle. Her hair has thinned and turned completely white, and her face has taken on the sharp, birdlike features typical of the disease. But Hana has Max's eyes, and no matter how fast she ages, her dark, piercing gaze is so filled with life it still breaks my heart to look into them.

Am I too heavy?" she asks me now. I manage a smile, thinking how I wish she were, how I wish it were Hana's strong, healthy arms supporting me. "No," I whisper into her ear. "Not at all."

She hugs my neck tighter. She hasn't always been so quiescent. Her life since the diagnosis has had its share of rebellious moments. She just accepts her fate better now, and as her body weakens her mind and heart grow and strengthen. I keep hoping for the same balance for myself. Sometimes I actually think I've found it, only to lose it again just before sleep or in the early hours of the morning. But it seems the more her heart opens up, the more mine hardens. By the time Hana leaves me, I'll have a heart of stone that refuses to break.

HANA

In the Quiet

Something woke me before dawn this morning—a tree branch scratching against the window, the sharp hoot of an owl, the whistling of the wind—but as I lay listening, there was only the creak of beams and rafters, then silence. My eyes adjusted to the darkness, the shadows slowly taking familiar shape. The brown-shingled house of my childhood holds everything in the darkness, each memory retained in cracks and crevices. For the past five years, I've slept downstairs in a small room next to my father's study, so I can get around the living and dining rooms, bathroom, and kitchen with ease whenever the ulcers on my feet and legs act up. Upstairs is my mother, Cate's room, my old room, a bathroom, and another guest room. And above that is the attic, reached by a pull-down ladder at the end of the hall. It's the large, comfortable house I've lived in since I was four years old.

I pulled the blankets up around me, and a long-buried memory from childhood surfaced: my pale pink, one-eyed stuffed dog that barked when his nose was squeezed. I went to sleep with him every night for years until he disappeared into the bottom of a drawer or the back of a closet. It was so simple then. I remembered how his short, sharp bark always reminded me I wasn't alone and there was nothing to be afraid of.

In the quiet I could feel my heart beating, the pulse and flow of blood that struggles precariously through my hardening arteries, like water unable to flow through the stem of a flower. Sometimes I feel a dull pain moving through my body, the muscles and organs scrambling over which will break down first. It's hard to believe that my body has become so fragile. God isn't supposed to make such mistakes. Sometimes, I can almost feel myself growing old, my body turning against me. And just when I'm ready to give up and wish for a way out of this cursed body, I feel a sudden surge of anger that wells up inside me, challenging me to a fight—a knock-down-drag-out fight to the finish.

Cate overslept this morning and I could see the fear in her eyes when she rushed downstairs to my room, barefoot and without a robe, praying I hadn't wet the bed again. In the white light of morning she seemed to appear out of nowhere as I counted the stars on my ceiling, passing time. And just then, in the telling light, I could also see how she had aged in the past few years caring for me—the strands of gray in her hair, the dark pouches below her eyes, the deepening furrow across her forehead that comes from worry. In her sheer blue nightgown, my mother's tall, slender silhouette appears thinner, yet not in a fragile sort of way but toned and even slightly athletic. I can't help but think she looks even more beautiful as she approaches her twilight years.

Cate leans over to stroke my forehead, and I smile. It has

become a habit for her to subtly check to see if I have a fever—
a light pat on the cheek, a quick hug, the casual brushing away
of a strand of hair from my forehead. I look into her tired eyes
and wonder if she ever imagines another life. One without fears
of fevers or waking up late. The freedom to go and do as she
pleases. Small prizes. A just reward after all these years. But I know
that wishing on all the stars in the sky won't change anything.
And if I can see so much about her in one early morning glance,
what does my mother see when she looks at me?

"Ready to get up?" she asks.

I reach out, fold myself around her tightly as if I'm being
rescued, pressing my face into the sweet, soap-smelling side of her
neck.

CATE

Fairy Tales

Our breakfast is usually very simple. A soft-boiled egg, with toast dipped in coffee, or oatmeal with low-fat milk and brown sugar. "Soft foods. A bland diet, easy to digest," Dr. Truman said sternly after our office visit last week, glancing up from his chart with just a hint of disapproval. He knows Hana has often disobeyed his direct orders.

"Soggy foods." Hana groaned. "Are you trying to kill me quickly?"

Dr. Truman shot a quick look my way. I've known Miles Truman since before I became pregnant with Hana. He and Max were great friends and he was the first doctor who noticed something wrong with Hana—how her stunted growth might be a sign of something serious. Miles urged us to take Hana to San Francisco and arranged for her to go through the first series of tests, which became a way of life for all of us. She has been poked, pinched, and probed in every possible way. An internist, Miles has studied long nights to become something of an expert on Werner's syndrome, so that Hana and I needn't travel to San Francisco every time one of her small emergencies—a fever or the recurrent ulcers on her feet and legs—arises.

"Just the opposite," Miles answered her. "I expect you to live for a long, long time."

His voice trailed off at the lie. But Hana is an old pro—she quickly picked up the ball before it bounced again in the wrong direction. "I plan to live a long time eating what I always do; nothing but pepperoni pizzas and strawberry milk shakes!"

Miles laughed. "Just follow the doctor's orders and keep up the good work."

"You know I will." Hana winked.

I can't help but think how much Hana and I resemble each other—not so much physically but in those invisible traits that show themselves at the most unexpected times. While her Japanese blood has always been obvious in her coloring and eyes, her quick retorts and infectious laughter come from me. It's then I see Hana is still my young and beautiful child, not this frail old woman. Even our smiles have grown more alike—the same deepening lines that spread outward from the corners of our eyes like rays from the sun.

Every morning when Hana eats her breakfast, she has to take a handful of pills. She knows the routine and follows it, if only to keep me happy. There's no pepperoni pizza, which would upset her stomach, and no milk shakes, which would clog her already thickened arteries. The pills range from round to oblong, small as a pea to large as a dime, in chalky whites, deep red, and two shades of green. This morning I have them ready at the side of her bowl and I watch Hana unconsciously play with them, fingering each one and stopping at the oval-shaped, bright yellow new one. She's restless, maybe because I've overslept and she wasn't able to get up earlier. Every day counts now, I tell myself.

Last week, after Hana's checkup, Miles and I left her alone to finish dressing. I could tell by the concerned look on his face he wasn't happy to see that along with wetting her bed and the tremors I'd begun to notice in her hands, she'd also lost weight. We both knew Hana had reached another, more debilitating stage of Werner's syndrome. The thought of it made me want to cry out loud. We had just stepped back into his office when I stopped biting my lower lip and suddenly found the courage to ask, "How long?" The words slipped out with the clear, fluid ease of water. In the beginning it was out of nervous habit that I'd ask him every time Hana had her monthly checkup, but as she began to age, I couldn't bring myself to ask anymore. I've known Miles so long he has become part of our family. He knows I'm not the type to beat around the bush when I need to know something. Until that very moment, I'd taken Hana's life one day at a time, believing that somehow time moved slower that way. But now, with her growing frailty, I needed to know. I needed to plan. If I could no longer slow time down, then I meant to make the most of every minute Hana had left.

As we stood by the door, he cleared his throat and gave it to me straight in his concerned, doctor's voice. "A year, maybe two, really functional years left. Then they become increasingly difficult. The body shuts down, as it does for all of us as we age, only faster—you know what it's been like for the past fifteen years, the cataract surgery, breaking her hip, the ulcers on her feet and legs. Now we have to be on the lookout for osteoporosis accelerating, along with diabetes, heart disease, and even tumors. About the only thing she's not troubled by is high blood pressure." Miles smiled sadly.

"What about Alzheimer's?" There it was, my greatest fear, out in the open, hanging thick in the air between us.

He shook his head. "Not a trace of it in Werner's syndrome patients."

I was so relieved I took a deep breath. Hana has a brilliant mind, and to lose it along with everything else seemed too unfair. Yet the irony also stabbed at me: her body would deteriorate while her mind remained active and alive. The image she carried of herself would never resemble the person she saw in the mirror. My little girl, my shining star, I thought, buried in the body of an old woman. My throat felt parched and scratchy. "So this old age disease doesn't carry all the old age diseases?"

Miles walked over to his sink and poured me a glass of water. "No, I guess not."

"It's a small gift," I said, my voice barely audible. I sipped the tepid water from the paper cup, really needing something stronger.

"I'm sorry, Cate, I wish I could give you better news." He wrote out a new prescription and tore it off the pad.

When I heard an outer door open, I rose quickly and reached for the prescription. "Thank you, Miles. You've always been a wonderful friend. We've been so lucky to have you."

What's this yellow pill for again?" Hana asks me now.

"For your liver, according to Dr. Truman." I knew he was concerned about her loss of appetite. I hand her the warm milk for her oatmeal, still feeling groggy myself. My daughter looks tired and ancient as she drowns her oatmeal in milk.

"Why do you think it's bright yellow?" she asks. Her voice is high and surprisingly strong. When she was a little girl, yellow was always her favorite color.

I shrug but begin listing reasons, spooning in mouthfuls of oatmeal to buy myself time and to hide the fact that I'm not up for games this morning. "So you won't confuse them with other pills? So it's not so easy to misplace them? So they'll brighten up your day?"

Hana smiles to herself and nods. "Yes, I think it has to do with how it makes you feel. If I take this bright yellow pill, I'll feel better—the ulcers on my feet and legs will heal, my hair will suddenly darken, and the wrinkles on my face will disappear along with the age spots. I'll be young again, and a handsome prince will sweep me off my feet, just like in the fairy tales." She twists a strand of snow white hair around her finger.

I pause a moment to see what Hana is really feeling. It could be anger or irony or just plain fear, but when I see the gleam in her eyes, I know that she's only teasing.

So I smile and reach over to her. "I'll take a couple of those yellow pills. I could use a good 'happily ever after.' "

Hana remains quiet. She stirs her oatmeal, her spoon click-clacking against the side of the bowl. "At least you've had your handsome prince," she finally says. "It's something I don't expect in this lifetime."

This time she isn't teasing. I can hear it in her voice, and see it by the way her eyes avoid mine. As a teenager, Hana had friends who were boys. She has been kissed, that much I know. I still remember the night she came in the door from her junior prom, flushed and happy. Barely four feet, eight inches tall, she was petite and still so pretty. No one would ever believe that less than seven years later she'd suffer from severe cataracts and her beautiful dark hair would begin to turn gray. Later, Hana told me she'd been kissed good night by Kenny Howe, and I kept thinking that maybe my daughter was just like any other sixteen-year-old girl going to the prom. Only she wasn't. She never made it to her senior ball because of a bout of pneumonia.

After graduating from high school, Hana went to Brandon College for a year, then to the University of California down in Berkeley. She seemed so fragile. I worried incessantly, while Max stayed focused and reassuring. "We have to let her go if we want her to come back," he said. "She has to have her fresh start. She needs to live a normal life, remember? And so do we," he added. Up until then, we were constantly watching for any signs of Werner's—the cataracts, the thinning and wrinkling of her skin, and the graying of her hair. I knew Max was right.

We visited Hana every month, and she saw doctors regularly at the medical center in San Francisco where we had first taken her. She and her childhood best friend, Laura, were roommates those almost four years, and had friends who came in and out of their apartment at all hours. Hana enjoyed being a college coed, and we tried hard to keep our distance. Whatever her life was like then, we knew it was important that it belonged to her. But she graduated and returned home to stay just after her twenty-third birthday, as the first outward signs of aging suddenly and mercilessly accelerated.

Fairy tales aren't always as good as they sound," I say lightly, tentatively. "Maybe the prince loses his looks, and then his job, and ends up overweight and mean-spirited!"

Hana's sudden high laughter pierces the air. "A prince can't lose his job, he inherits the throne from the king!"

I let out a small laugh and decide then and there that we need to get out of this house and go somewhere, if only for an hour.

Again, I feel something hard caught at the base of my throat as I struggle for an ending to this silliness. "It's my fairy tale, and if a prince can be changed into a frog, he can certainly get fat and lose his throne!"

Hana shakes her head and leans across the table. "Here," she says, dropping the yellow pill into my hand. "You need this more than I do."

HANA

Werner

The moments of restlessness are always the worst, those quiet pockets during the day when my mind wants to soar to faraway places but my body remains stagnant. For the past week, my swollen ankles and the ulcers on my legs have kept me immobile. I'm confined to sitting with my feet elevated, or moving around in a wheelchair. I look at the bright-eyed, dark-haired little girl in the photos on the piano in our living room and I can't believe she was once me. I sometimes close my eyes and I'm that little girl again, running down the beach, playing tag with the waves, my parents strolling behind. And I can almost feel the first startling contact with the cold water across my toes, how it surprised me, then drew me running into the waves. The more I lose control of my body, the more I need to remember what it was like to have had command of it.

While Cate does the breakfast dishes, I roll down the hall to my bedroom, trying to help out by at least picking up after myself and making my bed. I lean forward in the wheelchair to give a quick flip to the sheet and blanket. After they balloon up and fall over my pillow, I smooth them down and tuck in the sides, making perfect hospital corners. That's when I catch a glimpse of something shiny on the rug just underneath my bed. I push the wheelchair back just enough to bend over and pick it up; the gold earring Cate thought she had lost at Dr. Truman's office last week.

Dr. Truman has been taking care of me ever since I can remember. Along with a host of other doctors, he has watched the progress of Werner's syndrome from the time it was first suspected. Werner is what I'd rather call it. Personalizing the condition makes me feel as if Werner is something going through life with me, not against me.

I see Dr. Truman at least once a month for "preventive medicine," as he calls it, because Werner can affect multiple organ systems, everything from the immune to the connective tissue to the cardiovascular system. Miles Truman is a nice man, with the tall, gray-haired, well-scrubbed looks of someone you could entrust your life to. Born and raised in Daring, he left for college and medical school in Chicago, then returned with his wife. He wanted a small-town, hands-on practice, while his wife preferred life in the big city. Dr. Truman has one son, who lives with his family in Denver, and has been divorced for the past fifteen years. He's the kind of man every mother in Daring would want her daughter to meet and marry. But ever since my father passed away, it's my mother Dr. Truman pines for. I see it in every smile and gesture, even if he never says a word. He's like a schoolboy around her sometimes, exhibiting all the classic signs—from the awkward pauses to the avoiding of her eyes. And even if Cate seems oblivious to his attentions, I think it makes perfect sense that she should marry him. This way, after I'm gone she won't be so alone.

W hat I haven't told Dr. Truman or Cate is that I've been having bouts of insomnia lately, short spurts of sleep interrupted by hours of wakefulness in the dense quiet. I read, and when my eyes become too tired, I've replayed entire movies in my head, from *Breakfast at Tiffany's* to *Doctor Zhivago*, or listened to the all-night radio programs *From Midnight On* and *In the Wee Hours*. I've felt strangely close to all the low, whispery voices coming from the radio, as if we'd become intimate strangers who have found the same light in the darkness.

But I've decided the less said the better. The last thing I want is to take another pill to make me sleep. Sometimes I wonder what would happen if I just stopped taking all the pills. Would I dissolve like the witch at the end of *The Wizard of Oz*? Turn to ash and blow away? Anyway, they say the older you get, the less sleep you need. Though it's not sleeping I worry about but losing my memory or the ability to reason.

I'd seen it firsthand when I did volunteer work at the Evergreen Retirement Home. I'll never forget the vacant stares and the startled look of animal fear when I was first introduced to some of the residents. They appeared so lost and childlike. While my parents tried to talk me out of working there, worrying that it might be too depressing for me, I was adamant about finding out what the future had in store for me. The more they insisted I think it over, the more I resisted, even though I knew they were just concerned about my well-being.

It was Cate's best friend, Lily Polanski, who first suggested I do some volunteer work after I returned from Berkeley and had my cataracts removed. Cate has known Lily for over thirty years, ever since she returned to Brandon College for her teaching credential after I started kindergarten. Lily taught English at Redwood High, where Cate began substituting in the English department. So it was Lily who came to the house one afternoon with a handful of colorful index cards she'd taken off the bulletin board at the high school. "Pick a card, any card." She fanned them out before me. One pink card asked for a volunteer at the Children's Center. A blue card needed help at an elementary school. And still another, green card looked for a reader at the Evergreen Retirement Home. I held on to the green card; the idea of reading to others seemed appropriate after my cataract surgery. My mother, on the other hand, looked at the chosen card and had to be convinced.

"But you've always wanted to work with kids," Cate said that evening as she stood up and began stacking our dinner plates. "Why not volunteer at the Children's Center?"

"I'd still like to work with them sometime. I just think I'd rather volunteer at Evergreen for a while."

But why? I knew Cate wanted to say out loud. Why spend your precious days of youth with the elderly? Why stare the inevitable in the face? I could see the questions in her dark eyes as her lips pressed tightly together, the words balanced on the tip of her tongue. I avoided her eyes and didn't have an answer. I only knew that I needed to do this.

She cleared her throat. "Okay," she finally said, knowing I had already made my mind up.

My father rubbed the back of his neck and sighed softly. "Just as long as you know you can leave any time you want. You don't have to stay if it doesn't feel right."

I nodded, then stood up to help Cate clear the table, wondering myself just how long I would last at Evergreen.

I'll always be grateful to Dr. Truman for rallying to my defense one evening when they thought I was upstairs. "Hana's a fighter," he told them. "The worst thing you could do now is not let her deal with her life on her own terms."

If Cate were to ask me now, "Why volunteer at the Evergreen Retirement Home?" I wouldn't look away. I'd have my answer as clear as glass. Because of wonderful people like Howard Rice and Mrs. Mary Ellen Gravis, who both gave me those defining moments when I knew there was a reason God had put me on this earth.

I first stepped into the Evergreen Retirement Home, a large Victorian just off Main Street, fifteen years ago. It was a warm day in early summer, three months after the bilateral senile cataracts sent me home from University of California, Berkeley, and three weeks after my surgery to remove them. I remember the clarity of the light that morning, the beautiful brightness that made my eyes water. On the front porch of the grand, old house dripping with purple wisteria, I saw a group of elderly women and men sitting on benches and wheelchairs talking, while a few others sat with their eyes closed, their faces tilted toward the sun. There was something about the way they looked, so fragile and wise, both beautiful and sad at the same time, that attracted me. I felt my heart beating against my chest as I watched them, trying to imagine myself in ten or fifteen years.

I'll admit, I was frightened at the beginning. Some of the residents on the second floor were so old they just sat and stared, or lay in bed day after day, the nurses having to turn them from side to side to relieve their bedsores. Emanating from certain rooms I passed were the indescribable smells of rubbing alcohol and urine and, occasionally, something like the too sweet smell of rotting fruit. "Evergreen is simply a waiting room before we make our final journey," I heard one lady say. I almost walked out right there and then, thinking that I'd seen enough. Thank God I stayed, almost six years on and off, finding balance in the strength and vitality of other residents.

Evergreen was run by Gretchen Dodd. She was thin, sharp-featured, and in her late forties, neatly dressed in a blue skirt and sweater with a tightly wound personality, talking a mile a minute on the phone when I knocked lightly on her half-opened door. After she hung up, the interview took all of five minutes. I was hired on the spot as a volunteer reader, the one thing I knew I'd be good at. I was to come in two or three times a week for a couple of hours and read to one or more of the residents. "For some of our residents," she said, "it's all they have left to look forward to."

I nodded at the importance of my position. I had just gotten up to leave when Gretchen asked, "Oh, Hana, how old are you anyway?"

"Twenty-three," I answered. Other than the cataracts, Werner had kept his appearance to a minimum of a few gray hairs and the barely visible fine lines that had begun to spread from the corners of my eyes.

She looked again. "You're so petite, I thought you were younger," she said, turning quickly around when her phone rang again.

It's a short enough life," I had said lightly to Dr. Truman during my monthly checkup last week. "So I want to remember it."

Dr. Truman thinks memory loss is the least of my worries. "Your mind is as sharp as a tack. Let's take care of your body so that everything stays in working order." Then he smiled and told me about yet another prescription for some yellow pill to help me digest.

"So how's Werner doing?" I asked.

Dr. Truman adjusted his stethoscope around his neck and glanced over at Cate as I sat on the examining table, a thin sheet of tissuelike paper wrinkling underneath me.

"He's holding his own," he answered.

"Tell him to lighten up a bit. I need to get rid of these ulcers on my feet and legs. Still too much I have to do, and time's running out."

Dr. Truman laughed. "Did you hear that, Werner? Give Hana a break."

But Werner hasn't listened. I've wet my bed for the first time. I can't walk and don't sleep well, and the tremors have gotten worse. He's been a real son of a bitch this past week.

CATE

Waterford, Maine—1958

I want Hana to know that some fairy tales do come true. However, in my story, the prince arrived not on a white horse but in a gleaming, new black-and-white 1958 Thunderbird. I met Max on a Friday afternoon in Waterford, Maine, when the roar from his brand-new, twin-exhaust convertible turned every head along Waterford's Main Street. The top was rolled down, and a young man with a cap pulled low on his head sat confidently in the white leather driver's seat. From his radio came the smooth wailing of Elvis Presley's "Don't Be Cruel."

Waterford wasn't much of a town back then, nothing but a quaint, quiet Main Street three blocks long with a general store, a post office, small shops, the Waterford Hotel, and a restaurant. Tree-shaded residential streets in neat, square grids were lined with comfortable, picturesque white-clapboard and brick houses.

But I was a tourist in Waterford that muggy August day in 1958, trying to calm my restlessness with a long drive. I had just graduated with a degree in English literature from the University of California at Berkeley. I'd grown up in Boston, the only child of old-fashioned Italian parents—a calm, controlled mother and a well-known lawyer father who believed that raising his voice louder than that of whomever he spoke to would somehow justify everything he said. We lived in a brownstone filled with dark, heavy antique furniture, statues of the Virgin Mary, and the lingering fragrance of garlic and oregano. I went to an all-girls' Catholic high school but convinced my parents to let me go to Berkeley; I wanted to see what the rest of the world was like. "The real world's right here," my father said, though he knew I had made up my mind and finally relented.

For my college graduation, my parents flew out to California, where my father greeted me with a kiss on both cheeks and said, "Now you can come home where you belong." Desperate to earn a teaching credential in California, I was still trying to convince my father of the rightness of my decision when my parents boarded the plane back to Boston ten days later. Papa nodded his head slowly, pretending to understand, then said, "Boston needs teachers, too."

"Take care, sweetie." Mama gave me a quick kiss of reassurance. "We'll see you at Christmastime," she said, pushing my father along.

Two weeks later I was summoned home when my mother was badly injured in a car accident. Along with two fractured ribs and a broken leg, a concussion left a ringing in her ears. While my college friends were venturing out in different directions to pursue all the possibilities the world had to offer, I was suddenly right back where I started—the South End of Boston, with its indifferent, brownstone-lined blocks.

All that summer the heat was relentless, rising from the concrete and hanging heavy in the air. I felt restless and impatient about my future, while I took care of the household and worked a few mornings a week filing and bookkeeping at my father's law office. But on Fridays, when Aunt Sophia came up from Connecticut to visit Mama, I was free to do as I pleased.

One of those Friday mornings, on impulse, I drove up to Waterford. We had gone there on family outings when I was small, but it had been years since I'd been back. Compared with the hot, suffocating city, everything about Maine seemed fresh and new— the jagged shoreline that extended up the coast, the bobbing fishing boats berthed together, the small towns that resembled quaint villages out of books I'd read. It was everything Boston in the midst of an oppressive heat wave wasn't—a big enough draw for a young woman looking for a bit of diversion.

I returned to Waterford, curious to see if it was still the quaint town I remembered from childhood. I wandered around Main Street and, after a tuna salad sandwich and iced tea for lunch, found myself in a shop called Foley's Pet Store, watching a pen of playful kittens. At the sudden, sharp gunning of a car's engine I looked up and out the window but quickly dismissed the sharp-looking driver as some spoiled college boy from Harvard or Yale showing off the Thunderbird his parents had bought him.

I walked back to an aisle lined with fish tanks, their soft, gurgling bubblers humming in unison. I was mesmerized by the brilliant designs in yellow, orange, red, and blue hues that defined each tropical fish. I thought that only the endless possibilities of nature could produce such a kaleidoscope of colors, but I could see my mother making the sign of the cross and hear her say, "You see, Caterina, God certainly does work in miraculous ways."

Then, through the undulating water bubbling in the tanks, I saw the driver of the Thunderbird saunter in, dressed in a white shirt and dark slacks, his cap angled low on his head.

"Can I help you?" Mr. Foley asked. There was something awkward, almost hesitant in his tone.

"I'm just looking around, thank you." The young man sounded calm and even.

It was only after he took off his cap that I realized he was Oriental, the polite term we used back then. In California, I had embraced liberal Berkeley's cultural openness. After three weeks back in Boston, which was still closed to anyone outside its Catholic and Puritan world, this Asian-looking face made me miss California even more. I watched his solid figure move slowly to the stacked cages of live animals, saw him stick a finger through one cage and stroke a sleeping kitten, let an overzealous puppy lick his hand. The mixed breed pup threw himself against the cage, whining with excitement, his tail and hind end wagging frantically back and forth.

"Be careful there," Mr. Foley said, never taking his eyes off the young man.

He turned around and smiled. "You've got a wonderful store here."

Disarmed, Mr. Foley cleared his throat. "Yes, we like it. You need anything, just ask."

"Yes sir, I will." He nodded.

Mr. Foley cleared his throat again, then busied himself with a magazine, his eyes darting up every few minutes.

I couldn't help but let out a small laugh. The young man looked over and smiled.

I'll remember that smile until the day I die, his dark eyes catching mine in that first instant. People say you recall these kinds of things right before you pass on, those special moments in your life flickering before you like a silent movie, no words needed. It's one of the moments I hope for again, whether in dream or memory, and especially in death. I wish for a moment like it for Hana as much as for myself. Max had the most beautiful face I've ever seen, with a high forehead, straight nose, and slightly wavy black hair. While many of my Asian friends at Berkeley were shorter and slighter, compared with my five feet, seven inches, Max was four inches taller with broad swimmer's shoulders.

How he happened to wander into Waterford that weekend was just another stroke of luck. "I made a wrong turn," he explained early in our courtship, when every detail meant so much.

"And kept going?" I wondered.

"What can I say? You were the magnet pulling me there."

"That's it?" I asked, secretly pleased with his answer.

He smiled. "That's it. Fate brought us together."

I know differently now. What brought him to Maine was much less romantic than fate. He had driven across country from Los Angeles, having just finished a Ph.D. in history at UCLA. In Bangor he visited a grad school friend, and Waterford had been simply a wrong turn on his way back. But even that wrong turn was fate, Max said, so no matter how I want to remember it, he had his point.

Not long after her first kiss, Hana asked me, "What made you fall in love with Daddy?"

"His kindness," I answered. It was a quick and honest answer, but it made little impression on Hana. She was too young to understand that a little kindness could make all the difference when things became difficult.

"What did you do on your first date?" she asked, more interested in specifics.

"He bought me a cup of coffee."

"That's all?"

I laughed. "We met in a pet shop and he asked me to have a cup of coffee with him. That was pretty brazen, back in the fifties."

Hana rolled her eyes. "What did you do on your second date? Have tea?"

"Actually, he drove me to the beach and we sat and talked. It was very romantic," I added.

"Uh-huh," she said, already having lost interest.

Once in a while I try to imagine how different my life would be if I hadn't stopped that day in Waterford forty-one years ago. How fate could have been changed with a simple right turn instead of a left. No Max. No Hana. And I'm right back in the dark again— all the sudden cold fears of childhood overtaking me.

HANA

Mirror, Mirror

I sit on the sofa by the living room window, my feet elevated by cushions as I watch Cate working in the garden. It's part of our daily routine—she works in the garden, while I try to read or write to my best friend, Laura, who's now a brilliant criminal attorney in New York, where she has a busy, full life with a stockbroker husband and two daughters. Josephine and Camille are my godchildren, the only children I'll ever have in this life. Beautiful Laura Stevens, everyone's dream girl with her blue eyes, long, blond hair and her tall, thin figure. We've known each other since we were babies. We did everything together, from teething to having chicken pox. Our parents were neighbors and good friends. Laura even taught me how to kiss right before I went to the junior prom with Kenny Howe. "He'll be expecting at least a kiss good night. Just don't press your lips too tightly together," she instructed. When I made a face, Laura leaned over, rested her hands on my shoulders, and pulled me closer. She whispered to me, "Relax, Hana," my rigid body loosening up as she placed her slightly parted lips against mine. They felt soft and warm and I could taste the sweetness of her cherry lip gloss. Then she pulled away and said, "If his tongue slips into your mouth, don't worry, it's all part of it." I looked up at her blue eyes, trying not to think about Kenny's tongue in my mouth, yet grateful for the quick lesson. Now, I remember it with such vividness that a sudden, painful longing to see Laura fills me, and it's all I can do not to cry.

Sometimes, when all else fails, I listen to music—classical or jazz—Bach or Brubeck. Even in the cold, damp days of March, Cate's outside, imagining her spring garden in a few months' time, her face flushed pink from the raw wind. I shudder at the thought of such cold. Only when it rains does she stay in, gazing out the window at the low, dark sky, the grim, shadowy trees, the rainwater that runs in clear sheets down the slant of the road. Even then, I imagine it's a piece of each day that she can call her own.

Today I can't seem to concentrate on one thing. I'm discouraged because the ulcers on my legs and ankles haven't fully healed yet, and it's been almost a week. My joints have begun to feel stiff and useless. "In a few days. Be patient, Hana," Dr. Truman told me when he was here the day before yesterday to check on me. If it were true, I should have risen today and miraculously walked again. I'm tired of getting up each morning not feeling well, a dull ache that never seems to go away. When I accidentally glanced into the mirror this morning, I didn't turn away as I usually would. Instead, I looked long and hard and saw someone small and wrinkled staring back at me, with taut, age-spotted skin, dark, hollow pockets below the eyes, and gray tufts of hair sticking out in all directions. *What have you done with Hana?* I asked out loud. *Where did she go?*

I sit up on the sofa, then plant my feet on the cold floor, easing my weight forward as I try to stand. It takes only a moment of shooting pain in my ankles to know that I can scarcely stand, much less walk. And how will it be in a few years, when I'm confined to a wheelchair for the rest of my days? The thought circles around my mind as I fall against the sofa pillows. And, suddenly, it's Howard that comes to mind, and I can almost hear his deep voice urging me on.

Eighty-four-year-old Howard Rice, a onetime music teacher and violinist, was the best dancer at the Evergreen Retirement Home. With a one-to-four ratio of men to women, the ladies swarmed all over him at the weekly tea dance. When he escorted me to the front door after I'd read to him, some of the women laughed and liked to tease me with "You're giving us stiff competition, honey." Unlike the other men at Evergreen, Howard was always immaculately dressed in a white shirt, corduroy slacks, and cardigan sweater. His gray beard softened his deep-set, dark eyes and hawklike nose. I thought how he must have been very intense in his younger days with his serious, intelligent manner. On sunny days he liked to sit outside in the backyard under the shade of a large pine tree with me, while I read to him *Swann's Way* or *The Past Recaptured* from Proust's *Remembrance of Things Past.*

"Proust makes time stand still," he said to me. "Not a bad thing at my age!" He ran his large hand over his close-cropped gray hair.

I laughed. I had to admit there was something calming about the minute details of Swann's daily life.

We could never get through a few lines without stopping to talk. It took only a few meetings to realize that Howard was different from the rest, still deeply concerned with life around him. He hadn't given up, like so many others at the home had, and was intensely curious about everything. On one occasion, it began to rain and we scrambled inside to the community room and sat by the window.

"Before you begin reading today," Howard said, laying his large hands on the table in front of us, "tell me something about your life." I'd been reading to him for about two weeks, enough time for his curiosity about me to find its way into words.

"What would you like to know?" I asked him back.

Howard stroked his beard and looked at me closely before he said, "What's a vibrant, young woman such as you doing here at an old folks' home?"

I laughed. "I thought it might be a good experience," I said. "It's just temporary," I added.

"You should be out in the world, sharing your charms and meeting people your own age," he said, his dark eyes waiting for an explanation. "That's surely where I'd be if I were your age again."

There was no use complicating our new friendship with details about Werner. Other than being small in stature, I could still keep my secret. I didn't have the heart to tell him that being at Evergreen was just as much for myself as for anyone else. I was curious after the cataracts. I needed answers to questions I didn't even know yet. I wanted to know what to expect in the not so distant future, to see firsthand some of the mysteries of growing old.

"I met you, didn't I?" I said. "Some of the ladies here aren't too thrilled about my invading their territory."

Howard laughed. "Some of the ladies here can't remember what's their territory!"

Then I laughed.

"So you won't answer my question?" he persisted.

I looked into his gray eyes and saw kindness. "It's important that I be here now," I said, my voice turning serious.

Then both of us were quiet. I waited for him to continue, but he didn't. I knew Howard had never been married and had spent much of his life teaching the violin and traveling the world. He came to settle in Daring to be close to his niece, he told me, and to contemplate his remaining years among the redwoods. He entered Evergreen two years ago, when he fell and broke his collarbone, not wanting to be a nuisance for his niece and her family.

Howard smiled and changed the subject. "You're Japanese on your father's side, right?" he asked.

I nodded, flipping through *Swann's Way* and noting that we'd barely made a dent in the book in the past few weeks of my reading to him.

"Was he interned?" Howard asked.

I looked up at him. "Yes, he was. At Heart Mountain in Wyoming."

Howard shook his head. "I was proud to have fought in the Second World War, but I was never proud of what we did to our own Japanese Americans."

I tried to imagine Howard as a young man, tall and dashing in his uniform, as he fought for freedom and democracy, while my Japanese American father, who was still a boy, had lost the very thing Howard was fighting for.

"My father teaches history at Brandon" was all I could think to say.

"Totally understandable." Howard leaned back against his chair and closed his eyes, as he often did when I read to him. "He's still searching the past for answers."

I nodded. "He loves everything about the past and how we've come to where we are today."

"Perhaps he should pay Evergreen a visit. Lots of old relics right here in Daring."

I laughed.

"For whatever reasons brought you here," Howard then said, "I'm eternally grateful."

I smiled. "So am I."

Howard stood up and went over to click on the radio. A soft, sweet melody filled the room as he came back to me. "Shall we make the old girls jealous?" He held out his hand to me. "May I have this dance?"

And though the top of my head only reached his chest, I felt tall as he swept me across the floor with ease.

Cate looks up and sees me sitting by the window, raises her gloved hand, and waves. I smile and wave back. She still moves around like a much younger woman, kneeling for long stretches at a time, planting flower bulbs, watering the delicate roots until the day she sees the green shoots pushing through the ground, each a small miracle. My mother has always been the most beautiful woman I've ever known. More so because she isn't aware of it. I've heard Lily tell her, "Cate, I swear you must have blinders on, not to see how gorgeous you are." Then Lily would touch her own full head of frizzy, dark hair, look down at her own solid figure. "I'd kill to have your straight hair and even twice your waistline!"

Cate has no idea how often people are struck by the way she looks, turning and taking a second glance to see if their eyes are deceiving them under the bright fluorescent lights of the super-market aisles or in the dark, quiet corners of the library. She may think it's me they're staring at, which is something we've both had to live with, but I know better. Through the years I've come to realize that their furtive gazes begin with me—the four-foot-eight, birdlike creature—only to linger on my mother—the fair-complexioned, dark-eyed, auburn-haired beauty who's a full foot taller than I am.

We are so distinctly different in appearance that we create a kind of wonderment. What passes through people's minds when they see us together for the first time? That I'm the mother and she's my daughter? I can imagine the shock and dismay giving way to sympathy and compassion when they learn otherwise.

When the distinct signs of Werner began to show on my face in my twenties, Cate kept inventing new ways to distract me from curious looks, soften the surprised glances of those who knew something was wrong with this small, pinched person, even if they couldn't quite pinpoint what. As we walked down the street, I could see myself in their eyes. I was too small, too underdeveloped for my age. My face was aging but my body hadn't matured—there was something seriously wrong they couldn't quite figure out. Who could blame them when they quickly looked away?

We must have appeared to be a traveling sideshow, walking down the street, her arm possessively hooked through mine. But all through the years, she has never realized people weren't just staring at me but also watching her.

When I was a little girl I used to gaze into the bathroom mirror and wonder why I didn't look anything like Cate. I often wondered if I'd had a brother or sister, would my sibling resemble my mother? Every morning I checked to see if something had miraculously changed overnight, turning me suddenly into my mother's daughter. After all, there was evidence of my father, Max, in the shape of my eyes and in my straight, black hair, which I usually wore in a ponytail then. But Cate's presence in me remained a mystery. How I prayed for some trace of her when I looked into the mirror each morning.

"You have my lips and nose, kiddo," she finally said to me one morning, pouring milk into my cereal. She smacked her lips and blew me a kiss.

My father sat reading his newspaper before rushing off to work, rattling pages as he quickly turned them, sipping black coffee and eating toast with strawberry jam.

"Aren't you glad you resemble the Murayama side of the family?" he teased from behind his paper.

I was pleased to resemble Max, but I wanted some part of me to belong to my mother, too. I touched my full lips, staring first at Cate, then patiently waiting for Max to lower his paper so I could make a final assessment. Cate poured him another cup of coffee as I ate my cereal, never taking my eyes off him. Like clockwork, the paper lowered and he reached for his coffee, raising the cup to his obviously thinner lips.

I wanted to laugh with joy, jump up and hug both my wise, wonderful parents. It seems like a small thing to have stayed with me all these years, but it has.

That night I looked in the mirror and saw my lips, full and luscious, forming the smooth curve of a smile just like my mother's reflecting back at me.

CATE

Heart Mountain

When I finally told Hana the whole truth about Max and our second date, I swear I saw a glint of admiration in her eyes. She was sixteen, and I imagined it gave her a rare glimpse of a young, romantic mother and father she hadn't realized existed. Max had followed me back to Boston that weekend, and I had lied to my parents, telling them I was going out with an old Berkeley friend who happened to be in town. It seemed simpler than explaining to them I was going out with a Japanese man I'd met the day before in Waterford, Maine. I waited for Max down the street at the bus stop, anxiously listening for the roar of his Thunderbird, and I couldn't help but think of a conversation that I'd had with Papa after we'd seen the movie *Bridge on the River Kwai*.

Almost thirteen years after the Second World War, his conservative ideals still prevailed. "The Japanese had it coming. If it weren't for the bomb, we'd still be fighting that war."

"What about the Japanese Americans interned here in the United States? They were as American as we are," I said.

"It was for their own safety," Papa said, lowering his voice. "After Pearl Harbor there was too much anger in the air."

"An easy excuse for a terrible mistake," I said. "What if the president had interned all the German Americans because of Hitler, or the Italian Americans because of Mussolini?" It was a quick reminder that Papa's parents were immigrants themselves.

Papa shook his head. "You are too young to know what was going on. You think four years at that left-wing university out West gives you all the answers!"

"You better believe it." I laughed. He really believed that interning Japanese Americans had been for their own safety, and I knew nothing I could say would ever sway his thinking. But a moment later his face relaxed and he laughed along with me.

On our second date, Max and I drove out to the beach near Gloucester, where we wouldn't be seen. All the way there I thought I'd burn in hell for eternity for lying to my mother and father. I was convinced every person we passed on the road had seen us and would tell them. At the same time, I felt ashamed of myself for not having the courage to introduce Max to my parents.

But Max's quiet voice pulled me in, away from all these fears. We parked overlooking the beach, and while I didn't know where to begin, stumbling all over my words, he told me his life story easily. And so we paused only long enough, in the darkening light, to listen to the thundering of the waves below. What was it about him that I loved so much? I felt a soft rush of warmth inside as he spoke of his childhood dream of becoming a baseball player and, less happily, of his family's surviving wartime internment in Wyoming with other Japanese Americans. That very night, I knew I would marry Max. There was something courageous about him. He had left his family and friends and driven across the country in the new Thunderbird that he had worked four years, both as a teaching assistant and in an insurance office, to buy. He wasn't sure what he might find or how he would be received but knew only that here on the East Coast, Asians were still looked upon with reserve and apprehension.

"A Texas cowboy wanted to rough me up in a bar in Amarillo," he told me. "And I was almost shot in Arkansas by an irate farmer."

"Why?" I asked.

He paused. "Because his son was killed in Bataan."

Then we were both silent.

"Weren't you afraid?" I finally asked.

Max nodded. "Still am. But I wanted to see what the rest of America was all about. I couldn't just stay put in Los Angeles any longer."

"And what did you see?"

"There's always good"—he touched my hand—"as well as the bad. Better to face it than to run away."

All through our marriage, Max would surprise me with his ever-present optimism and determination.

Max was the youngest of three children. His parents were Issei who had immigrated to California from Japan as children. They lived in a blue, wood-frame bungalow on two acres of land they leased near Pasadena. In long glass greenhouses, his father produced prize-winning chrysanthemums and made a good living for his family. His older sister, Sumi, was married to a Japanese American dentist and had two children of her own. His brother, Tag, ran the flower business with his parents in Los Angeles. As children, they imagined other worlds in the greenhouses, from the Amazon jungle to magical ice palaces. They ran from one glass house to the other, three in all, one for each child. The scents of moist earth and fertilizer and sweet-blooming carnations and chrysanthemums flavored their childhood. Max spoke of it like a far-away dream.

Safely cocooned in the Thunderbird, I inhaled the aroma of his still-new leather seats mixed with a slightly salty scent of the ocean. A thin veil of darkness barely covered the sky.

"My brother, Tag, has always been the one with the green thumb in our family," Max said. "Even as a kid he had the patience to make things grow. He saw that beauty comes with time and patience. I wanted everything right away, then sulked when I didn't get it. I was the youngest, the troublemaker." He smiled, as if he were talking about someone else. "I was constantly breaking the glass panes of the greenhouses, smashing them with the baseballs I'd hit when we played in back of the house. I always dreamed I'd someday play professional baseball. I can't describe the joy of hitting the ball just right, making that connection and knowing that I'd smacked the hell out of it."

"What did your parents say?"

"They yelled and scolded, then finally gave up and took the money for the glass out of my allowance." Max suddenly stopped as if he'd said too much about himself. "And what about you?" he asked.

"I'm an only child. My parents hoped for more children, but it wasn't to be. 'God's will,' I heard Mama once tell my aunt Sophia. They've always wanted the best for me."

"All parents do."

"I guess so, but I always wished I'd had brothers and sisters to spread some of the concern around."

Max laughed. "Believe me, they always muster up enough for each child."

"Tell me about your sister," I said. I had always wanted one of my own.

"Sumi just had to put up with us. Having to deal with two younger brothers and be an obedient Japanese daughter wasn't easy." He smiled.

"You were all born in Pasadena?"

Max nodded. "And we never lived anywhere else, except during the war," he said. "When I was nine, we were interned at Heart Mountain. My only happy memory of Wyoming was playing fast-pitch softball or football starting in spring, right through the oven-hot days of summer. When we couldn't play outside during the freezing winters, I boxed with my brother and the other boys to keep warm. We just couldn't stop moving, it was all we could do."

When I asked him more about his camp experience, he shook his head and said, "When we played with other little kids in Pasadena, Tag and I were always the good guys. We fought for justice and killed the bad guys. Then one day the president declared me one of the bad guys, too, only I hadn't done anything bad. I saw my parents become old before their time at Heart Mountain. I was old enough to realize that we'd been imprisoned simply for looking different from everyone else."

"Was your parents' flower business still there when you returned home?"

Max nodded. "But it was in shambles. Rocks had shattered every pane of glass in each of the greenhouses. Only the frames still stood. Like many other families during that crazy time, my father made our Buddhist church the trustee of our property. I remember my mother whispering the word *skeletons* the day we returned home. Our next-door neighbor, Mr. Evans, had actually patrolled the grounds for us with his shotgun, or everything would have been destroyed. He's a man I'll never forget. The morning we had to leave, he told my dad not to worry, he'd take care of things. There wasn't much choice but to trust that he would do it. It was Mr. Evans who showed me that there's still a lot of kindness and fairness in the world."

Max stopped talking and gazed out over the water. I felt an unbearable need to touch him, to remind him I was there next to him. I touched the sleeve of his jacket, and he turned to me and smiled.

Then he cleared his throat and continued. "It took years to rebuild, but we were the fortunate ones. My parents worked hard all their lives and were lucky enough to find a way to hold on to their property. Most people weren't so lucky, they lost their leases and everything else they owned. A lifetime of work gone by the time they returned."

"How long were you away at Heart Mountain?"

Max rubbed his eyes. Even in gray evening shadows, I could see he was no longer smiling. "From the middle of nineteen forty-two to the end of nineteen forty-five."

The sea breeze was soft, the slap of the waves insistent, but Max's stories of Heart Mountain conjured arid desert visions in my mind. I wanted to understand it all. What was it like to be forced to give up everything and pack your entire life into two suitcases? Where did you sleep? How did you keep warm enough during the winters? Was there enough to eat? And, most important, weren't you angry that the country of your birth had turned against you? The questions rose to the tip of my tongue, but I swallowed them back down when Max opened the car door and stepped out into the warm night air, gesturing for me to follow.

Max stayed for three weeks in Boston and met my parents all of two times after I'd finally told them he was my friend from California. Then he returned to Los Angeles to work for an old professor as a teaching assistant. I stayed in Boston and worked at my father's law office. Our goal was to save enough money to start a life somewhere together. We wrote each other every week and saved every cent we made. Ten months later, at the end of the school term, Max returned to Boston and we were married at City Hall with two strangers as our witnesses, against the wishes of my parents, who had "nothing personal against Max" but simply wanted an easier life for me.

Two weeks earlier, when I broke the news to them about our marrying, it was Mama who spoke up first, for a change. "Marriage is a big commitment, Caterina. There are enough problems to deal with, without having to worry about the prejudices you might encounter as a mixed couple. Max seems like a nice person, but are you really prepared for the whispers and stares when you walk down the street?"

"And what about your children?" Papa asked, almost in a whisper. It seemed as if he'd lost his voice. He paced back and forth in front of the fireplace. "It's a difficult enough world, but to be caught between two cultures . . ."

"Just means they'll be blessed with twice as much," I finished his sentence.

"I don't suppose he's Catholic," Mama added. "What will Father Shaunnessy say?"

"His parents might be asking what their Buddhist reverend will say."

"Don't be sarcastic, Caterina," my father snapped. "I don't think you have any idea what you're getting into!"

They tried to bribe me with all the things they equated with an easier life—a new car, a trip abroad, an apartment of my own, money for graduate school. I found my voice and raised it just enough to make them realize I meant what I said. "I love you both, but I'm marrying Max, with or without your blessing!"

Max had been met with an anxious silence from his parents. There were no big scenes or loud words, just a weary acceptance of the fact that life was once again throwing them a curveball.

"They wanted to know why I couldn't just marry a nice Japanese girl." Max laughed into the phone from L.A.

"And what did you say?" I asked, gripping the receiver tighter.

"That I was marrying a nice Italian girl instead."

Mortified, my parents refused to attend our wedding. Their good Catholic daughter had gone astray at last, and they couldn't understand how or why.

Before we were married, Max and I talked about where we should live. He suggested we return to California. "There's an opening in the history department at Brandon College, up north, near the coast. It's roughly three hours from San Francisco. I'm sure you'll like it, it's beautiful country up there. The only skyscrapers are the redwoods. And we can make a fresh start on our own."

I had imagined that we would move to San Francisco or Los Angeles, to be near Max's parents. "It might be easier if we moved to a bigger city," I said, though I knew it was just as much for my sake as his. I knew the big cities might be more accepting—there were large Japanese communities thriving in both places and I'd thought we'd be accepted as a couple there. But unlike Tag, who had found a real satisfaction in growing flowers in the safe confines of his family's glass houses, Max wanted to be in open spaces and to be near the ocean. He couldn't wait to get as far away as he could from the arid Southern California climate. Max was still that little boy back in the camp who couldn't stop moving.

"In Wyoming," he had told me once, "our camp was surrounded by desert, and in the distance, there was the towering presence of Heart Mountain. Someone said it was over eight thousand feet tall. I looked out at it every morning and imagined it was a limestone monster that stood guard over us, never letting us leave."

I felt guilty then, realizing my parents were right. I felt ashamed of wanting to escape what people might say when they saw us together. And all Max wanted was to leave the past behind, to be far away from arid Los Angeles and parched Heart Mountain. He had always dreamed of being near the ocean, feeling the moist salt air against his skin, breathing in the briny scent of the sea. It was the freedom he had longed for, ever since he was a boy at Heart Mountain.

Max shook his head. "We don't need it to be easier, we need to build a new life. Our life."

Thank God I was too ashamed ever to say anything to him about my own fears. We moved to Daring, California, during the summer of 1959. It was as beautiful as Max said, with Victorian and brown-shingled houses, a river that ran under a stone bridge in the middle of the town, its bank thick with acacia and evergreen trees, and a main street lined with weathered stone buildings. And we were so close to the coast you could smell the ocean, and on foggy days, taste the salt in the thick moisture.

In September, Max started teaching at Brandon College right in town. It was then a small, private college with a growing student body and a faculty that included a handful of minorities. Brandon put the town of Daring on the map. We rented a small, one-bedroom bungalow within walking distance of the campus. While Max prepared his syllabi for the history classes he'd be teaching,

I unpacked and tried hard to make our small house a comfortable home.

"What's this?" I asked Max one afternoon when I opened a box in the living room. He sat at our makeshift dining room table, a piece of plywood balanced between two stools. I held up a black-and-white porcelain vase, which had the clean strokes of a black crane painted on it.

Max glanced over. "The crane is a symbol of good fortune. At Japanese weddings, friends and relatives fold a thousand origami cranes for the bride and groom. My mother wanted us to have it."

There we were, all alone, starting our life in a remote town, hours away from any big city. We were surrounded by the sea and giant redwoods. We had a statue of the Virgin Mary from my mother and a Japanese porcelain vase with a crane that meant good fortune from Max's mother. I followed the outlines of the crane with my finger for any extra luck it might bring us.

But the words that my parents had spoken would return to haunt us in Daring. For the first month, we tried to ignore the initial stares and occasional whispers of *slant eyes* and *Jap lover*. Once off campus, it was a typical small town—closed and tight-knit, wary of anyone or anything different. Not only did Max and I stand out when we walked down the street together but when I went out alone to buy groceries I was still an outsider. People seemed to stare and size me up by my differences. I walked in long, confident strides. And instead of shirtwaists, I wore capri pants with bateau-neckline blouses. My bangs and straight hair spelled radical when every other woman in Daring seemed to have a short bob.

A few weeks after we arrived, there was a loud bang against our living room window just as we were sitting down to dinner.

My heart jumped as Max sprang up to see what it was. "You stay here," he cautioned, but I followed him to the front door, praying nothing would happen to him. After a few moments, he returned carrying a small brown bag in his hand.

"What is it?" I asked.

Max's face was drawn and serious. He handed me a coarse burlap sack, dense and heavy with sand. "Someone threw this at our window."

"Did you see anyone?"

Max shook his head. "No one."

For days after, similar sudden attacks happened at different hours. Sometimes I heard the screeching of tires rounding the corner and at other times, nothing after the loud, dull blow. When I said we ought to call the police, Max said there was no damage or injury to report. I was a wreck by the time Max came home from teaching. One afternoon he returned to find me packing boxes.

"We're leaving!" I said, my voice tight and dry.

"We can't, Cate." Max sat down beside me.

"Why don't they just throw rocks or bricks and break the damn window?" I cried, my nerves raveled.

Max held me. "It'd be too easy. This way they can torment us to their hearts' content without doing any physical damage. We can't run away, Cate. Then they'd win. This is our home and I refuse to be pushed out again."

I weighed the Japanese ceramic vase in my hands, then stood up and placed it back on the mantel.

At last, Max called the sheriff and filed a complaint.

"Probably just some kids," the sheriff said. "You know the kind, pranksters." He looked away and rubbed his puffy cheek, then glanced over at me as he spoke, never once looking Max in the eyes.

After the sheriff's visit, whoever was throwing the sand-filled bags stopped. Days passed without problems, but just when I finally thought we'd settled into a life of our own, another incident tested us.

One mild evening as walked along Main Street after dinner, we were harassed by four or five teenage boys, James Dean wannabes, with hair slicked back and cigarettes dangling.

"Go back to Jap Land, where your kind belong!" one of them shouted at Max as we passed.

I stared fiercely back at them, as a couple of them pulled the corners of their eyes into small slits.

"You lost the war, Nip. You got nipped in the butt!" They all laughed.

I felt my mouth go dry, my stomach knot up. Did they think they were being funny, making such fools of themselves? I felt my anger taking over, the adrenaline rising inside, as if they were making fun of me.

Max kept walking, ignoring them. "They're just kids," he mumbled under his breath, though we both knew their hateful words had originated at home.

"How can you be so calm?" I hissed, angry with the boys for being so stupid and small-minded and irritated at Max for accepting it. I grabbed the sleeve of his jacket, but he pulled away.

Max stopped when we reached the corner and turned to me. "What would you have me do, Cate? Beat them up? Yell back at them? Then I'd be no better than they are. I've grown up with this, you haven't."

I looked away, fighting back tears. I knew he was right, but I couldn't stop feeling furious at a world that wouldn't accept someone as good as Max.

That night I stared into the bathroom mirror and saw my mother's auburn hair and fair skin, my father's deep-set eyes and full, thick lips. Would it have been the other way around, I wondered, if we'd been walking down a street in Japan?

HANA

In the Beginning

During the last few months, I've become more and more curious about my past, like Max, who always seemed to be searching for something. The more Cate wants me to live in the present, the more I seem to be holding on to history. How can I explain it to her? The longer I'm trapped in this wheelchair, the more I see my past as a way of forgetting the present. I find myself sifting through the years, putting things in order, looking for those moments that may reveal some rhyme or reason as to why I'm on this earth. My past is alive with memories, while the future is only an empty hope, a mysterious void.

My questions have been coming fast and furious, mostly when we sit down to eat or when we're walking in the park.

"What was it like to come here in nineteen fifty-nine?" I asked

Cate when we sat down to dinner last night. "And why Daring?"

"It was a small town, with a small-town mentality that took some getting used to. It was difficult at first, but we settled here because of your father's teaching position," she answered, placing a plate in front of me. On the table were two pieces of poached salmon, baked potatoes, and a bowl of peas.

"But he could have taught anywhere."

"It wasn't so easy in nineteen fifty-nine. There weren't that many teaching positions available. You had to go where there were openings." She cut open her baked potato and dropped a bit of sour cream into the slit.

"So he risked being the only Japanese in a small town during the late fifties? Wouldn't it have been much easier in some big city?" I asked.

"Yes," she answered, "but your father wanted to live on the coast. His childhood was filled with hot, dry climates. He wanted to live by the ocean. And he wanted us to have a fresh start."

I nodded my head and smiled. "Sounds just like him." I could see Max now, young and filled with conviction, ready to take on a new life by the sea.

Once more I was that child again walking along the beach beside him. He often drove us to Falcon Beach when I was young, and those summers at the beach are some of my happiest memories. My mother and I read and took long walks. Sometimes Laura came along and we spent all day building sand castles. It was a place where my tall, wavy-haired father became playful, where his imagination moved to stories of explorers and their discoveries. He could always see some great adventure happening before his eyes as he stared out at the ocean.

"Imagine the first ships that sailed over the seas to a foreign land." He smiled at me, inventing a tale. He pointed out to the endless sea, which on that afternoon appeared like a pale blue blanket. "Imagine a young captain named Hogan, who was commissioned to take a ship and crew and sail from America to Japan for the first time. Think of the fear he felt, not wanting to upset his family or his crew, yet not knowing what to expect each day as he stared out to the sometimes turbulent, unforgiving sea, praying that his ship and crew would survive the long, dangerous journey."

I was just seven or eight years old, filled with energy, and only half paid attention to his words, focusing instead on the rubbery, tubular-shaped pieces of seaweed that had washed ashore, searching for any hint of a seashell peeking up through the white sand.

"How young?" I asked, wanting him to think I was paying full attention.

He looked down at me.

"How old was the captain?" I clarified.

"Not even thirty," he answered.

My first thought was that he wasn't so young.

"Think of what it must have been like," he continued, "all the strange foods and mysterious smells, the different colors and customs in the way people looked and dressed. I remember how my own grandmother—your great-grandmother Miyoshi—thought Caucasians were barbarians with all the hair they had on their bodies."

I held my dad's hand tightly and could see how his skin was virtually hairless, while Dr. Truman's hairy wrist only appeared darker against the sleeve of his white doctor's jacket. "And would Captain Hogan fall in love with a beautiful Japanese girl?" I asked.

My dad laughed. "Yes, of course. Why go all that way across the ocean, if you're not going to fall in love?"

Then I laughed.

"What kind of world would it be now if these brave men hadn't sailed across the seas to make that first connection with other people in foreign lands?" He asked me this, talking more to himself than to me, running his fingers through his thick, black hair, his dark eyes squinting against the sun.

I suddenly stopped and thought about what my dad was saying. "Is that why you drove all the way across the country when you were young?" I asked. A glimmer of white shell in the sand made me let go of his hand, but I didn't run toward it.

My dad smiled. "It was to discover your mother."

I laughed and thought how I wanted to marry someone exactly like him when I grew up. We walked slowly onward until we reached the spot where I glimpsed the shell. I squatted and plucked it from the wet sand, a small, white shell shaped like a Chinese pointed hat, with a brown spiral encircling it. I ran down and washed it off at the water's edge, then ran back to my dad and placed the shell in his hand.

"—so you should eat more peas," Cate said, spooning more onto my plate, bringing me right back to the dinner table. "They're good for you. Lots of fiber."

I laughed. Occasionally such comments remind me that Cate is the older one—well past the age of fifty, when the word *fiber* becomes central to one's vocabulary. But I didn't have the heart to tell her that eating peas wouldn't help me now, and a rush of sorrow stirred inside of me.

"Tell me more," I said, as I shook off the gloom and lifted a forkful of peas to my mouth.

She took a bite of potato and smiled. "We had some rough moments when we first moved here. I was ready to hightail it out of Daring. I was already packing when your dad talked me out of it." She looked up and smiled. "He was right. When you came into the world a few years later, it made a big difference."

"Where would you have gone?" I asked.

"To San Francisco, or to Los Angeles to be near your grand-parents."

"They would have been ecstatic," I said, thinking of my grand-parents, Henry and Midori. I imagined the joy I'd have had play-ing in their greenhouses day after day.

"At one time, my parents would have given me big bucks not to marry your father." She laughed, a comfortable laugh that's grown deeper with the passage of time.

"Just think if you'd taken them up on the offer," I said. "How different your life would be."

Cate put down her fork and looked over at me. "Different doesn't always mean better. If I'd never married your father, we'd never have had you."

"That's what I mean. It would have been so much easier," I said quietly.

"I don't need it to be easier," she said, reaching over to me and giving my hand a squeeze. "I like it just the way it is. The way things were intended to be."

"You can't know that," I said, wondering what God intended when he saddled me with Werner, and my mother with me.

"Maybe not." She leaned back in her chair, and I could see a glint of pain in her eyes, for just a moment, before it disappeared. "But what I believe is that there wouldn't have been much point to it."

"To marrying Dad?"

"To my life," she said, looking over at me with a smile that carried a world of sadness in it.

CATE

Miracles

The day Hana was born brought two miracles. The first one involved the pure beauty of birth, which finally came almost four years after Max and I married. The overwhelming realization that this beautiful, dark-eyed, fair-skinned child with a full head of black, downy hair was a part of Max and me. She was so fragile, so beautiful. Suddenly sentimental, I understood that we had created her together, that part of us would live on through her and her children. Max loved to bathe Hana. He came home every day from teaching, rolled up his sleeves, and gently set her into the baby tub, her chubby limbs splashing in the warm water. I felt such joy every time I looked at her perfect fingers and toes.

And the second miracle was that Papa came to visit us for the first time since Max and I married. Mama had flown out from Boston for Hana's birth and stayed with us for two weeks afterward. Six months later Papa broke down in tears of happiness at the sight of his granddaughter's exquisite smile and sparkling eyes. He even went so far as to hug Max. From that day on, Papa sang Italian lullabies to Hana and was completely devoted to her until he died of lung cancer almost thirteen years later.

On Hana's third birthday, Max's parents drove up from Los Angeles to meet my parents for the first time. They had all been instantly charmed by their vibrant and energetic granddaughter, who appeared much more Japanese than Italian. Already at three she seemed to recognize the cultural difference between her two sets of grandparents. She sang "O Sole Mio" with my parents, and Papa chased her around the house, yelling out "Gotcha!" while he grabbed for air, as her giggles and screams rang throughout the house. But with Max's parents, she kept her voice calm and soft, even while learning to fold gold and silver origami cranes or eating her favorite plump pork and vegetable *gyozas* at the birthday party.

"Ravioli in another form," my father teased, standing in the kitchen popping another *gyoza* into his mouth.

"Only better," Max's mother, Midori, responded, without missing a beat.

Papa laughed. "Wait until you taste my Anna's spaghetti bolognese. You'll think you're in Italy."

"It's a place I always wanted to visit," Midori said softly.

Papa looked at Max's mother, and I could tell he wanted to hug her, the way he hugged Hana every time he saw her. "My little flower," he called his granddaughter, even before I explained to him that *Hana* meant the same thing in Japanese.

"What's going on in here?" Max's dad, Henry, came into the kitchen.

"Midori and I are going off to Italy," Papa boomed.

Henry smiled and said, "Have fun!"

I watched them having such a good time and thanked God for this child who had brought us all together.

I don't believe any little girl could have been better loved by her grandparents than Hana was. Max and I had hoped to have more children, but it never happened. "God's will," I could hear my mother saying yet again. Still, at one point, I worried about Hana being lonely as an only child, having been one myself. But more than that, I had my own selfish reasons for wanting more children, innately fearing the fragility of life, knowing that at any time something could go wrong.

But in that third year of Hana's life, there were no signs that anything might go wrong. She was a healthy, beautiful child in a yellow dress blowing out pink candles on a chocolate birthday cake. I remember it all as if it were yesterday—all of us surrounding Hana at the table—Louis and Anna, Henry and Midori, Max and Cate—a real family, frozen in a black-and-white photo that still sits atop the piano.

Papa died ten years later, just before we learned something might be wrong with Hana. It was a blessing in a way, since his death would have been much crueler had he known that the granddaughter he so loved would never live a normal life. Our lives, too, changed. Max and I were no longer just ordinary parents of an ordinary growing teenager. We both felt helpless at the time and somehow to blame, even before Hana was officially diagnosed with having Werner's syndrome in her twenties. The child we'd vowed to love and protect from her first breath would suffer because of a gene one or both of us might have passed on to her. The thought of it nearly destroyed us. I blamed myself for thinking once too often that she was a perfect baby. I'd read how the Chinese purposely demeaned their babies, calling them little pigs or scrawny dogs, in order to keep the gods from taking them away. I couldn't help thinking that I had somehow failed to protect my child.

I remember driving past St. John's Catholic Church more than ten times that first week after we learned something might be wrong. I ached to be in the cool, dark interior of the beautiful stone building. I wanted to be surrounded by the brilliant colors of the stained-glass windows, the kind and serene-looking gaze of the statues, the scent of burning candles. I wanted to kneel down and pray so hard that when I reemerged into the daylight it would have all been a silly mistake. I wanted a miracle to happen, but I couldn't park the car and go in, and I couldn't help thinking, Dear God, why have you forsaken us?

HANA

God's Children

I click on the CD player, slip in a disc of Gregorian chants, and the silent house fills with the perfectly modulated voices of the Benedictine monks. With my mother outside gardening, I turn up the volume until the speakers vibrate. Their unified voices create a kind of spiritual serenity in me, a calm I'm looking for this morning. The monks fascinate me. Every day of the year they sing their chants seven times, re-creating within the walls of the cloister they live in some of the oldest music we have. They have freely chosen a life of meditation, contemplation, and confinement. I close my eyes and listen to their praise, and their meditations on the power of faith. And in their perfect voices, I can believe that there is a God.

I was raised Catholic but went to public schools on weekdays and, beginning in the fourth grade, to catechism on Saturday mornings.

Being with Laura made it bearable to miss Saturday morning cartoons while sitting in a big, empty classroom with the handful of other public school Catholic kids. I was a fresh-faced little girl of nine and still seemingly healthy. My mother still went to mass almost every Sunday and prayed every night that I would grow up to be happy and strong. My father was never religious, and though he was raised Buddhist, he once told me he had ceased practicing any kind of religion a long time ago.

After the possibility of Werner came into my life at thirteen, my mother attended mass less and less. By the time I turned eighteen, she no longer went at all.

Every weekend while I was in elementary school, one of my parents drove Laura and me to St. John's, our local Catholic school right in downtown Daring. Sometimes, if Max dropped us off, he'd wait for us in the local diner, where he read the paper, prepared his classes, and drank coffee until returning to pick us up three hours later. And if Cate drove, she went to the library, ran errands, and once a month had her shoulder-length auburn hair trimmed at Sheryl Hansen's mother's beauty salon, the Right Cut.

The one good thing about catechism was that we weren't assigned seats like in regular school. Laura and I always sat next to each other. I couldn't get over how neat and tidy Catholic classrooms were—the blackboards washed, the erasers free from chalk dust, and all the desks in straight, uniform rows. A wooden crucifix hung at the front of the room, right next to the American flag. Every Saturday Laura and I sat at a different pair of desks and always sneaked a peek inside, lifting up the desktops and surveying the treasures beneath. Each desk was unique to the boy or girl assigned to it on weekdays—a collection of colorful pencils and erasers of all shapes and sizes, a multicolored ring, a handful of jacks, a pair of soiled sweat socks, stacks of baseball cards, the crumpled balls of returned test papers. From our very first catechism class, we were told repeatedly to leave the desks as they were, and never to take anything that didn't belong to us. But each Saturday, without fail, we learned that some parochial student had reported something missing the week before. Then the "it's a sin to steal" lecture, which we knew by heart, took up the first half hour of class.

"Why leave anything good in your desk if you don't want it taken?" a boy named Darryl Clark whispered from the back of the room, just loud enough for all of us to hear.

Laughter erupted, and he was made to stand outside the door of the classroom for the next twenty minutes. I thought it was an unfair punishment but was smart enough to keep my mouth shut in front of Sister Agnes, who was one step away from retirement and didn't put up with anything.

Each week we studied a chapter from our catechism book. And each year the cover changed color as we advanced. During the fourth grade, the cover was periwinkle blue, and we had to answer all the questions at the end of the assigned chapter before our class. Usually I wrote out the answers on Friday evening, so Laura could copy them from me on our way to class, holding her book low and steady on her lap so my parents couldn't see what she was doing. In turn, she brought Sweet Tarts, Twinkies, and Hostess cupcakes to share with me during our breaks.

"Here," Laura said one morning, "I brought you an extra cupcake." She handed it to me, and I broke it in two, keeping one half and giving the other back to her. Even at the age of nine, we looked after each other.

So what did you two learn today?" I remember Cate asking when she came to pick us up one morning. The good thing about Max picking us up was all he ever asked was "Are you two hungry?"

"We studied the commandments," I answered, already feeling anxious. "We're supposed to have them all memorized by next week."

Cate smiled and glanced toward the backseat. "I can help you with memorizing them."

Laura yawned, leaned over to me, and whispered, "Do you think we'll be home in time to see *American Bandstand?*" She swept her blond hair out of her eyes. She was taller than I, by several inches, and long-legged as a wild colt. If I hadn't loved her as much as I did, I might have been jealous.

But that fourth-grade year, we were both in love with the Monkees, who were singing on the show that Saturday. I glanced down at my watch to see if we'd catch the last half, the important part, when most of the popular bands came on. It was already decided that I would one day be Mrs. Davy Jones and Laura would be Mrs. Peter Tork and we'd live next door to each other in our big houses with swimming pools and tennis courts. The walls of our rooms were cluttered with foldout posters of them, cut from the teen magazines we bought with our weekly allowances.

"Hope so," I whispered back.

"So what *are* some of the commandments?" Cate glanced back at us again in her rearview mirror.

"Thou shall not kill," I said, remembering Ricky Hamilton yelling it out in the classroom when Sister Agnes asked who knew any of the commandments.

"Good idea," Cate said.

"Honor thy father and thy mother," I quickly added.

I could see my mother's smile in the mirror. "I really like that one."

"Thou shall not commit adult . . . adulthood?" I looked at Laura, but she only shrugged her shoulders.

Cate laughed. "You better start studying. You two don't want to flunk catechism!"

When Cate looked back at the road and fidgeted with the car radio to get the news, Laura nudged me and reached into her backpack. She smiled, showing all her perfectly straight teeth, and took out two new red and blue pencils for me to see, then whispered in my ear, "Thou shall not steal."

We looked at each other and tried to keep from laughing out loud. But mine was a nervous laugh, the kind of camouflage that erupts when you're too surprised to know what to say. Inside, my stomach had knotted up. Until now Laura had always been the adventurous one, but she'd never broken any of the Ten Commandments. I wondered what all this would mean. Would she burn in hell for stealing? Would I, for knowing and not saying anything? I lived with these questions for a week and prayed that Laura wouldn't do it again. And for the rest of the year, there were no more "it's a sin to steal" lectures from Sister Agnes. Instead we learned that God was all-forgiving. But I knew now that he would never answer Laura's prayers about becoming Mrs. Peter Tork.

A letter from Laura now sits unanswered on the desk. She hasn't returned to Daring since her parents died in a terrible train accident over ten years ago. I haven't seen my godchildren, Josephine and Camille, since then either—not since they were babies—which was more my choice than Laura's. What's the point of disrupting everyone's lives now?

Instead of visiting, Laura keeps me up-to-date with pictures. I see the girls growing up year by year in grinning photos—the missing teeth; the baby fat one year that's gone the next; the long and short hairstyles; the bright eyes and soft, unblemished skin of youth. An array of birthday and Christmas cards, crayon drawings, and scribbled letters has arrived over the years; Laura makes sure of that. "Dear Godmother Hana," they begin.

That makes me their god-grandmother," my mother said to me the other morning. She was standing in front of the refrigerator door holding a carton of nonfat milk in her hand, staring at the latest letters, photos, and drawings held up by colorful red, green, and blue magnets. I could see by the smile on her face that the idea pleased her.

"Guess so." I laughed.

"Sweet things," she added, tapping lightly on a photo of the girls, eleven and thirteen now, dressed as ski bunnies in Vermont over the Christmas holidays.

"They're the closest you'll ever come to grandchildren," I said, regretting the words as soon as I spoke them.

"It's close enough for me." My mother brought the carton to the table. She pushed a strand of her gray-streaked hair away from her face and poured some milk into her coffee.

"I didn't mean to sound bitchy." I sipped my orange juice slowly.

My mother laughed. "I know," she said glancing at me. "It didn't sound *too* bitchy."

"I'm not only getting old but cranky, too." I laughed.

"That makes two of us," she added.

I shook my head. "Never you," I said.

As I reached again for my glass of juice, my hand began to tremble. Quickly, I pulled it back and ran my fingers through my thin wisps of hair. Lately, the tremors have been occurring more often, and I don't want my mother to know just yet. One more thing for her to deal with, soon enough.

But, as always, my mother saved the moment. "As god-grandmother, I have a request to make," she said, then swallowed a mouthful of coffee. "Do you think Laura could give me a god-grandson?"

I looked up at her and caught her eyes, gleaming with mischief, as we both broke out in laughter.

I was sixteen when I first asked to see photos of Werner's syndrome patients, the hawklike nose, gray, thin hair, the ulcers and cataracts. I asked Dr. Truman if I could keep one of the photos and tacked it up on my bedroom wall. For weeks I said little and kept the photo to myself, studying it. I knew my parents were worried, but Miles was always there to reassure them. "Give her time. It would be a shock for anyone to see." He knew I would have to work it out on my own. One night when Cate came to say good night, I lay in bed perfectly still at first, pretending to be asleep. She lingered in the doorway and didn't say a word, simply stood there as if she were frozen in place.

She had just stepped back and was about to close my room door when I said, "The photo. That might be me in twenty years."

Cate stepped back into my room and came to my bed. "And it might not be," she answered.

I switched on the light next to my bed. "Will you still love me when I look like that?"

She watched me as if she were studying a painting. Then she leaned over to stroke my cheek and kiss me on the forehead. I had yet to have any outward signs of Werner. Then she softly said, "I'd love you if you had three eyes and a horn sticking out of your head."

Then I laughed and reached up to turn off the lamp. "Maybe I will by then."

Laura phones at least once a month. "Can I bring the girls to visit you?" she asked me again last week. "They're old enough to understand."

It suddenly comes to my mind that I've never sent a photo of myself to Laura. Since my college days, I've refused to be photographed. Once, when we were still in high school, I showed Laura the photo of the Werner's syndrome patient that I'd kept. She looked at it for a long time and said, "That'll never be you." And then she changed the subject. Thinking back, I see that it might have been easier to send her yearly Christmas photos showing her Werner's progress and how I *have* become that person in the photo—all in careful stages—the same way I've watched the girls grow up.

"I'd rather you didn't," I answered without hesitation. "I haven't been feeling too well." That's become my stock answer to her whenever she wants to come and visit. I love her like a sister and I know I'm being selfish, or afraid, or both. I wouldn't know what to say to those beautiful young girls, whose shock I can already see in their eyes as they look me over. And how would it be to see dear Laura in the prime of her life?

But this time Laura calls me on it. "Are you afraid they'll be frightened of you?" Her voice is firm and insistent.

"Wouldn't you, if you were they?"

Laura pauses, then says, "Who could ever be afraid of anyone as kind and sweet as you? Anyway, they know all about Werner, I've told them everything. And Josephine can use a good friend. She's had some tough times lately."

In her letters, Laura had hinted at Josephine's difficulties, nothing dramatic, just the angst of being a teenager, she had written.

"No wonder you're such a good attorney," I finally say.

"The best," Laura says.

"Do they know you've stolen pencils out of poor, unsuspecting Catholic schoolchildren's desks?"

Laura laughs. "I confessed it, wiped my slate clean."

"You know I love your girls," I say, suddenly feeling tired.

"More the reason you should meet them now. They're your godchildren."

For a split second, I want to give in, to see beautiful Laura, who is my oldest and dearest friend, again. I can hear the desire in her voice to see me, too, and the longing grips at me. But then my fear kicks in. We're all God's children, I want to say, but life doesn't always happen according to plan. What good would it do for the girls to see me now? It would only upset them, a woman who looks old enough to be their great-grandmother. To see them in the heart of youth would just be one more thing I'd have to leave behind. Photos and letters, an occasional drawing and card, it's all I can bear to have right now.

"Hana?" Laura says. "You there?"

"Yes, I'm here." I clear my voice. "Maybe you can bring them next month, when I'm not in this wheelchair anymore," I finally say, though I know that even Laura won't ever win this one.

CATE

Growing Up

As a little girl, Hana was filled with so much energy I worried that she'd burn herself out. The first ten years of her life were as normal as any other girl's, though she always seemed to do every-thing just a bit faster than other children. Skinny and agile, she ran faster and jumped higher; by the time she was three, she was reading words, whole sentences by four. Jumping rope and playing hopscotch and tetherball at recess bored her by the age of eight. At ten, she and Laura, who even then watched over slight Hana protectively, along with their classmates Martha and Jackie, rode their bikes up and down the street, inspired by the ads they'd seen of the movie *Easy Rider.* They were a gang of bikers, and Hana led the way. "We're making our way across America, just like Daddy did," she said when they stopped in for glasses of orange juice. On weekend sleepovers Laura and Hana immersed them-selves in Scrabble and chess games with Max coaching them.

"That's not a word," I heard Laura say one evening as they played Scrabble in the kitchen. They were at the age when they seemed to be spending more time together than apart. I wondered when something might cause a rift between them.

I waited to hear Hana's response. "Sure it is. *Arigatō* means thank you in Japanese," she said triumphantly. It was a word she'd just learned from her grandparents.

"It's not an *English* word," Laura protested.

"No one said it had to be in English." I could see from the smile on Hana's face that she had momentarily outwitted Laura.

I was just about to intervene, to say, "Hana, play fair," when Laura calmly said, "Okay then, the sky's the limit!" She paused and looked down to study her square tiles. Then one by one she lined them up on the board. *"Bonjour,* that's French for hello!" They sat back and both laughed out loud.

It was my first real glimpse into the dynamics of their friendship, how they motivated and challenged each other, how they weren't about to ever give up.

When her fifth-grade teacher called us about a small inattentiveness problem Hana was having in the classroom, Max wondered if she was bored, since everything came so easily for her, while I just held my breath. We each squeezed into one of the too-small chairs connected to desks and waited.

"I'm sorry to have to ask you to come here." Her teacher, Mrs. Aaron, smiled uncomfortably. She was an older woman with short, wiry gray hair and a solid, sturdy build. "Hana is an extremely bright girl, perhaps too bright for the rest of the class sometimes. She tends to finish her assignments way ahead of the others and then becomes bored."

Max just nodded his head as if he were agreeing with her,

then glanced over in my direction. I couldn't help thinking how all classrooms smelled alike—a musty, old books, chalk dust, worn gym clothes smell. On the black chalkboard behind Mrs. Aaron was a list of spelling words for the week—*redundant, specific, majestic* . . . I could see Hana closing her eyes and repeating each word aloud before she spelled them, one by one.

"Of course it's because Hana's so bright that she understands what takes the other children a longer time to grasp," Mrs. Aaron continued.

"Is that bad?" Max asked.

"No, of course not, Mr. Murayama." Mrs. Aaron peered down at us, as if we were children in her class. "We are considering having Hana skip a grade and wanted to see how you both felt about it."

"But then she won't be in the same school with all her friends next year," I said. "She'll have to go on to junior high ahead of them."

Mrs. Aaron straightened her back and crossed her arms in front of her chest. I imagined the kids saw this stance quite often, when she wanted to assert her authority. "Hana is small for her age, but it's not as if she would have any trouble adapting socially. I've heard you people are generally quiet and conforming," she said, looking at Max. "But Hana has a mind of her own. I'm sure she'll do fine in seventh grade."

Before I was able to say another word, Max lunged out of the desk chair and stood up. I could see the small vein pulsing in his forehead. "It's not a question of Hana's social skills, Mrs. Aaron. It's whether she'll be happy leaving her friends or not," he said, an icy reserve in his voice. "We'll think about her skipping a grade and call you."

"I didn't mean to upset you, Mr. Murayama. I just want what's best for Hana."

I stood up. Both of us were taller than Mrs. Aaron, which now gave us the advantage. "We'll call you as soon as we've come to a decision," I said. "Unless you feel my husband may be too quiet and conforming to deal with it!"

Max laughed all the way home. "I knew I married an outspoken Italian for some good reason."

The following year Hana accelerated to seventh grade at Jefferson Junior High School. After talking it over, Max and I felt the final decision was hers to make. She struggled with it for over a week, keeping to herself and talking on the phone to Laura and her other friends. She came to us one evening with her mind made up. "It's what I want to do," she told us. "I'll get to learn a foreign language and take advanced English classes."

"You're okay with leaving your friends behind?" Max asked her.

Hana shrugged. "I don't want to leave Laura, but I can still see her after school and on weekends. This way I'll be able to tell her what to expect when she gets to Jefferson."

"You know it'll be a big change," I added.

Hana hesitated, then nodded. "I think I'm ready for it."

I called up Lily and worried aloud on the phone. "What if Hana's not ready to go to junior high? What if she misses her friends too much? What if she can't keep up?" I could see Lily leaning against her kitchen counter, most likely rifling through a bowl of those red and yellow cellophane-wrapped butterscotch candies she kept there, letting me rant on.

When I finally took a breath, she made a sucking noise on her piece of candy and said, "What if she actually thrives and enjoys herself?"

I was not as ready as Hana was. She hadn't grown at all that summer and remained the same height as a seven- or eight-year-old. In elementary school, where all her friends were taller, her height had been less noticeable; she blended in with the kids from the lower grades, so she didn't seem strange or out of place. But when I dropped her off at Jefferson Junior High—a large, new redbrick building in the neighboring township of Blue Haven—it was like throwing a young lamb to the wolves. She was so much smaller than the other kids, I was afraid she'd be swallowed up. Gangly adolescents bounced around, chasing each other across the lawn, swarming like bees toward the main building.

Jefferson was the only junior high school within a twenty-five-mile radius, so students were bused in from all over. Hana's small-town safe haven with Laura and their elementary school friends was replaced overnight by all the bustle of a big city. Yet her independence surprised me, as it would so many times in the years to come. She walked straight toward the main building and never turned back. I sat in the car and quickly lost sight of her in the surging crowd, craning my neck and wishing I had walked into the building with her. I didn't drive off until I heard the anxious horn of another car waiting behind me.

Thank God, Mrs. Aaron was right about one thing; Hana had no problems making friends. She liked the variety of teachers and new classes, and no longer daydreamed through them. "I dream at night now," she said, laughing, when Max asked.

Before we knew it, new names filled the air during our dinner conversations. "Joanne loves the Beatles," or "Michelle doesn't get along with her parents," or "My English teacher, Miss Hughes, has assigned *Romeo and Juliet*." Max looked over at me and smiled. Hana's newfound happiness was a relief to us.

Still, I suspected Miles had begun to worry about why Hana wasn't growing at the same rate as other children. So far, her yearly checkups hadn't shown any abnormalities except in stature, but even though Miles never said anything, I could feel the hesitation in his voice as he declared, "All's well." But I refused to acknowledge that hint of concern. I wanted only to believe that Hana was growing up a normal young girl.

Then one afternoon Hana got off the bus in tears. "Those girls think I'm a freak," she mumbled to me when I'd finally gotten her to calm down and sit on the sofa.

"What are you talking about?" I asked.

She rubbed her eyes and blew her nose. "I heard some girls on the bus saying that I must be a midget since I'm still so short. That I'm probably not a dwarf since I'm too skinny and my legs are too long."

A quick rush of heat rose through my body. I pulled Hana close, shocked to hear my unspoken fears suddenly put into words I'd never dared to think. They knocked the breath out of me.

"Everyone grows at a different rate," I forced myself to say. "Don't listen to them. They'll soon see how much taller you are. Then they'll have to eat their words," I whispered between breaths, holding her tight and rocking her back and forth.

"Promise?" Hana asked.

"Promise," I answered, hoping that just saying the words aloud would make them come true.

When Hana was a little girl, we used to play a game called Promise. "Finish all your homework and then you can have dessert," I'd say, or "Do the dishes and then you can watch television."

"Promise?" she'd ask. "Promise," I'd answer. The promises I made to her were endless, but they never went beyond ones that I could keep. Everyday checks and balances. My daughter depended on these promises to find direction in her life, and it was my job to keep them. Now, for the first time, I'd felt uncertain. A shadow of doubt had crept into my heart, making me feel like a liar.

"When we first came to live in Daring," I told her, "all the neighbors who weren't faculty friends kept their distance, as if your father and I were contagious. But we just ignored their prejudice, pretending we hadn't noticed it. We knew our being together was right, no matter what anyone else thought. And guess what? Three months later Mrs. Cramer, a neighbor from across the street, brought us a tuna casserole, to welcome us to the neighborhood. She said folks were a little slow doing things around here, and she apologized for their bad manners. I gave her a hug because I figured if there were one Mrs. Cramer, there would be others, too.

"So you see, Hana," I said, "sometimes it takes longer for others to understand that however we look on the outside, we're all the same on the inside. One day at a time, sweetie," I told her. "Time marches on. Everything will be fine, just wait and see." Hana's beautiful dark eyes watched me, her skin still smooth as when she was a baby.

"Promise?" Hana whispered again.

This time I simply hugged her tighter.

But inside I was horrified that Hana might believe she was a freak and furious at those heartless girls, whoever they were, for being so callous. It had been ages since I'd thought back to those early days in Daring, when Max was mocked and jeered simply because he was Japanese. Fifteen years ago I walked down the street two feet away from Max and didn't dare say anything. And despite Mrs. Cramer, we didn't feel Daring was our true home until Hana was born. We had a sweet new baby, and the world was finally changing. And now it was Hana's turn to stand tall.

That was only the first of many times in the next few years that the cruelty of others would hurt her. I couldn't block all of the insults flung her way. I could only soothe her wounds with words that even I, as time went on, failed to believe.

HANA

Sticks & Stones

Lately, the memories seem to burn in the back of my mind, like flashbacks in a movie, the projector flickering in a dark room with the volume turned up. Even now on sleepless nights, the stray, hurtful words still ring out loud.

Look, here comes one of the seven dwarfs," a boy's voice cracked in the Jefferson Junior High cafeteria. I gripped my tray tighter as I passed his table.

"She's not a dwarf, stupid, she's a midget!" his buddy answered. I looked straight ahead and kept moving.

"A Ching-chong Chinaman midget!"

"I speak her language," another kid shouted. *"Moo goo guy pan!"*

They all laughed.

I remember the smell of the fried fish fillets, canned green peas, and applesauce, the roar of laughter and voices, the sudden, sharp pain in my stomach that made me want to throw up. I wanted to scream out at them that I wasn't Chinese, I was Japanese, and that they were too moronic even to know the difference, but I knew it would only provoke them more. I mumbled the words to myself, but no one could hear. Someone at another table made a farting noise, and there was more laughter. Without a word I walked quickly on, keeping my head bent low, wishing I could just disappear. Blood rushed up to my face. I set my tray on a chair and kept walking until I was outside the hot, smelly cafeteria, until the voices died away and I could take gasping breaths of fresh air, my heart pounding. "It's okay, okay, okay."

The next morning, instead of my taking the bus, my father drove out of his way to drop me off at Jefferson. He said he had to pick up some papers, but I knew my mom must have told him about the bus incident. When he pulled up in front of the school, he said, "Have a good day, kiddo." He leaned over and kissed me on my forehead, then added, "Don't ever be afraid to be yourself." His eyes were dark and knowing. His words meant everything to me because he knew what it was like to be singled out from the rest. Instead of jumping out of the car, I turned back to him and blurted out in a tearful voice, "They think I'm strange here because I'm so short and I'm part Japanese."

Max's hands rested on the steering wheel. "I'm sorry, Hana," he said, shaking his head slowly. "When will people learn?" he muttered softly to himself. Then he looked at me and asked, "What does your height and the fact that you're part Japanese have to do with who you are?" I could smell his sweet shaving cologne, see his dark tie rise and fall with each slow and steady breath.

"It's what they see," I answered. Some boys had paused on the sidewalk by us, looking at my dad's Thunderbird. I didn't want to leave the car and gripped the door handle tightly, hoping to keep the rest of the world out.

"What do you see when you look in the mirror?" Max suddenly asked, leaning closer to me. "*You*," he said again, his voice smooth and calm.

I stopped and didn't know what to say. At twelve years old, I saw a small, round-faced girl with long, black hair and dark eyes, who just wanted to be liked, even if I did look different from everyone else.

He gave my hand a quick squeeze, and for that moment I felt safe in the Thunderbird with him. "I see an intelligent, lively girl," he said. "They'll miss out, Hana, because they don't know any better. All that really matters is what the people who love you think. And, most important, what you think about yourself."

Then Max smiled and leaned over to kiss me again on the forehead. All morning, I tried hard to hold on to his quiet, thoughtful voice.

Sticks and stones will break my bones, but words will never hurt me." How many times did I whisper that children's verse to myself, rather than let those kids know how hurt I was by their ridicule and taunts? In a manner of speaking, I grew up at Jefferson Junior High School. I learned that, as much as I felt like just another kid, I wasn't. I was too small and looked too Japanese in a world where difference invited ridicule. I was reminded every now and then by boys and girls who didn't even know me. If that was a lesson in growing up, I should be ten feet tall now. It wasn't as if I didn't have any friends. There was always Laura, but she was still back in sixth grade at Daring Elementary. And Michelle, in my English and history classes, who got along with everybody. I didn't want to distress my parents more than I already had. But I was always a target for those kids who picked on anyone who was the slightest bit different.

It wasn't just me but all the others like me, all the kids who didn't quite fit in. We were like castaways on a desert island, learning early on to fend for ourselves, even if it meant that some of us were alone much of the time. There was a girl in a few of my classes who didn't have it much easier than I did, but for very different reasons. Her name was Sheila Wells, and she was tall and stout with large features and a bad complexion. Almost immediately after she moved to Blue Haven and attended Jefferson, I somehow became less visible. It was a sense of freedom that I rejoiced in.

But I felt bad for Sheila when I saw just how alike we were, how she kept her head bowed low to avoid eye contact with anyone else, hoping to will herself invisible as she walked down the drab, gray halls or through the crowded cafeteria. I could feel that same fear emanating from her, the silent words she chanted under her breath, *"Please leave me alone."*

And still I didn't befriend her, despite knowing that she was intelligent and well-read. During lunch she sat off in a corner, eating and reading alone. I was afraid if I were seen talking to her that the jeers would get worse. Two misfits together would give them too much ammunition. It wasn't until I saw her one hot, muggy Saturday afternoon walking by our house that I first spoke to her.

"Hi, Sheila." I raised my voice across the yard. It must have startled her, because she looked over at me wide-eyed, as if I was speaking a foreign language.

She hesitantly lifted her hand to wave, and I think I heard her say "Hello," but a passing car drowned out her voice.

I walked over to her, only to realize how ridiculous we must look together. At thirteen she was heavyset and already five foot eight, while I was a full foot shorter.

"Where are you going?" I asked.

She looked down at me. "To the library. To return these books." She tapped the black cloth bag that she always carried with her.

"Anything you'd recommend?"

She opened her bag and took out one of the books. "It's called *Death Be Not Proud* by John Gunther."

"What's it about?"

"It's a father's memoir of his son who's dying of a brain tumor."

"Sounds sad," I said.

Sheila nodded. "Yeah, it is. But it's also about his son's courage and humor in facing his death. So I guess it's about living, not just dying."

"Well, maybe I'll read it sometime."

Sheila smiled. "You'll like it, even if it does make you cry at the end."

She had a nice smile, something no one at Jefferson would ever take the time to notice. We stood awkwardly in the warm sun for a moment in silence, our smiles slowly fading. My shirt clung to my sweaty back as I watched Sheila walk down the block. I almost wanted to follow and say something else to her.

Back at school on Monday we were like strangers again. From the corner of my eye I saw Sheila approaching me, carrying a book in her hand, but I turned away quickly, as if to say, "Stop, go away!" She did. To this day I haven't forgotten how terrible I felt to have betrayed her, shying away from what might have become a good friendship.

In the end, I was no better than those boys in the cafeteria.

JOSEPHINE

In Name Only

My name is Josephine, which means "God shall add." I'm not sure what will be added, so I look up the masculine equivalent, Joseph, to see that it says, "God shall add a son." Both are less than inspiring. Lately, I've been fascinated with the meaning of names and places—the long and varied history that comes with each one. It sets people apart and gives them their individuality. I began studying the etymology of names a few weeks ago, though it may seem strange to other thirteen-year-old girls. During my lunch period, I whip out a book and start discussing the names of our classmates with my friend Annie. "Did you know that Robert means 'bright or famous,' " I say, choosing to unravel the mysteries of the most popular boy in our school. It makes perfect sense, how you can see this faint glow of light always surrounding him.

Annie makes a sighing sound like she doesn't know what to

do with me. "They'll think you're even weirder than you really are," she says, glancing over to a group of popular kids.

"Thanks a lot," I say, knowing that Annie is really the one who fits into the weird category. She's so superstitious that she keeps an acorn in her pocket wherever she goes, explaining it brings good luck and ensures a long life. And she even went so far as to tell me that if you take a test with the same pencil you studied with, that pencil will remember the answers. As far as I know, it hasn't worked for either of us.

My younger sister, Camille, can't understand why I'll spend hours reading everything from baby name books to history books searching for meanings and connections. It's a hobby of mine, I tell her. She looks at me and rolls her eyes. But I still let her know that Camille means "unblemished," like her smooth, fair skin and straight blond hair. She's beautiful and takes after my mother.

I'm tall and skinny, with skin that keeps breaking out with angry patches of pimples that I can't help but pick at and, to top it off, I've just gotten braces to correct an overbite. My mother calls it the "awkward stage" that everyone goes through, but I bet it's a stage she skipped. I have my father's darker coloring and his chestnut-colored, wavy hair, which I usually tie back into a pony-tail so it's out of my way.

Instead, I've decided to identify my name with another story. I like to tell people that I'm named after Napoleon's wife, the empress Josephine, who also had dark, wavy hair, because it gives me an immediate sense of history, one much more romantic and exciting than my own. When it became apparent that Empress Josephine couldn't give Napoleon an heir to the throne, he divorced her and married Marie Louise of Austria, but not before buying Josephine Malmaison, a small estate near Paris. She lived there for the rest of her life, always trusting Napoleon and never doubting his love for her. When his heir was born, Napoleon brought his new son to Malmaison for Josephine to see. After all, she understood he needed a son to take over his empire. Napoleon had had no other choice but to divorce her, so she never stopped loving him, even begging to go into exile with him on the island of Elba, only to die before she received his response.

My parents, Laura and John, have Camille and me, but we weren't enough to keep them together. I wonder if it would have been different if one of us were a son—an heir to the empire. My dad moved out and lives in an apartment a few blocks from us now. If I'd really paid attention, I guess I would have seen it coming. Even when he was still living at home, they hardly saw each other. As a stockbroker, my dad always left the house very early, while my mom, more often than not, worked until very late at her law office. Somewhere along the line, they stopped long enough to look, only they didn't recognize each other anymore.

"Where did Daddy go?" Camille asked the first night he was gone, almost nine months ago. She came into my room and looked young and scared.

We're different, Camille and I, soft and hard, day and night. At least that's the way people see us. I'll readily admit, she accepts things at face value much easier. I tend to question more, probe beneath the surface before I can feel really comfortable with people or new situations. I thought I didn't feel anything after my dad left; after all, he lives within walking distance. But I began to miss the small, inconsequential, everyday things I never really paid attention to before—the low timbre of his laugh, how he was always checking to see if his tie was straight, and even the annoying way he pulled on my ponytail to get my attention. These are the things that have changed the most, even with weekend visits.

I felt a sudden sisterly love and put my arm around Camille. "They're taking a break from each other." I repeated the words I'd heard them say.

"So you think he's coming back?" she asked. Her blue eyes widened, and I could see she was anxious, just by the way her fingers played with a strand of her blond hair.

I shrugged. "Maybe," I said. But deep down I knew he wasn't coming back. Unlike Napoleon, who still had feelings for Josephine, my parents are like two strangers who move quickly and silently around each other.

Since my dad moved out, my mom's been acting kind of strange. For the past few months, all she's been talking about is taking us back to visit our godmother Hana in the Northern California town where she grew up. Camille and I have heard about Hana ever since we were little. Hana this and Hana that. You'll love Hana, my mother always says. There's a photo of them together when they were girls, around fourteen, not much older than I am, but it looks as if Laura's standing next to a much younger girl because of their height difference. Still, if you stare into Hana's eyes long enough, as I have done, you'll see that she's much older and wiser than she appears.

Later, when we're sitting in the living room, I look up the name Hana, but find only Hannah, meaning "grace" or "the mother of Samuel," the prophet from the Old Testament. I can only imagine all the stories attached to it.

"Hana means 'flower' in Japanese," Laura says, when I question the spelling of her name. I'm immediately taken by the idea that a name can also mean something else in another language.

I flip through the book and find my mother's name again. Laura means 'laurel,' which is a wreath or crown. There's no need to look any further for a more inspiring meaning, since it's a name that suits her just fine.

A few years ago, Mom carefully explained to us that Hana had some kind of disease that makes her body grow physically old, even though she really isn't. My dad was in the living room, watching the news. We were in the kitchen setting the table, and it was a rare night when Mom was home from the office early.

"How much older?" I asked.

She pulled out an onion from the refrigerator. "Twice as fast as the normal rate."

"How did she get the disease?" Camille asked, placing a blue napkin at each plate.

"It's genetic," she said, slicing an onion. "It's a gene that she was born with."

"When did she start looking old?" I asked, pouring milk into our glasses.

Mom turned around, the knife in her hand. "The first symptoms began in her twenties."

"That must be strange," Camille said, "knowing someone who's going to suddenly grow old before your eyes. I wonder what she looks like now."

"I haven't seen Hana in a long time," Mom suddenly said, dropping the onions into the frying pan. They sizzled and filled the kitchen with a sharp aroma I always liked.

"Why not?" I asked.

Mom paused a moment and didn't answer. Then she turned from the stove and said, "You were babies and it was hard to travel." Then, realizing we haven't been babies for quite a while, she added, "Then my work seemed to dominate everything. And there were times when Hana wasn't feeling too well."

"She must look really old now," I added, putting the milk back into the refrigerator.

"Yeah," Camille echoed.

Mom nodded her head. When she turned back to us, her eyes were moist and red, which she blamed on the onions.

CATE

The Thunderbird

There are defining moments in my life that have changed me forever, when I knew nothing afterward would ever be the same. In addition to marriage, birth, and death, the *big three,* there were unexpected events when even the air around me changed and I had to learn how to breathe all over again.

At first, the thought of my healthy child having something wrong with her was so outrageous I was sure the doctors had made a terrible mistake. How could God pull such a cruel joke? Max and I barely slept the night after leaving the doctor's office. "We need to run more tests," the doctor said. What did that mean? I asked. And what was this Werner's syndrome the doctor mentioned? Our San Francisco hotel room suddenly seemed small and suffocating. We lay apart from each other in bed, listening to the soft breaths from Hana's cot on the other side of the room. It seemed as if she were breathing for all of us.

The next day, we drove back to Daring. I kept glancing into the backseat at my bright and happy girl, wondering how this could be God's will. How he could have finally given us Hana, only to take away her chance for a happy life of her own. It was too unfair. Max stared straight ahead, as if the road had pulled him into some kind of trance. Halfway home, when we finally stopped at a rest area to use the bathroom, Max spoke for the first time since the three-hour drive began. "Who wants something to drink?" A weak smile formed on his lips.

"I do," Hana piped up. "A Coke?" She looked at me for approval.

"A Coke it is," Max said before I'd even had a chance to answer. He pushed the car door open.

"It will spoil her dinner," I said automatically.

For the first time in our entire seventeen years of marriage, Max shot me a look that glimmered with pure resentment. "Does it really matter?"

I felt as if he'd struck me. Of course it matters, I thought, but the words lay flat and heavy in my throat. I wondered if he could possibly blame me for Hana's illness. I leaned over to touch his sleeve, but he got out of the car before I could reach him. Even now, so many years after that initial shock, I wince at the distance that pooled between us that afternoon. For weeks after, the closer I tried to move toward Max, the farther he withdrew.

Soon we were feeling the burden of rising medical bills. Hana needed a barrage of blood tests and X rays that took us to San Francisco three times that first month. And while our insurance covered certain areas, most of the genetic testing was too new and experimental to be included.

For two months we hid the fact that there might be something wrong with her, reluctant to disturb her life; after all, she was only thirteen and still seemingly healthy. When Hana began questioning all the tests she had to take, I remember saying to Max, "We can't hide it from her anymore."

"What's wrong with me?" she asked. "Why is Dad always so sad?"

"They're just taking some blood tests to make sure everything's all right. Your checkup showed some abnormalities, and they just want to be thorough," I soothed her.

But we hid the truth from ourselves as well, hoping she would prove the doctors wrong and grow into a strong young woman. Max and I had to lie, so that we could face Hana and not break into tears, and so that we didn't have to feel so sorry for ourselves. Some nights I prayed to God that it was all a mistake, while on other nights I couldn't pray at all.

When the bills started coming in, I picked up more substitute teaching jobs; Max taught an extra class and worked longer hours at the college tutorial center, then came home exhausted. Most nights we were too tired to talk, or even to grieve, and we both simply fell into a heavy, druglike sleep.

It took Hana finally to say the words I'd held back. Halfway through the third month after all her tests, she and Max were in the living room late one afternoon when I heard her suddenly ask him, "Are you mad at me?" I stood at the kitchen doorway and listened, heard the rustling of the newspaper as he lowered it and looked up at her. Even with his back to me, I could imagine the worry lines deepening across his forehead as his eyes widened.

"Of course not," he answered softly.

"You're always unhappy." Hana's voice grew stronger. "Is it because of all the tests I have to take? I can stop."

Max cleared his throat. "You haven't done anything," he answered. "I've just been working too hard."

"Are you mad at Mom?"

"No."

"Well, you're mad about something."

I knew Hana was not about to let it go until she received some kind of answer. For a long moment, neither of them said anything. Then Max folded the paper and stood up. "Come on, let's go for a drive."

From the time she was a little girl, Hana loved it when Max drove her around in the Thunderbird with the top down. She'd wave to neighbors and strangers alike, or hold her arms up high above her head, daring the wind to blow her away.

"Mom, we'll be back by dinner," Hana yelled as the door banged shut behind them.

When they returned from their drive that evening, Max had answered all her questions. "I told her something may be wrong," he said, when they walked in, not looking me in the eye. Hana appeared pale and shaken.

I turned from her to glare at Max. "How dare you?" I snapped. "How dare you tell her without me!" I wanted to slap him for his silence, for betraying me by not allowing me to be there and hold my daughter against all her fears. It was a decision both of us should have made.

But Hana stepped between us and hugged me tightly, her fragile body trembling against mine. "It was me, Mom. I made him tell me."

What's wrong with me?" she asked that night in tears.

"The doctors aren't sure yet," I answered, deciding then and there that I would never keep anything from her again. "They thought it might be a problem with your pituitary or thyroid gland or something called Turner's syndrome, but the tests have returned negative. They also suspect a disease called Werner's syndrome."

"What's that?"

"It affects your aging and growing process."

"Will I die soon?" Her voice strained. "Because I don't want to die."

I sat on Hana's bed holding her, trying to give her answers I didn't know myself. I took a deep breath, trying to be calm, my throat dry from my own fear. "No, you won't die soon," I soothed. "The doctors aren't even certain it's Werner's syndrome. You'll still have plenty of years ahead of you."

"How many?" Hana pulled away from me, her dark eyes wide with fear. "I want to know how many."

I shook my head and felt frantic inside. I had no idea. "I'm not sure, the doctors will have to tell us that."

"I want to know," Hana said again. She had Max's strong will and determination.

"Years and years," I said, hating God at that moment but pleading with him anyway. *Please, God, at least twenty or thirty years. You have to give her that long.*

"How many?" Hana persisted.

"Thirty years," I guessed. It was a foolish thing to say when I couldn't know. My face flushed with the lie, and I felt a swell of anger rise up inside—anger at myself for having lied, with Max for putting me in such a position and, most of all, anger at God, who had abandoned us.

I could feel Hana's body shiver in my arms, then slowly calm. At thirteen, she must have felt as if thirty years was a lifetime away. It was, after all, a small piece of hope for her as well as for me. She relaxed in my arms then, until her breathing slowed and I knew she was asleep.

That same night, moments after we'd turned out our lights, Max whispered, "Maybe the doctors are wrong. Maybe Hana's fine." We lay in bed without touching, as we had ever since we returned from San Francisco three months before.

My wordless groan told him I believed otherwise.

"I'm sorry I've been acting like a jerk," he added, his voice breaking.

"You have been." I turned and looked for him in the darkness.

He breathed in and out heavily, as if struggling for air. "She seems so normal."

"And it's up to us to make sure her life stays as normal as possible." I'd been telling myself this every day as I stood at the kitchen window watching Hana outside with the neighbors' kids. She didn't look so different, maybe smaller, but all kids take their own time growing. She was still bright, funny, and apparently healthy.

"Yes," Max answered, a calm returning to his voice.

"I need to know that you can do that, because if you can't . . ." My voice trailed off. It was an ultimatum I never thought I'd deliver.

"I can," he whispered in the darkness.

I took a deep breath so I wouldn't cry. I could tell Max was watching me now, straining in the dark for the familiar. Then I felt his body inch toward me, closing the space that had separated us, his warm hands reaching out for me.

Two weeks later, Max left for work in the Thunderbird very early in the morning and returned that evening at the wheel of a green Ford sedan.

"I was able to get a very good price for the Bird from a guy who came up from San Francisco," he said. "It'll help with the bills."

"Oh, Max," I said, trying to hold back tears.

He smiled tiredly. "It's time to grow up."

"What will we tell Hana?" She loved the Thunderbird as much as Max did.

"That we needed a bigger car." He ran his fingers through his hair and sighed.

It wasn't a lie. I thought of the many times I had cursed that car as I tried to get groceries out of the narrow backseat or tied another scarf around my hair when the top was down. But I loved the Thunderbird because it was so intricately tied to Max and his sense of freedom. I loved the Thunderbird because it had brought Max to Waterford, Maine, that day so many years ago. I didn't say another word, just hugged him tightly until he pulled away. "I think I'll lie down for a while before dinner," he said. The sudden loss of his warmth left me feeling desolate. I watched as he walked out of the kitchen and upstairs to our room, the door clicking shut behind him.

We'd turned the page on our fairy tale. From that day on, we were in the fight together. To me, and to Hana, even without his gleaming black-and-white Thunderbird, Max was still a prince.

HANA

The American Dream

I roam from room to room in my wheelchair. I'm not sure what it is that suddenly reminds me of the photograph of the Thunderbird, but it's imperative that I find it, like a thirst that demands water. The wheelchair becomes a nuisance when it refuses to turn, or is too wide to enter narrow spaces. I can't believe that wheelchair-bound TV detective played by Raymond Burr on *Ironside* could ever have solved a case without his sidekicks doing all the legwork. But then I think again—*he* was the one who solved all the cases.

When I look back, I see that Werner became real for me the day my father sold his Thunderbird. Before then, I knew only that I had something wrong but no one seemed to have the answer. Werner was just one test after another, and for a long time it was a mystery disease that—except for my short stature—I had yet to feel or see.

"Tell me more about Werner's syndrome," I asked Dr. Truman six months after seeing the doctors in San Francisco. All the other tests I'd taken had returned negative by then. Cate wanted everything out in the open, for which I've always been grateful. No more surprises. She had stepped outside, and he and I remained in his office alone. Unlike his examining rooms, which were always so antiseptic, his office was as comfortable as someone's living room.

"If it *is* Werner's syndrome, you may not see obvious signs of the disease until you're in your twenties. There have been varying cases," Dr. Truman explained. He sat down in the leather chair next to me and straightened his tie. "Then it may first appear subtly in the way you look, your hair turning gray, the skin on your face changing."

"I'll get old?" I asked, matter-of-factly, as if it were all happening to someone else.

"You'll begin to age." Dr. Truman cleared his throat.

"But not right now?" I asked.

"No, there won't be any outward signs for another ten years or so."

"And then I'll die?"

Dr. Truman's eyes widened at my question, and he shook his head. I could see flecks of gray in his hair. "The aging process isn't that fast, Hana. You'll have many years after that."

"Do you think it's Werner's syndrome?" I asked.

Dr. Truman hesitated. "We can't be sure yet," he answered.

"How many years?" It was becoming my new chant in life.

Dr. Truman hesitated again. "If you take good care and we monitor everything regularly, a good thirty years or more," he finally answered.

Only then did I take a deep breath, my knuckles white from grasping the arms of the chair I sat in, relieved that what my mother had told me was true.

As the days passed, Werner became more of a looming mystery. Not until my twenties would I suddenly and rapidly begin to age, and that seemed very far away. While my parents anguished, I was more frightened by the way they were acting than by the disease itself.

I'll never forget that evening when Max came home without the Thunderbird. Even as I heard him saying, "We need a bigger car now that you're growing up," I felt as if I'd ruined everything. I tried hard not to cry in front of him and, rather than upset him more, I ran out to the garage, where my tears flowed freely. That ugly, green sedan was the direct result of my being sick. I knew he had sold the Thunderbird to help pay for all the tests I was taking. And that made me feel much worse than the disease itself.

"I hate you, I hate you, I hate you!" I remember yelling at the car, kicking it over and over, and slapping the hood until my hand stung and reddened.

From the moment I understood how much the Thunderbird meant to Max, I had treasured it, too. Not that I wouldn't have appreciated it on my own, but you do that for the people you love, learn to enjoy what they enjoy. I can still feel the wind in my hair as we drove down the street. When he was behind the wheel of that car, my father was somebody else, someone who cherished the freedom it gave him to go anywhere he pleased. And I've never been able to forgive myself for taking that freedom away from him again. First Heart Mountain, and then me.

Cate keeps most of the older family albums in the hall closet, neatly stacked on the second shelf, just within reach. I begin at the top and work my way down the pile, all the vibrant red, green, and orange colors of Life Savers. The photo I'm looking for was taken over thirty years ago, and with each page I turn, I keep hoping it will suddenly appear. What I do find are scalloped-edged black-and-white photos of Cate and Max, so young and carefree I can hardly recognize them. There are also photos of my grand-parents when they were young, my grandfather Louis when he arrived from Italy as a boy, my grandmother Midori in a kimono at the Los Angeles Cherry Blossom Festival, each a bit of history frozen in time.

But the photo I'm looking for isn't there. I stack the albums neatly back on the shelf and close the closet door. When I straighten up, my head spins and a flush of heat suddenly charges through my body, as if someone has filled my veins with warm water. I lean back in my chair, dizzy, and don't know if I should yell for Cate. I imagine her rushing in from her gardening, laying her ungloved hand on my forehead, feeling the heat of a raging fever. But just as quickly, the warmth subsides. I'm relieved I didn't call out and make a scene over what must just be another side effect of the pills I'm taking, to be cataloged along with the irreg-ular heartbeat, loss of appetite, dizziness, the muscle spasms and rashes. There's a slight twinge in my stomach, too, a reminder of the ulcer I had a few years ago. If Werner doesn't kill me, I'm sure all the pills I'm ingesting soon will.

The last place I look is Max's study, in his desk, where Cate sits to pay the bills at the end of each month. I push myself over, pull open the bottom drawer, and it's there that I'm surprised to find a beige-colored album among my father's things. I flip quickly through it; the photo I'm looking for is on the third page. It was taken with Max's new Polaroid camera, which endlessly intrigued me as a girl. After he peeled back the outer strip, I sat stone still and watched the picture materialize little by little, like a bit of magic before my eyes.

Only now, as I stare at the photo, all the colors have faded and we appear pale in the bleached background. But there we are, me six years old, sitting beside my smiling father in his beautiful Thunderbird, waving for the camera. He was young and happy, and enjoying the American Dream.

CATE

In the Garden

For most of the morning Hana has been sitting by the window watching me as I work in the garden. I wave and we exchange smiles but she remains there, my small, birdlike creature framed in the large picture window. There's a concentrated expression on her face, as if she's trying to memorize everything she sees. I know she's unsettled this morning and hasn't been sleeping well, even if she doesn't say a word. I can see it in her eyes. After lunch I'll insist we go to the park for a walk, no matter how much she fights me. She hasn't left the house for a week. Today I won't take no for an answer.

Two years ago we went walking along some rougher terrain on a hillside behind the house that Hana could see from her window. "Let's climb up there," she had suggested. I looked out the window to see the hillside ablaze with wildflowers. Against my better judgment I agreed, hoping for a moment of normality. The sharp, sudden animal cry of pain Hana gave as she tripped and collapsed on the ground still haunts me. She lay there in excruciating pain with what we later found out was a broken hip caused by osteoporosis. Dear God, how could I have been such an idiot to let her talk me into taking that walk? What was I thinking as I ran to the nearest house for help? That it takes so little to lose someone you love. That all the years it takes to nurture and learn and grow can end without a moment's notice. That a simple misstep could break bones or stop a heart from beating.

I realized that day as the ambulance carried us to the hospital that I'd learned to alleviate all the minor physical symptoms—the sores, the swelling, the unexpected fevers. What there weren't directions for was how to carry the emotional burden. On good days like today, I can remove myself just long enough to grasp the fact that I'm one of the few mothers who will see her own child grow to old age. I share that burden with her and have to summon up all my strength to make Hana's days as comfortable as possible. On my more frequent bad days, I can't help but curse a God who would have a child grow old and die before her mother.

All the dreams that are lost for Hana settle in my heart like a dead weight. Sometimes at the park I see such sadness in Hana's eyes when she watches a young mother playing with her child, and I can barely contain my own grief. This is coupled with the guilt, and the understanding that much of my grief is for myself, for all the joys that will never be part of my life.

A rush of cool wind whispers against the back of my neck. I push my trowel into the cool earth, bringing up another scoop of dirt that quickly grows into a small mound around the hole I'm digging. In the garden I feel most comforted, most in control, though Mother Nature has a mind of her own. It's something I've learned to live with; a healthy tree suddenly withers and dies, while a small blossom pushes its way out of a crack in a concrete sidewalk.

"The earth can be a most fickle mistress," Max's father once told me. We were walking past one of his greenhouses and he pointed to an area outside where he was trying to grow tomatoes and summer squash. "I can make flowers blossom, but vegetables refuse to grow for me." He laughed and shook his head, as if surprised every time he told someone about it. While my father was always too busy to garden, and rarely set foot in our small Boston backyard, Henry Murayama saw life come from the earth and he never failed to be amazed by it.

"Look," he said, in his quiet, measured way. He pointed to the rows and rows of white and yellow chrysanthemums that filled his greenhouses. "Life."

Every spring I watch for each new bud as if my own life depended on it. The return of this brief beauty brings me fresh hope. In my garden, I leave problems behind and step into a world governed by seasons. Here, I face the persistence of birth, life, and death. I look up, and a choir of robins and cedar waxwings warbles around me, fluttering from tree to tree. I look down, digging and scooping with a rhythm that warms me through. I pat the last trowel of dirt down smoothly, the surprise underneath covered with dark, rich earth. I dig another hole, and another, planting each with different bulbs of dahlia, calla and day lilies.

"Hello there." A sharp greeting interrupts my thoughts.

I turn around to see old Hank Greenwald walking his dog. "Hi, Hank. Have to get these bulbs in before lunch."

"Hana okay?" he asks.

"She's fine," I say, adding a quick wave before turning back to my work.

Hank shuffles for a moment at the edge of our front lawn, then finally mumbles good-bye and walks on with Taco, his Chihuahua. Hank has known Hana since she was a little girl. When she came back from college and was finally diagnosed with Werner's, he took it upon himself to inform neighbors of her good and bad days. I no longer mind as I used to, when everything was so raw. Now I'm grateful he saves me the effort of having to explain Hana's illness. I usually tell him just enough to satisfy his curiosity. But a conversation with Hank might last a good half hour, and I just don't have the energy this morning.

I hear the birds rustling under the photinia shrubs, staking their claim on a dry, sheltered spot. Overnight, new buds have sprouted into green leaves, while others blaze red like flames from the shrubs. Digging deep into the cool, damp earth has always brought me a calm I wish I could share with Hana, but she never took to gardening. Like Max, she never had the patience to wait for a shoot to sprout from the ground. Hana prefers instant gratification, and who can blame her? A bouquet from the florist reminds her at once of the happy summers she spent with her grandparents on their flower farm.

The first time Hana went to the flower market with them, she returned and told me excitedly, "You have to go next time, Mom. It smells like every kind of flower in the whole world!"

"And what does that smell like?" Midori had asked her, a pleased grin forming on her lips.

Hana thought for a moment and sipped her juice. "Like God's garden."

I shake my head now and smile at the thought. When I glance up again, Hana's no longer by the window.

HANA

Another History

To the right of our front porch steps is the flag holder my father put up when I was just a little girl. Every once in a while, it catches my eye as I look out the window, and I can't help but smile. Every Fourth of July, Max went to the garage, unfurled the flag he kept neatly wrapped in a plastic bag, and placed it in the holder. I loved the way the flag sounded as it fluttered in the wind—the dull slapping of air that reminded me of a balloon bumping against the spokes of a bicycle.

Max was always so proud to be an American, despite what happened to his family during the war. When I was twelve, he began to tell me about the Heart Mountain internment camp, at first saying only that he'd been too young to feel the full effects of his imprisonment. "Not like your grandmother and grandfather," he had said. "It was more difficult for them. The past isn't something they like to speak of. For them, it's best forgotten." He said this to me without anger or sternness in his voice, but I knew instantly that it was a subject I shouldn't bring up with them.

I loved visiting my grandparents and their flower farm in Pasadena, where I enjoyed hours of entertainment as I roamed up and down the aisles of the humid glass greenhouses. I never told Max that my grandmother Midori had already told me about Heart Mountain, that the years she spent there were like a bad dream.

It was the summer I was nine years old. I had gotten up before dawn to go to the flower market with my grandparents for the first time. The air still smelled of night, a smoky richness of damp soil, when my grandfather Henry loaded his brilliant, long-stemmed yellow and white chrysanthemums into the bed of the truck. We sat three abreast, driving down the dark, quiet streets while most of Los Angeles still slept. Even my parents were back at the house sleeping.

My grandmother poured coffee from a thermos and handed it across to my grandfather.

"Hot," she said.

My grandfather nodded and sipped from the cup, steering with one hand down the freeway he'd driven three times a week for almost fifty years.

"Good," he replied.

I noticed how they spoke in a secret code of quick one-syllable words and simple gestures. From another thermos she poured me a half cup of hot chocolate.

"Careful," she said to me with a smile. I held its warmth between my hands and drank cautiously so I wouldn't spill. Tasting chocolate and the sweetness of sugar on my tongue, I was wide awake in the dark.

The flower market was a long, open building where growers had their own stalls and sold their goods to the retail florists and flower stands all over Los Angeles. It glowed with life in the shadowy early morning light. My grandfather was well known for his chrysanthemums and could easily have had orders sent out from the farm, but he made the early morning trips himself to maintain the sense of community he had established long years before. Many of the growers were Japanese, their businesses handed down from one generation to the next. My grandparents greeted them all as we carried green plastic buckets filled with flowers to our stall. It was like stepping into another, more exotic world. "*Ohay-ōgozaimasu,*" good morning, rang out in Japanese, followed by a string of words that sounded like music to me. The vibrant red, yellow, and purple of the irises, lilies, and snapdragons blazed in the hazy white lights. I breathed in the sweet, pungent fragrances of gardenias and lilacs that perfumed the air and made me dizzy. My grandfather hurried ahead of us, eager to get on with his business, but my grandmother lingered with friends at several stalls, bright and talkative in the early morning.

"This is my granddaughter Hana." She introduced me as we passed by.

"Max's daughter?" a woman asked, clipping the ends of long stemmed carnations.

"Yes."

"*Kirei.*"

My grandmother bowed quickly. "She says you're pretty," she whispered to me.

"Do you know everyone here?" I asked.

"Many of us were at Heart Mountain camp together. We know each other very well, good points as well as bad points." My grandmother laughed quickly before turning thoughtful and serious again. "When you live through such a shameful time, you must find a way to survive. We had only each other."

I remember nodding, not really understanding what Heart Mountain meant at the time. I knew it was a place my father and his family had gone to when he was a boy. I was just happy being with my grandparents in that big room filled with so many sounds and scents, seeing them move confidently through a world that obviously belonged to them.

JOSEPHINE

Life Lessons

Today in third period history, our teacher, Mrs. Keller, began discussing a new unit on the Japanese internment camps. I still can't understand how we could have internment camps here in America. "Can you believe what our government is capable of?" I whisper to Annie, sitting next to me. She looks at me quickly with her don't-bother-me-now gaze and stares attentively toward the front of the classroom. Annie has her heart set on going to Yale or Stanford, and nothing is going to stop her. Sometimes I wish I had her direction. Mrs. Keller is saying something about a camp called Manzanar, the full, round sound of its name pulling my gaze back toward the front of the room. All the while, I can't help wondering what the name means.

———

During lunch, Robert of the "bright light" fame actually nods to me on his way back from the milk line. I watch him walk toward the group of popular kids he hangs out with as they clear a place for him to sit at their table.

"Don't even think you could be part of his group," Annie says. "They don't pay attention to people like us."

I want to say, speak for yourself, but I know that she's just repeating what I already know. Annie and I will always be on the sidelines, watching from the outside, the last chosen to be on any team.

"Just wait until we're grown-ups," Annie says. "We'll show them!"

"Yeah," I say, raising my voice with confidence, but all I really know is that I haven't a clue how I'm going to get any farther than where I am.

When I get home, I look up the word *manzanar*, which is Spanish for "apple orchard." It's funny how one thought connects to another and triggers something else. I try to picture what it must have been like—fruit once blossoming where there were only rows of colorless barracks waiting to greet all the uprooted Japanese Americans. I close my eyes and try to imagine a ghost wind carrying a sweet cider scent across the camp, reminding them that there was once life there.

CATE

Drunken Birds

I hear a quick rustling of leaves and look up from my digging just in time to see the robins and cedar waxwings flying toward our neighbor's pyracantha bush. Its branches bounce under their weight, the pungent clusters of blossoms quiver, filling my heart with dread. We had a pyracantha in our backyard, its branches laden with berries the autumn Hana turned eleven years old. It was unusually cold that year, and the berries clung longer than usual, fermenting on the branches. The birds flocked to them and became so drunk on the berries that they swooped and dived like kamikaze pilots, straight into the plate-glass window overlooking our deck. It was like a scene out of the Hitchcock movie *The Birds.*

Life and death lessons come to us at the most unexpected times. This was Hana's first experience with death, and we were both unprepared for it. I was in the kitchen when the first bird slammed against the glass like those sand-filled bags thrown against our window when Max and I first moved to Daring. A chill traveled through my body as I remembered our helplessness.

Hana raced downstairs and went out the back door. "Wait!" I yelled at her, but she was already gone. For a split second I was angry with her for not listening. I ran after her, my heart racing, only to see her squatting on the deck, holding the small brown body of a robin, its black bead eyes staring up toward the sky.

We striped the window with masking tape in an effort to divert them, but it didn't work. In the course of that day, four robins and one cedar waxwing broke their necks with hard, flat crashes of their small skulls against the window. Hana watched as their bodies convulsed after impact—thin, dark lines of blood trickling from their beaks as they quivered and fell still. Unafraid, she gently cradled them in her hands, as if she could will them back to life, or at least provide them with a last bit of comfort.

"Why are they doing this?" she asked, her voice tight with anguish.

"It's like drunk driving," I said. "The birds eat the fermented berries and become too disoriented. They see their reflection in the glass and think it's the sky."

We went back inside and spoke in hushed tones and waited with a kind of dread, wondering if it would happen again. Then Hana began to cry, slow tears flowing freely down her cheeks. "What will their families think when the dead birds never return home?"

I shook my head. "I don't know."

Just then we heard another loud impact and the window's reverberation. "Dear God," I whispered.

"What kind of God would let this keep happening?" Hana said, her voice strained. "I hate a God that would do this." She jumped up and rushed out the door to the back deck.

I stood up but couldn't move. It's all part of God's greater plan, I suddenly heard my mother say. It was what she always said when she didn't really have any answer to a question I asked.

We buried five birds in one afternoon. One other bird had just knocked itself silly and survived. It stood motionless for the longest time, its head bent forward as if it had fallen asleep standing up. And just when Hana was going to go see if it was dead or alive, the bird staggered forward. I grabbed her arm. "Look," I said. It slowly walked the length of the deck, at first barely able to lift its wings. When it finally got off the ground, after several unsuccessful attempts, Hana was ecstatic. "The bird's flying!" she yelled, as if she were witnessing a miracle.

It's going to have one hell of a hangover, I thought to myself.

But this time she came back in carrying a brown robin with a red-orange breast. "It's so small," she said, stroking its downy feathers in the palm of her hand. His head flopped to one side.

"Let's bury him, too." I emptied the matchbox from the shelf by the stove, and she laid the bird gently inside.

"Will this happen every year when the berries get ripe?" Hana asked.

I shook my head, wishing Max were here to explain things in his calm way. My heart jumped with each thud against the glass. Life was too fragile. How could this fit into God's plans?

"It doesn't make sense," she said.

"I know."

We buried the tiny bird among the other mounds of freshly turned earth. Hana made another small cross out of plastic straws, five in all, that looked like a row of addition signs. We stood side by side, and I quickly mumbled something from the top of my head, "We send this bird into the kingdom of God." Hana remained silent, her head bent, her eyes closed. Afterward she turned around quickly and walked toward the toolshed. I went inside to start dinner. A few minutes later, I heard clipping sounds from the yard and saw Hana from the kitchen window. She had taken the gardening shears and was cutting down the pyracantha bush.

I stopped what I was doing and hurried out to help her.

HANA

Laura

In the bottom drawer of Max's desk, I also find my 1975 yearbook from Jefferson Junior High. I open the hard, laminated cover and flip through the glossy pages of smiling kids with braces and long, unruly hair staring up at me from the black-and-white photos. When I come to the dog-eared page with my photo, I study the smiling girl with the full cheeks and long, black hair as if she's someone else. I imagine Max did the same thing as he sat here and gazed at the young me. I flip through the pages and stop when I find Laura's photo, her face smiling up at me like a long-lost friend. It has been over ten years since I've seen her, but I feel her presence here in the room as if it were yesterday. My fingers brush her long, blond hair, the smooth curve of her cheek.

During my second year at Jefferson, I was reunited with Laura and my other friends from Daring Elementary. I still remember how intensely happy I felt then. I had a best friend again, who knew me for who I was. Over the summer, Laura had had a growth spurt and stood almost a foot taller than me. The first week of school we walked down the long, green hallway lined with gray lockers, and I paid little attention to the stares or wisecracks. We were dubbed the Princess and the Pea. Once, when Laura heard some girls making fun of us during study hall, she went over and told them, "You're right, Hana *is* a princess, and I don't mind being her pea at all!"

It was during a sleepover on my fourteenth birthday that I first told Laura that something might be wrong with me. We were sitting on top of our sleeping bags and she was eating popcorn and deciding what nail polish color to use.

"Laura, I need to tell you something."

"So tell," she said, not looking at me.

"You know how I've been feeling tired all the time?"

Laura reached for more popcorn. "My mother says we get those dark pillows under our eyes when we don't get enough sleep."

"Laura!" I said, hard and flat, demanding her attention. She looked up at me. "Well, my doctors in San Francisco think there might be something wrong with me, that's why I'm still so small. I might have this disease. It's called Werner's syndrome. It'll make me grow older much faster than normal." I said it all in one quick stream of words, glad to have finally gotten it out.

Laura kept watching me, her blue eyes narrowing, trying to decide if I was playing a joke on her or not. "What do you mean?" she finally asked.

I swallowed hard. "Well, if it is Werner's syndrome, it means there's something in my body that'll make me grow older twice as fast as you. I'll be an old lady way before you." It seemed like such a silly thing to say that I almost wanted to laugh.

Laura stared at me and became serious. "Is that why you were taking all those tests?"

"Yeah."

"You'll look older? Sooner?"

I nodded. "And I'll most likely die a lot sooner, too." I was surprised at how easily the words came out of my mouth, as if I were talking about someone else, a tragic character from *Anna Karenina*, the novel I was reading.

"And the doctors can't do anything about it?" she asked, putting the bottle of Cherry Mist nail polish down.

I shook my head. "They don't know that much about Werner's syndrome yet. They aren't even sure I have it. The signs of it don't really show until I'm in my twenties."

"But they discover stuff all the time," she quickly added.

"Yeah, they do."

Tears filled her eyes as she listened to me. I don't know if she really understood what I was saying, since Werner wasn't really evident yet, and it sounded like something out of *The Twilight Zone*. I remember the Jim Croce song "Operator" playing in the background.

"Are you in any pain?" Laura finally asked, her blond bangs falling across her eyes. She whispered the words as if she were in pain.

I shook my head. "Right now, it's hard to believe there's anything wrong with me," I said, "except that I'm small."

"Will you grow any taller?" she asked. Laura had grown to five eight by the time she was twelve.

I shook my head again. "This is it." I could see Laura's eyes glance quickly up and down my body in wonderment. Until that moment, I still hoped I might reach five feet. We looked like a circus act walking down the street together, but it never seemed to faze Laura. Without knowing what possessed me, I said, "Wanna see?" I unbuttoned my pajama top to show her my breasts were still two flat nipples. Laura was so thin and gangly herself, I couldn't imagine she was much more endowed.

Laura laughed and wiped the tears from her eyes. "Breasts are overrated, especially when you have to run the mile in P.E. Who needs the extra baggage?"

We laughed, then listened to the music in silence, neither of us saying anything else about Werner.

That night, we slept side by side in our sleeping bags on the floor of my bedroom. It smelled of popcorn and nail polish. When we turned off the light, moonlight filled the room with a strange white glow. We whispered words back and forth until we were too tired to talk. Just before I drifted off, Laura reached over and took my hand in hers, holding it tightly.

CATE

Ghosts

I look up at the window but Hana hasn't returned. I imagine she's retreated to Max's study, where hundreds of books, mostly concerning Asian and European history, ancient civilizations, subjects he loved to teach, line the bookcases. A voracious reader, Hana takes after him. Rarely did I ever see either of them without a book in hand or close by. I remember, early in our marriage, asking Max what was it about the past that intrigued him so.

"How can we appreciate the present and our future if we don't understand the past?" he responded thoughtfully, then looked up at me with a smile of pure joy. "The more I learn about other cultures, the more I see how much we're all alike."

I knew at that moment why he was such a good teacher, because even if he had to say the same thing over and over again each year to new groups of enraptured students, it was a subject he never tired of.

I prune the last of the rosebushes. Sometimes I find myself surprised it's just Hana and me living here together. At the oddest moments, I still feel Max's presence. It's strangely comforting, yet painful at the same time. Is this what it means to be haunted?

The evening Max died three years ago, it was so sudden I never had a chance to say good-bye. He came home from work, walked up the stairs to the bedroom to change before dinner, and never came back down again. When I went up to get him, Max was half slumped on the bed, almost in a kneeling position, his tie on the floor, his shirt unbuttoned. I knew he was dead the moment my fingers touched the back of his neck, the warmth already waning, the last of his life seeping away. I stroked the back of his gray head, leaned over and kissed him just below his ear.

I've tried to imagine what he might have been thinking the instant the blood vessel burst in his head. Did he realize that death had come? Did he call out my name, or did blinding pain take away his voice? Did his life flash before him in black-and-white photos like you see in the movies? For weeks after, I felt numb, his presence still everywhere. I tried to remember our last conversation, what words he had gone away taking with him. I couldn't. I lay in bed night after night playing it all back in my head, until one sleepless night I turned on all the faucets in the house. Hana must have thought I'd gone insane, and rightly so, though she didn't say a word. Just the sound of all the rushing water seemed to calm me, and with it, Max's last words came back to me.

"Where's Hana?" Max had asked. He kissed the back of my neck, his lips dry and cool. I still long for those kisses.

I was making meat loaf, potatoes, and vegetables. "Upstairs, I think." Words said without thinking. Did I even look back at him? See how tired he was? His hair had grayed considerably the year before he died, and there was a slight puffiness to his face that came with age.

"I'll tell her dinner's almost ready," he said, his voice sounding weary.

But he never did.

What were Max's last words to Hana? All I could think was that she'd have to reach back even further, to that morning, before he left the house, to find his voice again.

I was unprepared for the cold, sudden shock that my life with Max had ended. It was much too soon. After spending more than half of my life with him, I couldn't believe that he would no longer walk through the back door every day, the sound of his calm voice like a cool drink of water. After his death, I couldn't catch my breath. Grief made it hard to swallow, to talk, even to think. During all those sleepless nights after Max died, I still had one-sided conversations with him in my head. "Where are you?" Frightened, I touched the empty space in our bed. Who would be left to take care of me? It seemed like such a selfish thought, but in the darkness all my fears surfaced in flashes of self-pity. Suddenly it was my responsibility alone to stay healthy and alive for Hana. And then one day, she too would be gone. These thoughts circled my mind like a swarm of stinging bees.

Lily came over and stayed with us the first week after Max died. "What about Ben?" I pulled myself together enough to ask. Her easygoing husband owned the Daring Hardware Store.

"Don't worry about Ben. Now that the kids are out of the house, he wants nothing more than to be alone with the 'sixty-four Sting-Ray he's rebuilding," Lily said. "He won't even notice that I'm gone."

Lily took over the household, ordering me to get some rest,

as if I were one of her students. She made our dinner and kept Hana company, while I went upstairs to lie down. With the curtains drawn, I lay in the shadowy room and tried not to cry, emptying my mind of all the voices and memories, but they kept coming back like unwanted guests.

I took care of Hana in silence, going through the motions I knew by heart. I couldn't bear the thought of losing her too, of being left behind. I kept waiting to hear Max's voice whisper in my ear that it was all just a bad nightmare.

But it was Hana's voice that called me out. One evening after Lily went home, as we were clearing the table after dinner, she said, "God made another mistake. I was the one who was supposed to leave first." I heard the anger and grief in her words as they came out hard and flat. Her face was sad and serious. And then my sorrow rose up and a great, warm flood of tears fell and, for the first time in months, I slept through the night.

I shake the thought away, forcing myself to stay in the present, turning on the water and picking up the hose to water the barren rosebushes. Come late spring, when their green buds begin to emerge, I'll have Hana right here with me to explain how important this garden is to me.

HANA

My Father's History

I feel Max's presence most strongly in his study. The worn leather chair, the large old desk, and his favorite pen still in the top drawer. All the hours he spent among his books, preparing his classes, writing papers on the ancient civilizations of China and Persia, extracting the wonders of the world and the peoples who lived thousands of years before us. Sometimes I still hear his voice. When I was a child, he told me stories of Alexander the Great, Marie Curie, and Marco Polo, but it wasn't until I'd studied the internment camps, in seventh grade, that I saw for the first time my father's own history.

I finally began to understand what his family had gone through, how they were herded together like cattle and sent away to relocation camps in the middle of some barren landscape, name tags clipped to their coats as if they were pieces of merchandise. I learned that eighty-five men from Heart Mountain, the largest number from any camp, refused to mark yes to questions asked on a "loyalty oath" to America. They were branded resisters and sentenced to a state penitentiary for three years, while hundreds of other Japanese American men fought and died for their country.

That was just a few months before I found out about Werner. Max's family had been silent for so long, I was stunned to learn that this was part of my history, too. I couldn't understand how he could have folded away his past so completely.

But it wasn't until I was twelve that I questioned Max about Heart Mountain for the first time. I came downstairs after reading a chapter in my history book on the Japanese internment camps to find him correcting papers in his study. "What was it like at Heart Mountain?" I asked, leaning lightly against the doorframe.

He looked up and rubbed his cheek in thought, then put down the papers. "Let's go for a walk before dinner," he said.

I could hear my mother in the kitchen talking to Lily on the phone about a class she was substituting.

"We'll be right back," I yelled to her as we stepped out into a mild May evening. The sun was just falling behind the redwood trees in the distance.

"Let's go to the creek," he said.

It was a place in the nearby woods that we both loved. At the end of our block was the dirt trail that led to the creek. The air was sweet and pungent from the pine trees.

I looked up at Max, a glint of gray showing around his temples. "What was it like at Heart Mountain?" I asked again, eager to know more.

"It was a prison," he answered, his voice tight as he kept walking, leaves crackling under his foot. "There were nine guard towers and fences with barbed wire surrounding the entire compound. After the Japanese bombed Pearl Harbor in nineteen forty-one, everyone of Japanese ancestry was suddenly caught in the web of suspicion. President Roosevelt ordered all Japanese Americans living on the West Coast to be confined in internment camps, under the guise of protection. We were all forced to sell or leave behind everything we owned and had worked so hard for, only to be herded into camps in the middle of nowhere. All because the government thought we were dangerous, simply because of our heritage."

"But you were Americans." My voice rose higher. We walked onto the well-worn trail, lined with pine and eucalyptus trees, that led us to the creek, where the clear water flowed all year round. We could hear the birds fluttering in the trees, the soft songs of the crickets already playing.

Max nodded. "We were. We always were, no matter how the government tried to make us feel as if we weren't. Your uncle Tag and I played baseball and football, dreamed of hamburgers and milk shakes. Uncle Tag even tacked up a poster of Veronica Lake above his cot. At the same time, we ate rice, spoke broken Japanese to our parents, and occasionally lit incense at a makeshift shrine to honor our ancestors. It was part of our heritage. Did that make us less American?"

I shook my head no and leaned over to pick up a fallen branch.

Max stopped and licked his dry lips. He was tall, and still lean and athletic for a man in his forties. I could see his Adam's apple move up and down as he swallowed. He took off his glasses and rubbed his eyes. "We live in a world in which to look or act different is to inspire fear and provoke anger." He looked at me, and his eyes were kind and tired. "People seem to make the same mistakes over and over again."

"I'm sorry," I said softly, poking the fallen leaves with the branch. "If you were old enough, would you have signed the loyalty oath?" The sudden dark, dank coolness of the tree tunnel we were walking through made me shiver. I gripped the branch tighter in my hand.

Max leaned closer and smiled. "Do you know about that?"

I nodded. "It was something you signed to prove your loyalty to America."

He smiled, then turned serious again. We walked on in silence and continued down a path to the creek. I could hear the water rippling and smell the damp earth.

Max stopped when we reached the creek, where he watched the water for a while, then said, "There was a young man, Danny Ito, the older brother of my school friend Bobby, who refused to sign the loyalty oath." He paused. "Danny was eighteen, old enough to be drafted. The two questions on the loyalty oath asked, first, if he would fight for the United States and, second, if he would forswear allegiance to the emperor of Japan. Danny marked no and no to the questions and wouldn't change his mind, even at the urging of all his family and friends. 'Why do I have to prove I'm loyal?' I remember him arguing, 'I'm as American as any one of those guards out there! If they'd treat me like an American, I'd fight tomorrow. And I've never sworn allegiance to the emperor, so why should I revoke something I've never done!' "

Max helped me down the embankment, and we sat on a flat rock at the edge of the creek. The sound of the water was comforting. Then he continued, "Late one afternoon, when Bobby and I were about ten, we were walking around the camp minding our own business, still full of energy after winning a baseball game with some other boys. Before we knew it, we'd walked to the far end of the compound by the water pumps, lost in the excitement of our win. Bobby was swinging the bat, and I was punching my mitt like we were major leaguers." My father stopped and leaned over to dip his cupped hands into the cold, clear water, drinking a mouthful and letting the rest trickle through his fingers. "It was a warm day and there was a dry wind blowing. Out of nowhere came the smell of cigarette smoke, which we picked up and followed like a couple of hunting dogs. When we reached the last tar-paper barrack, we heard a low moaning sound and men laughing. We looked around the building to see three guards hitting and kicking somebody slumped on the ground. When he shifted his arms to cover the back of his head, we saw it was Danny they were beating."

"What did you do?" I asked, my voice breaking.

"Before I had a chance to think, Bobby ran toward the soldiers swinging the bat and screaming, 'Leave him alone, or I'll kill all of you!' The soldiers laughed at first. I ran after Bobby and heard the dull thud of the bat making contact with one of the soldiers. It all happened so fast, I didn't really see who he hit, but the next thing I knew, Bobby was falling to the ground, still clutching his bat. Then something hit the side of my head and I went down, too."

"Were you all right?" I asked, incensed that they would hit a ten-year-old boy.

Max touched his cheek. "Only the memory of it hurts now. Well, it's about time I told you about Heart Mountain. You're old enough to understand it now."

I nodded.

"Anyway, I heard a soldier say, 'Damn it! The kid broke my nose.' Danny was trying to get up, and Bobby and I were already on our feet swinging at the guards again. I don't remember ever feeling so angry in my life. It made me fearless. 'We're Americans, too!' I screamed. After all, I had just as much right to be here as they did. Tears were streaming down my cheeks and I was ready to be slapped down again, but instead one of the soldiers said, 'They're just kids. Let's get out of here.' And they took off. I can still see Bobby wiping away the blood from his nose with the back of his hand. We helped Danny up and to the camp clinic. He had a couple broken ribs and cuts and bruises. Less than two weeks later, he was taken away to prison."

A rush of wind moved through the pine trees. I swallowed, then asked, "Did ojī-san sign?"

"Your grandfather was too old for the draft anyway. He only wanted his American-born kids to be free, so he would have marked yes and yes to the two questions, along with most of the people at Heart Mountain. I honestly don't know what I would have marked if I were Danny's age. That day, I was ready to fight those guards, my fellow Americans. I felt the anger and injustice of it, just the way Danny did."

"What happened to Danny afterwards?" I asked.

"Danny and the other men, who were called no no boys, were sent to the camp at Tule Lake, where they were registered as resisters and sent to prison. Bobby and his family went along with him and were also seen as resisters, though they stayed at Tule Lake. Danny and the others were freed and finally pardoned in nineteen forty-seven. I never saw Bobby again until we were young men and he looked me up on his way through California from Seattle. I remember we were shy and uncomfortable with each other at first.

" 'How was Tule Lake?' I asked him.

" 'No better than Heart Mountain,' he answered.

"But it changed Bobby, somehow. He was nothing like the young, happy-go-lucky boy swinging the bat that day after the game. He looked old and defeated. It wasn't until we began to talk about baseball that the young Bobby I knew returned. You see, Heart Mountain, Manzanar, Tule Lake, and the rest of the camps were nothing more than prisons. They stole years of our lives away from us, leaving an entire generation of Japanese Americans voiceless."

Then all we could hear was the rippling water just below us, creating a sleepy, lulling effect. I thought of how the creek flowed down to the river that ran through town, and eventually found its way to the ocean. We both remained quiet as my father's words echoed through the soft evening air and I leaned over and hugged him tightly.

JOSEPHINE

A Wish

Today, I walked home from school rather than taking the bus to ballet lessons. "Mom's going to be mad," Camille warned as she hesitated, then finally boarded the bus by herself. I watched it pull away, leaving the dizzying fumes of exhaust behind. Then I turned down busy, bustling Broadway, passed the clothing shops and the small cafés, the video stores and newsstands. It made me feel calmer, like all the turbulence of life—the crowds and noise and confusion filling the air—was on the outside and I was just watching it all. People moved quickly, scattering like bugs down the crowded street. I took in everything—the square-jawed construction workers who drilled and hammered, a harried mother who pushed her sweet-faced baby by in a stroller, the homeless man who sang and danced then spread open his palm for handouts. I knew Camille would never understand if I tried to explain what I was feeling to her. I didn't quite understand myself. I watched it all from a distance, feeling strangely separate, yet excited by the intricacies of life.

I started feeling like this a few months ago, when my father came over for my thirteenth birthday dinner and we were all together again. A family. I watched how each one of us hardly noticed the others. It was as if we were all as invisible as the people I saw walking down Broadway were. My parents never once looked at each other across the table. And Camille hardly paused long enough between her eating and talking to realize that no one was even listening to her.

"What's wrong?" I asked, at first under my breath and then louder. "What's wrong with everyone?" It was as if I couldn't hold the words in.

My mother looked at me, her fork in midair. "There's nothing wrong," she said, trying to sound convincing.

My father and Camille just stared at me as if they were watching a movie.

"We might as well be eating alone the way we all sit here avoiding each other!" I let my fork drop with a loud clink against my plate.

"What's the problem, Josie?" my father asked, trying to keep his voice even. After all, it was my birthday.

You are! I wanted to scream. I felt the blood rush to my head, and then it was as if time slowed down again and, when I looked into each of their concerned faces, I realized that I was the one who didn't belong, not them. I stood up, excused myself, and went to my room, even as their voices called after me.

Later, when my mother came in carrying a tray, I pretended to be studying.

"I brought you a piece of birthday cake and some milk," she said, setting the tray down on my desk. "Are you okay, Josie?"

I nodded but didn't say anything. A single yellow candle was pressed into the chocolate frosting.

"You know you can always talk to me," she continued. "I know it's hard right now with your dad living somewhere else, but it'll get easier, I promise." Her voice sounded small and uncertain.

For a moment I wanted to throw my arms around her, tell her that I didn't know what was wrong, that I felt strangely out of place no matter where I was or who I was with. But when I looked up into her clear, blue eyes, it was as if I didn't know what to say.

"I'm fine. I'm just tired," I finally said.

Mom reached into her pocket and pulled out a pack of matches. With a quick snap of a match, she lit the candle. "Make a wish," she said.

"It's not my birthday yet," I said, watching the orange flame flicker then continue to burn.

"You're going to be thirteen, you're entitled to more than one wish." She laughed.

In one quick motion I blew out the candle, wishing that my life would miraculously change for the better, as the wisp of smoke curled upward and disappeared.

"Good." She smiled, then she leaned over close to me and I could feel her warm breath against my cheek. "It's going to be okay," she whispered into my ear, kissing my cheek before she pulled away. "Maybe we can go visit Hana sometime soon," she added.

Then I felt the hot tears pushing against my eyes and I nodded again, because I knew if I said something, the words wouldn't stop. I'd have to tell her that I felt like the loneliest person in the world, and that everyone at school, even Annie, sometimes, thought I was strange. I might even have slipped and told her how angry I was at both Dad and her, making us believe we'd always be a family. But I didn't say anything; I just stopped talking, secretly hoping my wish would come true before I disappeared into myself again.

CATE

Dreaming Water

This morning when I overslept, I was dreaming of Max, but I forgot all about the dream in my rush to see if Hana was all right. Now, in the quiet of the garden, it returns to me like some tender memory. We were a young couple again walking on the white sands of Falcon Beach, six-year-old Hana in a red T-shirt running ahead. Max was tanned and broad-shouldered, so relaxed and confident that I felt shy and tongue-tied. There was so much I wanted to tell him about the three years since he'd been gone, but he leaned over, put his finger to my lips, and then pointed toward Hana.

"She's doing well," Max said. "I knew she would love being back here at Falcon Beach."

"As well as can be expected," I said, forever the pessimist, even while dreaming, but the roar of the waves drowned my words out.

Max leaned closer to me, the warmth of his breath grazing my ear. "She's happy," he added.

This time I simply agreed. "Yes."

"Are you happy?"

"As well as can be expected," I said again, remembering the long nights after his death that I found myself sleepless, compulsively turning on and off the bathroom faucet just to hear the sound of running water. Max had the habit of leaving the faucet running, whether he was brushing his teeth or doing the dishes. "It soothes me," he said, whenever I reminded him to turn it off.

After Max died, Miles worried about me. "You couldn't help it," he said. "The aneurysm was a time bomb waiting to explode. It could have happened anywhere, at any time."

Still I kept thinking, if only I hadn't been downstairs cooking when Max had his stroke, if I'd just gone upstairs and checked sooner, I might have called an ambulance in time.

"Miles is right." In my dream, Max stopped and looked at me. He had read my thoughts, and for a split second I felt violated. But when I looked into his eyes, I saw myself as a sixty-two-year-old woman again, being gazed at with love and longing by a twenty-eight-year-old Max. "I want you always to be happy," he said. "You deserve happiness."

"I've had happiness." I wanted him to put his arms around me and press his body against mine. And he did.

Max smiled and pulled gently away to look at me. "You'll have more. Life surprises you when you least expect it to." He pointed to our young Hana again, running in and out of the waves. She was deliriously happy and waved for us to join her.

Seagulls circled above us. The roar of the ocean grew, drowning out Max's words, though I knew he was speaking to me. I could see his lips moving, the calm, knowing smile I've always loved.

"What?" I called. "I can't hear what you're saying." I grabbed his arm tighter, anxious now, somehow knowing he was about to leave me.

Then Max put one arm around my shoulders, pointed again, and it was a grown-up Hana, beautiful and vibrant, running toward us. This was how I had always imagined Hana would look at thirty-eight, free from Werner's syndrome, tall and fresh-faced with her large, clear eyes and lovely dark hair. I wasn't a bit surprised. Without hesitation, I left Max behind and ran toward her.

Max was sixty-three-years old when he died. Toward the end of his life he began to talk more of his days at Heart Mountain, almost fifty-five years before. The memories seemed to flow back into his consciousness with a strange vividness. The camp stories came, sporadic and unexpected, during dinner conversations or on our walks with Hana in the park. It was as if the smallest thing— the smell of rice vinegar or a hot, dry summer day—would spark a memory, a feeling that brought back those three desolate years of heat and cold, the long days of life within the confines of a barbed-wire fence.

"You know what I dreamed of during all those years I spent at Heart Mountain?" Max asked me suddenly one evening when he and I went for a walk. "I dreamed of water." The fog had rolled in, and there was a fine mist falling. I lifted my collar against the sharp wind. "Even though they pumped water in from the Shoshone River, it never seemed enough to me. Our skin cracked and flaked from the lack of moisture. I couldn't get enough water, drinking it, swimming in it, showering in it, listening to way the last of it sucked down the drains of the makeshift shower stalls. They even dug a big pit in the ground for a swimming hole. But in the Wyoming desert, those endless summers were so arid and dry. When the wind blew it was like a hot blast from a furnace. Dust was everywhere." He looked at me as if he could feel that heat again. "It's something you can't forget. It burns inside of you."

"And the winters?" I asked.

It had begun to rain lightly. Max stopped walking and looked up at the darkening sky. "Bitterly cold. There wasn't any insulation in those tar-paper barracks. We packed newspaper in the cracks, trying to keep out the freezing wind. The five of us slept together on the floor rather than in our separate army issue cots, trying to keep warm with the heat from our bodies."

I mumbled, "Terrible," under my breath.

"It *was* terrible," Max repeated. "Some people died of the cold. Mostly the elderly or the young. They'd close their eyes and never wake, their hearts just stopped. But the summer heat and having that thirst with you day and night was unbearable. You couldn't quench it. I saw it drive one old man mad. One afternoon, he just began running through the compound screaming, '*mizu, mizu.*' 'Water, water' rang through the camp. Then he tried to climb over one of the barbed-wire fences near our barracks. I heard two clear shots from one of the guard towers, and the old man dropped. His blood soaked into the dust and stained the ground."

There was nothing I could say that wouldn't sound frivolous. It began to rain harder and I pulled my coat close, holding tightly to Max's arm as we walked on. It stung me to think that it hadn't been so long ago that I was afraid to walk down the street arm in arm with my own husband.

There are things you never notice until too late. Or maybe I did notice but simply dismissed it as an idiosyncrasy, a habit accepted along with the vow of "till death do us part." Not until Max had been gone a full year did I recall that he never drank down a glass of water without first licking his lips—an unconscious ritual of appreciation.

Like Max, Hana loves water. When she was barely three years old he taught her to swim by jumping with her into a neighbor's pool and letting her go. I rushed toward the edge of the pool, but Max held his hand up to stop me from grabbing her. As Hana's head dipped below the surface and she began to sink, I screamed. Then her tiny body suddenly buoyed upward, and her head emerged from the water. Water has never frightened her the way it does me when my feet no longer touch a solid surface. I panic and the struggle sinks me but, even at three, Hana trusted the water to make her float, dog-paddling back up to the glassy surface, where Max was waiting.

Summer days were spent swimming at the pool or at Falcon Beach until the year she turned twelve and a sudden and powerful fatigue began to plague her. All that early summer Hana was listless, wanting nothing more than to lie on the living room sofa and read or nap. This wasn't the child who usually had enough energy for two people.

"I thought you wanted me to read more," she retorted when I said she should be playing outside in such gorgeous weather.

"I want you to do so many things in life," I answered.

"There's plenty of time," she said, and closed her eyes again.

Without saying anything, I called Miles to set up an appointment for her. I remember that summer as the real beginning of the end of Hana's childhood.

I place a dahlia bulb into the hole I've dug, shovel dirt in after it. Buried treasure. Another morning is over and I should be happy with all I've planted, but lately I've begun to wonder if each day will be Hana's last and it sets a dark cloud over everything. I can see Miles shaking his head at me, clicking his tongue and saying,

"If you worry about tomorrow, you'll miss today." I smile to think of his unconscious bits and pieces of wisdom. But I know he's right, each day from now on means so much more.

When the final dahlia bulb is planted, I stand up slowly, feeling an ache in my knees and a kink in the small of my back. It takes a minute before I can stand straight. Another reminder that I'm not getting any younger. A few more years of this and I'll have to buy my flowers at a stand. For now, working in the garden is a part of each day that gives me such pleasure. I pick up the trowel, grab the rake and watering can, and stand there surveying what I've just planted. This bare and skeletal garden will be blooming in a few months' time, and I relish the thought.

I stretch, arch my back, then glance down at my watch to see it's just about lunchtime. A pot of soup waits on the stove, along with some fresh bread I picked up earlier. I wonder what Hana has been doing with herself. Even if she's unsettled this morning, I know it's important for her to have some time to herself. With our lives so intertwined, we have found our own moments of silence.

I open the back door, stamp my feet three times on the top of the back steps, loosening dirt and pine needles. There's something pressing in the back of my mind, a longing that this not be just another day of waiting. I've lost too many days to the fear of what might happen, what *will* happen. Hana is going to die. It's a hard and bitter taste to swallow. *Oh dear Hana*, I think to myself, *how do I let you go?* When I open the back door, the savory fragrance of vegetable and barley soup wafts from the kitchen. My stomach suddenly growls with hunger. I put down my tools, hang my jacket on the hook, change my shoes, and hurry in to be with her.

HANA

Everything Counts

I'm in the kitchen slicing bread when the back door opens and I can hear my mother stamp her feet three times on the top step before entering and closing the door. Every day when she comes in from gardening, there's a smile of contentment on her face. I can see her in the back porch, where there's the dull clank of her gardening tools as she returns them to the storage closet. She hangs her jacket, tucks her gardening gloves into the left pocket, slips out of her mud-splattered boots into a pair of old brown loafers.

I decide to make myself useful, since I haven't read or written a word all morning. The soft chants of the monks still hum in my ear, and I stop a moment in front of the refrigerator door to stare at the smiling faces of Josephine and Camille. A spark of regret moves through me, about having turned down Laura's offer to visit. Then I push myself over to the stove and heat the pot of barley and vegetable soup Cate has waiting before slicing some cheese to go with the bread.

I can't help but think of Mrs. Gravis and how she would sometime become restless in her wheelchair all day. During my first year at Evergreen, I read to Mrs. Gravis for an hour every Tuesday and Thursday. At first she simply sat in her wheelchair and stared at me. The nurse told me to talk to her as if everything were normal. "Mrs. Gravis had a stroke. Her body is paralyzed but her mind isn't. She can't speak to you, but she can hear and understand every word you say to her." I could only imagine then what Mrs. Gravis was going through, isolated within her body.

"Hello, Mrs. Gravis," was my usual greeting. I felt awkward talking and receiving no response, my voice echoing through her tiny, sterile room and landing flat on the gray linoleum floor. I felt the blood rush to my head, a warm flush coloring my face. I wondered if Mrs. Gravis could feel my fear and embarrassment. The left side of her face drooped slightly from the stroke, but she was still a handsome woman, always immaculately dressed in rose-colored sweater sets and skirts, or a flowered robe with matching slippers. I could see, even when she was ravaged by age and a stroke, that she must have been stunning when she was young. Another thing that set Mrs. Gravis apart from the others at Evergreen was that her room always smelled of lavender, so that if you closed your eyes for one precious moment, you might believe you were sitting in a garden.

"Let's pick up where we left off." I cleared my throat and rummaged through my bag for the copy of Agatha Christie's *Ten Little Indians*.

I didn't know what Mrs. Gravis liked to read, but her eyes appeared inquisitive and intelligent. I wanted to read her something entertaining, yet complicated enough to keep her focused and interested. I quickly realized that mysteries grabbed attention and were fun to read aloud. The more I read to Mrs. Gravis, the more I became familiar with who she was and how she thought. She stared at me, and I learned to focus on her eyes, which followed me around the colorless room and eventually began to speak to me in the same manner as words. Just by the blink of her eyes or the slow tapping of her right index finger, she conveyed her feelings. Blinking once meant yes, twice, no. One tap meant she liked the book, two, she didn't. My reading to her made a world of difference to both of us. I brought something to her closed world, and she showed me what strength and determination was. I looked forward to our time together, and I could see by the gleam in her eyes that she did, too.

Every once in a while, Mrs. Gravis would sit up straight and tall in her wheelchair and a soft moaning sound would come from her. A secret language I slowly learned to understand. The first time it happened, I stopped reading in midsentence, filled with panic. The low, mooing sound emerged from her one, two, three times, a tiny line of saliva drooling from the side of her mouth. I thought she was in pain and buzzed for a nurse. Someone quickly came and helped Mrs. Gravis back to her bed, her eyes losing their light as they lingered on me. As the weeks went by, and I came to know Mrs. Gravis better, I realized she was trying to say the word *move*, that she had had enough of sitting in her room and wanted out. From then on, when I saw the restlessness in her eyes and heard the soft moo coming from her thin, dry lips, I put down the book I was reading and wheeled her outside to the garden. And sometimes, if she were feeling well, we even ventured down the block and into the real world.

Everything all right?" Cate asks, stepping into the kitchen and bringing with her the outside smells of damp earth.

I nod and force a smile. "Fine."

There's no need to tell her how I really feel. It would only cause her more worry. How I can't seem to concentrate on any one thing today for more than a moment, how it seems as if the rooms are closing in on me, how I feel like all the medication is making me lose control.

"I didn't feel like reading or writing any letters," I say, "so I decided to try cooking instead."

"Smells good," she says, lifting the lid to check the boiling soup.

"It should, you made it."

"You helped."

I look up. "I hardly think measuring a half cup of barley constitutes cooking!"

"Everything counts." My mother laughs.

As she washes her hands at the kitchen sink, she turns toward me. "I was thinking that we'd go to the park after lunch. Get some air."

I slice another piece of bread. For the past week, I've been fighting my mother about going out. I haven't had the energy and, with the ulcers on my feet, she'd have to deal with me, and the wheelchair, too, lifting it in and out of the trunk. She's not getting any younger herself. I look at my beautiful mother and feel such grief for all that I've put her through. But this morning, wheeling myself through each crowded room of the house, I felt as if I was suffocating. Like Mrs. Gravis, I feel the word *move* is a low moan rising out of me.

"Sounds good," I say, not looking up to see the smile of surprise that has most likely crossed my mother's face. Instead I concentrate on placing the bread and cheese onto the plate, fanning the pieces into the petals of a flower, as my grandmother Midori once taught me.

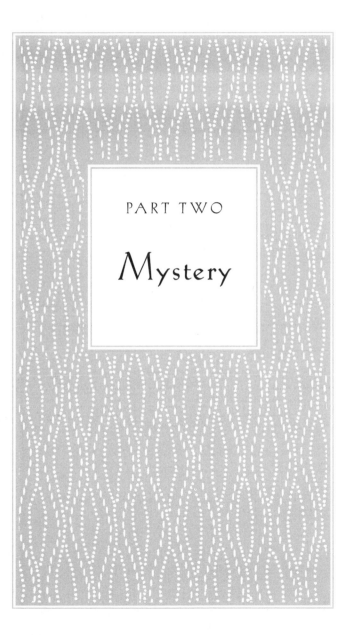

PART TWO

Mystery

CATE

What I Want

Just before we leave for the park, I glance quickly into the hall-way mirror. Hana is already safely seat-belted in the car when I run back in for her sunglasses. I look again, startled by what I see—a woman who has lost all trace of vanity. I shiver at the thought that this is the way Max saw me this morning, even in a dream. My eyes are dull and lifeless, my once dark hair is streaked with gray, and my pale, dry lips could use some color. I snap open my purse and dig around for lipstick, then run my fingers through my hair in the hope of giving it some kind of luster.

What I suddenly want at this very moment is a long, hot bath with not a care in the world. I want to luxuriate in the embrace of the water, drop rose-scented bath beads in, and run more hot water every time it gets the least bit cool. I'd stay for hours and hours, reading magazines and eating chocolates, my skin turning pink and soft to the touch. And I long for Max's touch, for his hands on my body, stroking my thigh, my arm, his hand finding my breast, pressing his body against mine. The wanting is like a dull ache that comes to me at the most unexpected times. I close my eyes and take a deep breath, then look up and catch a glimpse of myself in the mirror again. I hate myself for wishing such a thing when I know Hana is waiting for me in the car. I grab her sunglasses and am out the door again.

What I really want is a miracle. Miracles take place every day, I think to myself as I'm driving us to the park. Cures for cancer, the AIDS virus, Werner's syndrome—all possibilities. I can even close my eyes in sleep and talk to a handsome, young Max again, press my face against his neck and ease my longing. I can glimpse what Hana would look like as a beautiful young woman. I can even stop time for just this afternoon and let myself believe that Hana will one day bury me—throw a pale, white rose into a dark hole dug into the earth, tears streaming down her healthy cheeks.

HANA

Mistaken Identity

My mother and I haven't gone on an afternoon drive in months. The farthest we've ventured is to the store, the park in town, or to see Dr. Truman. At lunch she suddenly looked up and told me we were going to McClaren State Park, rather than Daring Park close by. Ever since my father died three years ago, and my grandmother Anna two years before that, we've only been to San Francisco a few times, and that was for tests. Flying to Los Angeles is too strenuous for me now, and besides, since my grandfather Henry passed away, my grandmother Midori has been too frail to have houseguests. I've tried to persuade my mother to take a few days' holiday away from me, go off somewhere and get a suntan, reassuring her that Lily would gladly stay with me, but she'll only smile and say, "There's no other place I want to be." But now here we are on the road again, and it's been a long time since I've seen her so happy.

When I was little, we used to visit McClaren Park on weekends. During the summer, we usually spent time at Falcon Beach and also visited my grandparents either in Boston or in Los Angeles. I loved them equally, though they were as different as day and night. My mother's parents, Louis and Anna, especially my grandfather Louis, with his large, imposing presence, seemed to fill every room they walked into. My father's parents, Henry and Midori, had the opposite appearance. They would shrink into themselves in a room full of people, staying in a corner as if that's where they belonged. I always wondered if it had to do with their internment at Heart Mountain, as if they could never really trust the world around them again. Yet, whenever we were all together as a family, my grandparents complemented each other in those strange ways that opposites often do.

"Yin and yang." My father laughed.

Still, I knew how much it meant to my mother and father that their parents had found a balance in each other's company.

After my grandfather Louis died of cancer the year I turned thirteen, our lives became quieter, more serious. It was as if a certain light had gone out, and when Werner was introduced into our lives a few months later, we fell deeper into that darkness, emerging slowly with visits to my grandmother Anna in Boston and my grandparents in Los Angeles.

The first time I rode on an airplane by myself was the summer I first heard about Werner. My grandparents asked me to come and stay with them in Los Angeles for a few weeks after the initial series of tests was over. Before then, we had always taken vacations as a family. Two weeks seemed like an eternity, and I remember feeling like I'd finally grown up, even if it wasn't physically noticeable, since I was still a tiny mouse of a thing, no taller than a nine-year-old. At the San Francisco airport, there were crowds of people, and finally a muffled voice that came over a loudspeaker announcing my flight. My parents stood at the gate, waving nervously as I walked away from them. Even then, I couldn't understand how I could be their child. They stood so tall and glamorous, my mother with her pale, smooth skin and shoulder-length dark hair, dressed in cool beige linen, while my father's black hair was newly flecked with gray that gave him a distinguished, college professor look. I can still see the look of grief in my mother's eyes, as if she might be losing me forever. I waved furiously as my parents were swallowed by the crowds, then looked away so I wouldn't cry; after all, I was thirteen and certainly grown-up enough to ride on an airplane all by myself. A stewardess appeared next to me, grabbed and held my hand, as if I were half my age, whispering softly to me, "You'll be just fine. I have all kinds of wonderful things to keep you busy until you see your grandparents."

Once I was strapped into my seat, the stewardess returned and squatted beside me with crayons and a coloring book of animals from around the world, a deck of cards, and a pair of captain's wings that she pinned onto my white sweater. "There you go, sweetie, that should keep you busy for a while."

I looked at her and smiled. She had no idea how old I really was. "Thank you," I said politely as she patted me on the head. I felt a rush of irritation move through me but had learned that it was simpler to play the role rather than explain that I was older than I appeared. It took years before I finally let people know the mistake they were making.

"You're such a well-mannered little girl." She smiled. "Just press this button if you need anything. This one right here." She pressed a gray button on the armrest, and a tiny overhead light flickered on and then off again with another click.

I nodded that I understood, and she smiled as if she'd accomplished her mission. "Just start coloring and I'll be back to check on you before you know it."

I knew she meant well, but I couldn't help myself. "Oh," I said politely, "I'm allergic to crayons."

She looked at me, puzzled, then reached out to take back the box of crayons. "Well, let's see what else we have."

I watched the stewardess hurry down the narrow aisle, touching the tops of the seats to balance herself. I leaned forward and dropped the coloring book into the slot in front of me, then took out the copy of *Gone with the Wind* that I was reading, and couldn't wait until we landed in Los Angeles.

W̶hen I walked off the plane, refusing to hold the stewardess's hand, my grandparents were waiting. They stood to the side, my grandmother waving when she saw me, calling just once, "Hana!" They hugged me carefully as if I might break and looked at me with sad, loving smiles, unable to believe that something might be wrong with me. And even though I knew my life had changed, I was too excited at having flown all this way alone to feel anything but happiness in seeing them.

But it was my grandfather Henry who made a special point to spend more time with me. He had always been a small, slight man, grown shorter still in his later years, his shoulders and back stooped from all the hard work growing his beloved flowers. He had often looked up at my father and asked him proudly, "How did you get so tall?" Yet, although he never said a word about my condition, I could see the grief on his face, the secret glances that came my way, as if making sure I hadn't disappeared right before his eyes. So, ironically, it wasn't until I began taking all the tests that our time together took on a different quality and we became closer.

"Come along," he said, as he led me out to the greenhouse each night that I visited. He knew how I loved staring up into the night sky, hoping to see stars, inhaling the humid warmth and dank smell of earth mixed with the sweet fragrance of the chrysanthemums. He brought out two wooden chairs and dusted them off with his rough, callused hand, and we sat in the doorway just outside the glass house, our backs to the dark forest of blooming flowers. Then he switched off the lights, and in the moonlight we could see the entire night sky above us. The stars glimmered in the darkness and crickets chirped through the silence. It was our special time together and sometimes we wouldn't exchange more than ten words all evening.

"This is one of the moments in the day that I love best," he said one evening. Leaning back, tilting his head, he looked at the sky.

"Me, too," I said, copying his every move. That evening my grandfather was unusually talkative.

"It goes on forever," he said, staring upward. "Life is a mystery."

"Yes," I agreed again.

"We have to accept life as it's given to us." He reached over and took my hand. "Right, Hana?"

"Yes, Ojī-san," I answered easily. I had learned a few stray words of Japanese over the years, but whenever I visited my *ojī-san* and *obā-san* I wished I knew more. By their example, my grandfather and grandmother had taught me the meaning of respect and diligence, the strength to persevere.

"No need to be afraid, ever."

"No, Ojī-san."

My grandfather stood and stepped back into the moonlit greenhouse. He clipped a yellow chrysanthemum from one of the long boxes and presented it to me. "For my flower," he said, bowing to me.

I stood up and accepted his gift, then bowed low back to him, just as my father had taught me.

JOSEPHINE

Out of the Blue

Last night, I thought Mom would be angry with me for skipping ballet, but out of the blue she announced we were going to fly out to California this weekend. We had just eaten dinner and were clearing the table when she said, "As soon as you're finished, I want you both to go upstairs and pack. I was able to get us last-minute tickets and we're going to see Hana tomorrow morning for the weekend."

"To California?" I asked, in disbelief.

Her high laugh sounded slightly nervous. "That's where Hana lives."

Camille swept her blond hair away from her face and stood by the table, looking a little stunned.

"When did you decide this?" I asked. I still didn't believe her. My mother's never done anything like this before. Most of the time, we can't go see a movie without weeks of preparation, especially when she's working on some important case. Then we can barely speak to her.

"This afternoon," she answered. "Just this afternoon," she said again, as if convincing herself.

Then I believed her. There was something about the tone of her voice that suddenly made it real, a tinge of weariness I hadn't noticed before.

"We're going to California," Camille piped up all of sudden, as if it were a line from a song.

"Pack light." Mom smiled. "We're going to be on the move."

I wanted to laugh because it sounded strange, like we were on the run, that somehow our lives would never be the same.

"What about school?" Camille asked. "Are we going to miss any days?"

Mom looked up a moment, her thoughts apparently already on to something else. "A day or two. You can both make it up when we get back," she said.

It was certainly all right with me, but I never thought she had it in her, to leave her precious job and let us skip school, even for a few days.

"Does Hana know we're coming?" I asked.

Mom licked her lips. "It's a surprise," she answered. "Now go pack. We have a very early flight."

It feels like we've been traveling for days, getting up just past dawn, then going to the airport to catch a plane, which we nearly miss because Camille forgot her hairbrush and we had to find an airport shop to buy one. "Well, would you rather have her complain about it for our entire trip?" my mom asks, as a form of explanation. Then, after we arrive in San Francisco, we wait in a long, slow line to rent a car so that she can drive us three hours to a place where the trees are taller than the buildings. Daring, California. I ponder the name, but I'm too tired to dig the name book out of my bag. I wonder if Daring is someone's name or if, back in the Gold Rush days, it required a certain daring to scale its rough terrain, thus acquiring its name.

"Let's go, Josie," Mom says, waking me from my daydream.

We make one stop at a corner market for yogurt, candy bars, and potato chips for the drive up. I beg Mom to stop in San Francisco for even an hour longer, but she refuses. "We've come all this way and we can't even see San Francisco," I argue. "It's so insane!"

"We didn't come to see San Francisco," she says in her calm lawyer's voice, which I hate sometimes. "I want to get to Daring before dark." End of conversation.

While I sit up front with Mom, Camille is in the backseat and has already closed her eyes again, her head tipping to the side.

"I wish I'd stayed home," I mutter like a spoiled child. It isn't true at all, but lately I either clam up or can't seem to contain the words coming out of my mouth. Everything makes me want to scream. It's like I have this volcano inside of me that erupts all the time. Sometimes things are fine, and at other times I look for ways to give my mom a hard time. Lately, I haven't seen my dad enough to throw any tantrums, so my poor mother gets the brunt of them. Sometimes I feel bad, sometimes I don't.

"Sit back and enjoy the scenery," she says, unfazed by my outburst. "Breathe in the fresh air, it's good for you." She reaches down and adjusts the radio to a classical station.

I roll down the window, and a blast of cool wind fills the car. I exaggerate taking a deep breath of fresh air and blowing it out again. And even though I know she has a point, I put on my earphones, pick at a pimple on the side of my face, and don't say another word.

CATE

At the Park

We drive north about twenty-five minutes to McClaren Park, complete with picnic areas, a carousel, a lake where you can go rowing, a small animal farm, and a rhododendron garden that blooms with the most amazing white, pink, and purple flowers in early summer. It feels as if we haven't been here in years, instead of months. The scent of eucalyptus reaches us first, sharp and pungent, on the cool breeze. The long, curved leaves crackle under the weight of the wheelchair. In the distance, a blanket of fog hovers over the ocean.

Hana is in good spirits as I push her wheelchair down the path toward the carousel, one of her favorite places in the world when she was a little girl. I'm afraid I've been acting like an over-protective mother, bundling her child in too many clothes so that she resembles an Indian papoose. I'd carry her on my back if I could. But I worry, knowing how susceptible she is to every bug.

With her compromised immune system, a simple cold could easily lead to pneumonia. Complications could arise from the smallest thing, a tiny cut or a wayward germ.

I lean over and say, "If you're too hot, we can unzip your jacket."

Hana smiles. "I have enough clothes on for Antarctica!"

I laugh, help her off with her down jacket as we look down the slope at the carousel, the tinny sound of the mechanical music floating up toward us. It's amazing to think that it's played that same song for over thirty years. From the distance, it sounds hollow and strained, while the turning carousel is a blur of colors in motion.

"Remember when you used to saddle up?" I ask.

Hana pulls her baseball cap low. "I'm afraid my riding days are over," she says.

When Hana was small, she liked to ride the white horse with the red and gold saddle. She named him Trigger. If someone else was riding him, she'd wait and wait to take her turn. No amount of coaxing could get her to ride any other horse. As soon as Trigger was free, she ran to him, and Max or I helped her up. She'd lean over to stroke the wooden mane and whisper something sweet into his ear. Her feet never reached the stirrups. When the carousel jerked back and started up again, I couldn't help but laugh at how the music always wheezed and took a moment to catch up. Hana would grab on to the silver pole and ride off across the purple sage, never once turning back.

I push Hana's wheelchair down to level ground. There's only a handful of small children riding the carousel now, all preschool age, their mothers holding on to them and talking to each other as they circle around.

"I wonder what happened to Trigger?" Hana suddenly asks.

"Retired him to breed?" I answer, though I find myself also searching for him among the freshly painted palominos and pintos as the carousel turns round and round. But I can't see him, and imagine they must have retired him after so many years of service.

"Guess even Trigger had to kick the bucket," Hana says.

We keep watching, hypnotized by the rushing horses, the shrieks of laughter from the children riding them. After what seems like ten minutes, the carousel slows, and comes to a full stop. I push Hana around, glancing at each stationary horse, but it's plain to see that Trigger is nowhere in sight.

HANA

Trigger

Trigger is dead. The idea surprises me. I thought he'd last forever, like the tin can music. My mother won't give up at first, creating a carousel effect of her own as we circle around and around the standing horses. She scrutinizes each one, then sighs and gives up, bringing the wheelchair to an abrupt stop.

"He's not here," she says, defeated.

"No," I say. "He's in horse heaven."

Her fingers graze the side of my cheek, and I reach up and grasp her hand. A bell rings, loud and grating, as the music winds up and the carousel begins to turn again, slowly at first, before picking up speed.

Let's get something to eat," my mother says.

I look up at her astonished. We almost never eat outside food anymore. She takes great pains to prepare only low-fat, high-fiber meals. Dr. Truman has commended her more than once on how well she keeps to the regimen. "You're really amazing," he said a few days ago, when he came by to see whether the swelling in my ankles had gone down. They were standing in the kitchen, where my mother poured him a cup of coffee. He didn't realize I'd overheard, and I saw him touch the small of her back.

"Like what?" I ask.

"Popcorn. Popcorn is healthy," she says, like a child.

"Just what I've been craving," I say. "I'll stay right here and watch the herd. You get the popcorn."

My mother hesitates for a moment, then sees that there's no danger in sitting amidst mothers and children and wooden horses. The concession stand is no more than thirty feet away.

"I'll be right back," she says, backing away.

"I'll yell and scream if anyone tries anything," I tease.

She smiles. "You better."

Mothers and their children are in a category all their own. There's no bond so strong in the entire world. No love so instantaneous and forgiving. I watch these mothers and know they would give their lives for their rosy-cheeked babes, much as my mother has done for me. But these babies will one day leave their comfortable nests, fly away and seek their own lives, whereas I have stayed home to roost.

A little boy begins to cry, no longer wanting to be strapped to a horse going around in circles. "It's all right," his mother coos as the carousel turns out of my sight. When they come around again, she has unstrapped him from the horse and is holding him, bouncing him up and down, lifting his hand and waving it to whomever will pay attention. When they come to me, I lift my hand and wave back.

"Say hi to the nice lady," I hear her tell him. But he's like a puppet in her hands, doing what she tells him without any concept or understanding. When they are out of sight again, I lower my arm, wishing my mother would hurry back.

Which she does, carrying two red-and-white-striped boxes of popcorn. She takes long, fluid strides, and in that moment watching her, I have yet another revelation. Another detail I want taken care of.

"Do you want to stay here?" she asks.

I shake my head. "I've heard this tune once too often."

"I'm with you," she says.

Cate guides my wheelchair away from the carousel, down a path to a small meadow. Tall grass and eucalyptus trees surround us, and it seems a perfect place to talk about my latest notion. She sits down on the grass in front of me. Between us, there's the crunching of popcorn, which tastes even better than I remembered. A soft breeze is blowing, and it feels so good, as if the day was created for us.

I gaze out at the trees for a long time. "Do you think you'll ever marry again?" I suddenly ask. My mother has too much life left in her to be alone.

She turns to me in surprise, still holding a piece of popcorn between her fingers. "No," she answers, even before she's had a chance to digest the question. I can see by the surprise on her face that the thought has never entered her mind. Her response comes without hesitation, with perhaps a slight edge of irritation in her voice. But I don't care. I haven't time to beat around the bush.

My mother takes another moment and then adds, "I really can't imagine being married to anyone other than your father."

I raise my hand against the sun, as if I'm saluting someone. "Why not?" I ask.

"Because I can't," she says, her words quick and terse.

I pause for just a moment, then say quietly, "You should think about it. I don't want you to be alone." I reach down and squeeze her arm, and I see her watching me as my hand trembles just the slightest bit. "Dad would understand."

An overwhelming sadness crosses her face. She shakes her head and whispers back as if telling a secret. "I'm not alone."

"But you will be, one day."

The look on her face keeps me from adding the word *soon,* but I think it, and suspect she does, too.

My mother forces a small laugh and dodges the topic. "One step at a time," she says. "We're at the park today. I'll think about dating some other time."

"You're right." I smile. "No hurry, we can start looking to-morrow."

She looks at me, and I can see the seriousness of the moment has left her face. "Popcorn made me thirsty," she says, standing up and brushing off her slacks. Again she hesitates, then says, "I'm going to get us some water."

I watch her walk away and suddenly feel frightened. "Mom?" I say.

"I'll be right back." She smiles.

"Promise?" I ask. A word saved since childhood.

She blows me a kiss. "Promise."

JOSEPHINE

Driving

In the end, Mom's right, the drive north to Daring is beautiful. Once we leave the city and cross the famous Golden Gate Bridge, we both seem to relax and enjoy the ride. To each side of the freeway are rolling green hills that eventually give way to large, towering trees. Not a sight we often see in Manhattan. I leave my earphones on but turn down the music so that I can hear Mom softly humming with the classical piece on the radio. I glance over at her now and then, but she keeps her eyes focused on the road, especially now that the fog seems to be drifting in fast, leaving everything slightly out of focus. Mom looks different since Dad left—thinner and older around the eyes. I turn back to see that Camille is still asleep, and I think it's a wonderful time to tell my mom something nice after all she's been through.

But when I look back at her again, I can see that her thoughts are elsewhere. She looks as if she's listening to something serious, as if she's deep in conversation and doesn't like what she hears. Maybe she's thinking of all that she's left behind in New York. Like Dad. In a fight I once heard them having, he said she didn't really care about anything but her work. There was a moment of silence when I thought she wasn't going to say anything back. But then in her cool, lawyer's voice, she said to him, "I love my daughters more than life. Can you say the same?" And then it was silent.

I decide it's not the time to disturb her after all. Instead, I turn up the volume to the music of Vertical Horizon and look out the window as the trees slowly disappear into the milky whiteness.

CATE

Losing Control

Even from this distance I can tell something is wrong by the way Hana is sitting. Call it a mother's intuition, living with a child day in and day out. If you really pay attention, everything is right there, in a look, a gesture, or the sound of the voice. From this angle, Hana appears to be slumped over the side of her chair. Dear God, I think to myself, let her be all right. I run across the meadow as fast as I can, dropping the bottles of water along the way. I was only gone for ten minutes, at the most. But then that's all it would take, if her heart stopped beating, if an aneurysm burst, or if some organ failed. My own heart is beating so hard I feel as if it might jump out of my chest. By the time I reach her, I'm panting, fear catching my last breath.

"Hana?" I gasp, relieved when she turns my way. She watches me and doesn't reply. Her wide-eyed look shows me she's distressed, but she doesn't seem to be in pain.

"What is it? What's wrong?" I lean over, wanting to embrace her, but she puts her arms out to stop me.

I step back, giving her room. "What's up, kiddo? I bought us some water," I say, realizing that I dropped both bottles somewhere out there in the meadow. Feeling foolish, I point to where I see the plastic glimmering in the sunlight.

Hana is quiet, her face flushed. "I've had an accident," she mumbles.

I quickly reach for her again, wondering if she really is in some kind of pain and trying to keep it from me.

"I'm all right," she says, as she lifts the jacket that's lying across her lap, and I see the dark, wet stain that has spread across the crotch of her pants and down her thighs.

Another lifetime ago, Hana was a brilliant student. She spent a year at Brandon before she and Laura were both accepted at Berkeley. I knew it was a dream come true for her. She loved history but decided to major in English. She read day and night, wrote long, complicated essays on the Romantic movement and Virginia Woolf, flourished in the world of academia. Her phone calls home were filled with excitement and future aspirations. "I may be able to be Professor Heiden's teaching assistant for a semester after graduation," she said. "I've been thinking that teaching is the direction I want to go." Max and I couldn't have been happier for her.

She and Laura lived on the third floor of a six-story stucco building, each apartment with a small balcony that also seemed to double as a closet. Each time we drove down to visit as the school year progressed, we'd look up to see more bikes, clothes, and boxes piled up outside. Hana and Laura's two-bedroom apartment overlooked a small, unattended yard, with a couple of old chairs that sat in the middle of a patch of dying grass. The apartment was decorated in an Asian, Middle Eastern, hippie motif—lots of big red and purple pillows on the floor, beads hanging from doorways, and tie-dyed curtains. We were deliriously happy for her, never daring to think too far into the future. But for that short time, I tried to believe that my prayers had been answered, and that Hana would have the chance to achieve some of her goals.

So Max and I were more than surprised when she came home from Berkeley unexpectedly one April weekend. We were just sitting down to dinner when we heard the front door open and her "Hello?" The sound of her voice, weak and strained, told us something was wrong. Hana rarely came home except for holidays. When we drove down to visit her, we always felt like intruders. Now Max and I hurried to the living room to see Hana standing there between two suitcases.

"Hana," Max said, a smile in his voice. "We didn't expect to see you for another month."

I stepped toward her. "What a nice surprise." She looked tired and thin. Her eyes avoided mine.

Hana tried to smile, then looked quickly to Max. "Can you please pay the taxi driver? He's bringing in one more box for me."

Max gave Hana a quick hug first, then went out to take care of the cab fare. I hesitated for a moment, then wrapped my arms around her. I smelled the sweat of travel on her pale skin, her hair slightly oily and in need of washing, but she felt small and warm in my arms, and her body relaxed the longer I held her.

"What's wrong?" I whispered.

Another long pause. "I'm having trouble with my eyes," she finally answered. "It's Werner," she said softly.

171

"Werner," I said to myself. The word lay thick and heavy on my tongue. After all these years waiting, I was still surprised. "The cataracts aren't supposed to develop so soon," I muttered. I pulled away and looked at her, lifting her chin so I could see the dark eyes I knew so well. And, for the first time, I saw the hazy film covering her lenses, the cloudy edges that reminded me of a moon just before rain. Miles had told us that cataracts would be an early symptom of Werner, but part of me kept hoping it would never happen. Hana had just turned twenty-three. She was at the height of her beauty, with straight, long black hair and dark, piercing eyes.

"For how long?" I asked.

Hana looked away. "For the past six months, but it's only gotten really bad in the past month. I was hoping to finish the semester."

"What did the doctors in San Francisco say?"

"That I should have surgery to remove them within the next few months."

I swallowed. I didn't like the word *surgery*, no matter how simple a procedure it was. I knew this meant that Werner would begin making his presence known in a more aggressive way. "What about school?" I managed to ask.

Hana stepped away from me now. "I think I'll be able to graduate anyway. I have enough credits."

"If not, you can always finish next semester," I said, knowing that by then Laura and all her friends would have graduated without her.

"It's okay," she reassured. "I talked to my professors."

"You should have called," I said. "We would have driven down to get you."

"I said it's okay!" Hana said sharply. She looked at me and then sighed. "I didn't want it to be a big deal, so I took the bus.

Laura wanted to drive me, but she has a paper due."

I nodded. It was a big deal. I felt the tears welling up and looked away when Max came back in.

"All taken care of," he said, glancing my way, then taking Hana's hand in his. He didn't ask her any questions. "Let's get you something to eat. You hungry?"

Max didn't wait for an answer, but led her to the kitchen with the same matter-of-fact manner he'd used in teaching her to swim and ride a bike.

During the months leading up to her cataract surgery, I read to Hana every night. She never mentioned the teaching assistant position again. Every time I saw the cloudy veil over her beautiful eyes I bit my lip and blinked back tears.

"So, what book do you want to hear tonight?" I asked.

"Anything," she said. "I just like to hear the words read aloud."

She closed her eyes as my voice filled the room with Willa Cather's My Ántonia. I knew she was following along, just like when she was a little girl, seeing the characters in faraway places with her mind's eye, reaching back and trying to understand how her life had come to this.

Now I can't help but blame myself for Hana's accident. As her mother, I should have known better. As her caregiver, I should be aware of these things. At home I'm constantly asking of she needs to use the bathroom, wants a glass of water, or if she's hungry. It's part of a routine that shouldn't be broken, even if it does get on her nerves sometimes. "I'm fine" is her standard answer, two words that can be said a multitude of ways to convey her mood, depending on her tone and which word is accentuated. When

Hana was a little girl, she could go for hours without having to use the bathroom. She'd sit quietly through a movie or an afternoon of shopping without a complaint. Only when I suggested we make a stop before going on would she nod her head in agreement.

Hana's only other "accident" was more than a week ago, when she awoke in the morning to find she'd wet her bed, lying atop the moist, warm stain that looked like a spreading bruise.

"I'm sorry, I must be losing control," she'd said to me, in a voice that was more accepting than upset.

"It's just one little accident," I'd answered. But inside, I was the one who was upset. I knew that every small mishap meant some part of my daughter's body was weakening, shutting down.

Now, it's two little accidents.

The fog has quickly rolled in from the ocean as I settle us back into the car, teary-eyed, muttering, "Where are my keys?" all set to drive us home when Hana says, "Please, Mom, it's all right."

"It's not all right!" I choke out, now in tears. "This is absolutely ludicrous. What was I thinking, leaving you all by yourself?"

"You were thinking we needed something to wash down our popcorn," Hana answers. She looks at me, her face calm and serious.

Now I'm crying for real, forehead propped against the steering wheel, hot tears streaming down my cheeks. I feel ridiculous and scared and sorry my sweet Hana has to sit beside me in wet pants, and yet I'm the one who's crying.

"Don't give up on me," I hear Hana say, then feel her hand touch the back of my neck, "because I haven't."

I look up from the steering wheel, stung by embarrassment. One thing is certain, at this moment, Hana is clearly the wiser of the two of us. "I'll never give up on you," I say. "Just don't give up on me."

"No chance." Hana laughs. "Especially when I need you to drive me home."

I laugh, then reach into my pocket for a tissue. Sometimes I wonder who's taking care of whom here. I wipe my eyes, blow my nose.

"Let's go home," I say, starting the car with a roar.

HANA

Winter Bones

To see my mother cry is rare and unnerving. She maintains a brave front while caring for me, as if I belong in this life, no matter what Werner has to say about it. She hides more sorrow than any person should have to endure. Every night when she goes to sleep, I know that she hopes I'll be with her the next day. And every morning when she wakes up, I know there's a split second between dream and reality, when she wonders if I'm still here.

After my mother left to get the water, I closed my eyes for a minute against the weakening sun and listened to the wind blowing through the eucalyptus trees. Here, close to the coast, the fog rolls in so fast it's startling, leaving everything in shadows. So, for the moment, the warmth felt comforting and I thought of Mrs. Gravis and Howard and my grandfather Henry, and how they liked to be outdoors whenever they could, receiving the warm embrace of the sun, as Howard once said. Then, before I knew it, I was sitting in a pair of wet pants, watching the warm, dark stain spread down my legs.

And all the while, it felt as if my mind didn't have anything to do with my body, like I was watching someone else's body malfunction. I once overheard my grandmother Anna say to my mother that everything in the body breaks down when you get older. "Your body no longer listens to your mind. You simply can't move as fast as your mind wants you to," she said. "It's as if winter gets into your bones." The image stayed with me all that afternoon. Winter in your bones. Winter bones. The gnarled branches of trees in winter. It sounded like the beginning of a Robert Frost poem.

Lately, I've encountered all four seasons in my bones—the brittleness of summer, the wetness of spring, the cold of winter, and the dull ache of fall. With differing degrees of grace, I've dealt with the physical symptoms of Werner, everything from bilateral senile cataracts to a broken hip, from arteriosclerosis to the ulcers on my feet. But losing control of my bladder has had a completely defeating and depressing effect on me.

The first time, a little over a week ago, I woke up and felt a wetness in the sheets beneath me. My mother had just come into my room, and I didn't know how to explain what had happened as she helped me up from bed. When she saw the dark, wet shadow on the cream-colored sheet, her eyes widened in surprise before she forced a smile.

"I'm sorry" was all I could think to say. "I didn't even know it happened. I must be losing control."

She touched my cheek, pulled my blankets away. "You don't ever need to say you're sorry to me," she answered, helping me up from the bed. "It's just one little accident. Now let's get you into the shower."

As the warm water fell on my pale, bony body, I looked down at my almost flat breasts and sparse white pubic hair, the protruding ribs, skinny arms, and legs scarred by recurring ulcers. Perhaps the dark marks were the beginning of some melanoma. What next? I felt a sourness rising and vomited, right there and then. "Werner, what are you doing now?" I asked aloud, my arms braced against the shower wall. "Isn't it enough?" I began, but couldn't finish the sentence. I started to cry, the water washing the tears from my face. Lately I've spent a lot of time crying in the shower, and wonder if that's where my mother also sheds her tears. Over the years we've tried to spare each other as much grief as we could. But this was the first time I had lost control of my bodily functions, and it must be a sign of things to come. I had seen it at Evergreen, and now I was losing hold of the one thing I most wanted to keep: my dignity.

When I came out of the bathroom, my mother was already in the kitchen making breakfast. I smelled the coffee brewing, heard the toaster pop up with a tinny ding. I went into my room to find my shades wide open, a bright morning light streaming in, and my bed already freshly made up, everything perfectly tucked in as if nothing had ever happened.

For the nights afterward, I was afraid to go to sleep. I couldn't help wondering if I might lose control again, or if I would have to wear those grown-up diapers I'd laughed at when I first saw them advertised on television. I prayed to God that it wouldn't happen again. I had to believe what they told me in catechism, that God would never abandon me, even if I didn't attend mass every Sunday.

Days passed. Mornings came without incident, and I thought my prayers had been answered. Werner hadn't won this round yet. I woke up in a kind of rapture when I found my bed perfectly dry. When my mother saw the smile on my face, I could see the relief in her eyes. By the end of the week, I began to believe that my accident had been a one-time-only event, and I treasured that gratifying thought.

Until this afternoon.

JOSEPHINE

Getting There

There it is!" Mom says suddenly, startling the dull, stale air of the car. Camille leans forward from the backseat, and I straighten up and pull my earphones down around my neck.

"Where?" Camille asks. My sister is the type who has to be the first to know everything.

"It used to be green, but it's salmon-colored now with green trim." Mom points to a big, old-fashioned Victorian that's half lost in the fog.

"That's where you and Uncle Jake grew up?" I ask, surprised at my sudden interest.

"That's it," she says, slowing down as we pass the house. "It looks so much smaller now," she says to herself. She stops the car for a moment and stares at it.

To me, it looks old and complicated, with a bay window and an attic room at the top. It's the room I would have liked to have had if I grew up there. Back in New York, Camille and I each have our own small room. When we visit Dad, we stay in his guest bedroom, which smells new like paint, like no one ever stays there for long.

"Was that your room up there?" I ask, pointing to the attic.

"No." She laughs. "Neither Jake nor I wanted to clean out all the junk up there, even if it would have made a great room."

"Can we see inside?" Camille asks.

"No, stupid." I glance at her. "Other people are living there now."

But before it erupts into an all-out name-calling, Mom says, "Josie, don't call your sister stupid," while Camille shoots me one of her evil-eye stares.

"Well, it's simply common sense," I say, deciding it isn't worth a fight.

Mom continues down the block, slowing and turning into the driveway of a large, brown-shingled house. "And this is Hana's house," she says, turning off the engine. "Wait here."

We watch her go to the front door and ring the bell. I can tell she's nervous by the way she keeps straightening her blouse, pulling it every which way when she looks just fine. After a few minutes, she shrugs and walks back to the car.

"No one's home," she says, slamming the car door closed.

"You mean after we've driven all the way to no-man's-land, they're not home? I thought you said they're always home." I need to rub it in. For dramatic effect, I climb into the backseat to hunker down next to Camille. Not that she'd ever take my side, she'll stay neutral, watch from the sidelines.

"So we'll wait," Mom answers. "They'll be back soon enough."

I can tell by her voice that she's not so certain, that she's getting weary of her spur-of-the-moment trip. I want to say I told you so, but it lingers on the tip of my tongue and I don't. I look out at the hazy darkness that surrounds us and wonder what we're doing here.

"What if they've gone somewhere," Camille suddenly asks, "and won't be back for the weekend?"

"Then we'll check into a motel and have a little vacation," Mom says.

"Here?" I say.

She nods. "Yes, *here*. Anyway, they couldn't have gone far, not with Hana in a wheelchair, unless something happened—" She stops and I can hear an edge of defeat in her voice.

Then something shifts inside of me, like something hard melting right below my heart. It makes me feel so sorry for her that I say, "No, you're right. They should be back any minute now. I can feel it."

Mom turns around and smiles at me. Even in the fading light, I can see how much she appreciates what I've said. "Thanks, Josie," she says.

It's not so hard to say something nice, I think. I want to say something more but the moment's gone. What I'm really feeling again is that it's *so* stupid for us to be sitting in a rented car thousands of miles from home, waiting to see our mysterious godmother, who has some kind of old-age disease, when my mother's obviously having some kind of nervous breakdown.

CATE

Underwater

I drive home with my eyes glued to the road, my hands gripping the steering wheel tightly as the fog comes in, thick and swirling. It feels as if we're in the middle of a cloud. Halfway home, we can barely see the road in front of us, except for what my headlights illuminate through the haze. The towering pine trees are lost in the gauzy white mist. I watch the yellow markers in the road, glancing at Hana every once in a while to make sure she's all right. She looks small and fragile, staring out the window at nothing. I want to take her in my arms and hold her, tell her everything will be all right, though I'm not so sure it will be. And right there and then a sudden sinking feeling fills me, like I'm drowning, even as I breathe in great mouthfuls of air.

"Are you okay?" Hana asks.

I take one more breath. "I'm fine," I exhale.

When I was six my father tried to teach me to swim. We were at his private club in Boston, where they had an indoor swimming pool. It was a long, Olympic-size pool, divided into lanes for members who swam every morning. I remember how muggy it felt in there, the smell of chlorine stinging my eyes. My father jumped in with a big splash, the dark hairs on his wide chest rising in the water.

"Come on, Angel, jump in," he urged.

I stood at the edge of the pool in my brand-new cobalt blue bathing suit, dark spots of wet where the water had splashed on me, and couldn't move. I was terrified the water would swallow me up.

"Daddy's right here," he said, waving me in. "You have nothing to be afraid of."

I looked down at him in the water and wanted more than anything to jump in, knowing he would save me. So I jumped, holding my breath with my eyes squeezed shut, sinking into the cold, quiet void, only to feel my body suddenly buoyed back up, my father's large hands holding me out of the water, saving me.

I want to save Hana in just the same way, but recently I feel her slipping from my grip.

HANA

Details

I stare out the car window and watch the fog become thicker and thicker, like white tissue paper hiding a gift beneath. It happens right before my eyes, houses and trees losing their definition, their edges blurring so quickly I blink and they're no longer there. I feel the same about Werner lately, only going in the opposite direction, aging my body in sudden, devious ways, a surprise around every corner. The symptoms are overlapping, taking over. One day I know Werner will rise up with the final blow, a seizure or organ failure, just when I think everything has balanced out.

The last time I saw Howard at Evergreen, he began talking about putting his life in order, so that when he was gone nothing would be left undone. He looked tired and distracted.

"Are you feeling all right?" I remember asking.

He looked down at me and smiled. "I'm a bit preoccupied this afternoon," he said, stroking his beard. "There's a number of things I need to put in order."

"Can I help?"

"I wouldn't bore you with all the details." He laughed. Howard had a deep, solid laugh, which I loved. In the two years I knew him, he never again asked why I volunteered at Evergreen, he simply enjoyed our time together. "Just clocks to be set and letters to be signed before the day ends."

"Shall I read?"

Howard shook his head. "I'd rather talk for a moment."

I nodded. "What about?" I asked, knowing that music and books were his favorite topics.

Howard smiled. "About something I want you to have." From a bag beside his chair, he took out a recorder, made of rosewood, he said, which his father had given to him. "When I was a boy and first heard the sweet notes coming from it, I knew that music would be my life."

"I can't take this," I said, holding the reddish brown recorder. It felt light and smooth in my hands.

"Of course you can. I can't think of anyone else I'd rather give it to. So wherever you go, dear Hana, you'll always have music close by."

I felt tears pushing against my eyes.

"You *will* leave Evergreen?" he asked.

I nodded yes, which seemed to make him happy.

"Good," he said. "This isn't the place for someone like you. Go out in the world, and live in the heart of life, and think of your old friend Howard once in a while."

Then I laughed. "Yes, sir."

"I mean it," he said.

"I know."

Howard died a few weeks later without ever knowing about Werner. I've kept my word as much as I could. The heart of my life takes place here in Daring with my mother, and every time I play his rosewood recorder, I think of Howard, much more than once in a while.

Lately, I've begun to think about putting my own things in order, the many details Howard spoke about. Despite what most people would think, it's not as depressing as it sounds. Like a wedding, I want my death done right—the music, the flowers, and all the people who are invited. I don't want Jell-O molds and sponge cake; I want sushi and crème brûlée, exotic and exciting. These thoughts come at the most unexpected times. A few weeks ago, Mom and I had just finished lunch when I had another revelation.

"I've been thinking," I said seriously, "that I'd like to be cremated, not buried in the ground."

We had yet to speak of this, and I know it was unfair of me to blurt it out. My mother sat back in her chair as if the wind had been knocked out of her. "But then how would I . . . ," she said, and her voice trailed off.

I knew the first thing that came to her mind was where would she put all the lovely flowers she'd bring to my grave?

"You know how claustrophobic I get," I said lightly, trying to extract a smile from her. "All you have to do is sprinkle me around your garden, instead of bringing flowers to the grave. I'll be surrounded by them every spring," I said, in a silly, lighthearted banter. I really meant it.

A sound came from her, more of a cry than a laugh.

I reached over and said, "It's what I want."

She nodded.

Howard was right, there are just as many details to dying as there are to living.

JOSEPHINE

While Waiting

I stare out at the murky light, watching the eerie shadows of the trees dance back and forth as nightfall begins to settle in on Daring. It's not only cold but also kind of creepy waiting in the dark in this driveway. Mom grips the steering wheel with both hands as if she's driving, staring out at nothing, while Camille plays with her Game Boy, the light from the flickering screen catching my eye over and over again.

Only the thought of missing a few days of school makes this all bearable. I wonder what Annie will think when I don't call and I don't show up on Monday. What will she think if I don't return at all? Last year, quiet Kristin Miller went away with her family to Thailand for a year, and when she returned she was a different person, sporting spiky, cropped hair and a tattoo on her left upper thigh. She bragged that her parents never knew she'd gotten it. Tattoos were cheap in Thailand, and with the help of her soldier boyfriend, who thought she was eighteen, Kristin had an eagle tattooed on her thigh. She showed us in gym class, lifting her shorts as the girls gathered around. "It hardly hurt, except for here," she pointed to the dark, beady eyes. "Now when I look at it, I forget all about being back in this shithole," she said, letting go of her shorts as the blue material covered it again.

What if the same thing happened to me? I think. My life could change like Kristin's, right here and now in Daring, California. It doesn't seem likely, but I still smile secretly at the thought. It might not be something as permanent as getting a tattoo, but change comes in all shapes and sizes. It doesn't matter how I change, I think, as long as I return to New York as anyone but myself.

Camille reaches into our sack of goodies and rips open a bag of potato chips and I can hear her crunching, even with my ear-phones on. I pull them down and I'm just about to suggest we go find the closest diner for a burger, then the nearest motel that has HBO and call it a night, when a car slows and pulls into the driveway behind us. The blinding headlights fill our car with light. Camille and I pop up from the backseat as my mom turns around and says, "She's here."

CATE

The End of the Day

By the time we return home, a thin veil of mist still keeps every-thing just out of focus. It's already dark and we're both exhausted. My only thought is getting Hana bathed and into some dry clothes. I can't imagine how uncomfortable she must be, but she doesn't let on. She's so quiet it frightens me. In fact, there's a strange serenity to our drive home, blanketed in the fog, the hum of the radio filling the car and Hana smiling into the whiteness. The restlessness she felt all morning has disappeared. Going out to the park seems to have brought her some calm, despite her accident.

"Who's that?" Hana suddenly says, pointing to a car I almost don't see, parked in our driveway.

"I don't know," I answer, slowing down to get a better look. It's not a car I've ever seen before.

"You expecting a date?" Hana asks.

"Not unless you set it up," I answer.

It's rare that we have many visitors, even in the daytime, so I can't begin to imagine who might be visiting now, at dinnertime. In the past year, we've seen Miles and Lily most frequently. Hana feels uncomfortable with too many people around now. Many of Max's and my old friends have kept in touch by phone or cards, but making sure Hana is comfortable is all that matters to me now.

"I don't recognize the car," she says.

"It's not Miles," I say; I would know his white Lexus anywhere, even in the dark of night. His previous car was a white Volvo and before that, a white Saab. I used to think it was just an eccentricity, but now I know it's for the more practical reason of being seen in the dark. Miles is one of the few doctors in the world who still makes house calls, day or night.

"Then who would be visiting us now?" Hana asks. "I can't see anybody like this." Her voice has an edge of apprehension to it. She shifts in her seat, and I'm reminded of her discomfort.

My eyes strain to see in the hazy fog. "Don't worry, I'll get rid of them," I add, reassuringly.

As we pull in behind the midsize, dark-colored car, our head-lights illuminate the inside. I see someone sitting in the driver's seat, and two heads poke up from the backseat. The front door of the car swings open, and a lean, long-legged driver steps out, shielding her eyes against the glare of our headlights as she walks toward us. In the white hazy light, she approaches us, finally coming into focus so that I can see she's well dressed, with stylish, shoulder-length hair.

Hana sits forward but doesn't say a word. It takes me a minute to recognize the face I'd seen almost daily during Hana's childhood. She's thinner and older, and perhaps a bit pale in the harsh white glare, but after more than ten years, it's unmistakably her.

"It's Laura," I say, surprised.

"Yes, it is," Hana whispers back.

HANA

Reunion

I knew it was Laura from the moment she stepped out of the car. No one moves like her, with the quick snap of assurance that she's had ever since she was a little girl. Even when she was in trouble at school, or at catechism, she didn't show fear like most kids would. Her eyes would glaze over as she was being lectured and she would drop her head and retreat somewhere within herself. What adults thought was remorse, I knew was simply boredom.

The years quickly dissolve the moment I glimpse Laura's face illuminated in the headlights. I can feel the blood circulating through my body down to my legs, and I want to get out of the car and run to her as fast as I can. I click open the car door, and only then, in all the excitement, remember the ulcers and the swelling of my ankles. And the fact that I'm sitting on an old beach towel my mother found in the trunk so I wouldn't wet the seat. Instead, I stay in the car and wait.

My mother gets out and greets Laura first. "I can't believe it's you," she says, hugging her tightly.

I can hear a symphony of crickets and smell the sweet night air. Seeing my mother and Laura together after so long, both so tall and beautiful, I can't help but think of what a perfect mother and daughter they would have made. The thought like a small ache moves through my body.

Laura says something that I can't hear, and in the next moment, she's coming around the car toward me. There's hardly enough time to panic before she swings the door open, and it's like being at the flower market with my grandparents again, as she brings the scent of lilies and narcissus into the car with her.

"I took the chance you'd be mad at me for coming," she says, bending over and kissing me on the cheek.

I touch her face, making sure she's real. Laura hooks a strand of her blond hair behind her ear and looks at me. For a split second it seems as if we're frozen in time. I can't imagine what she's thinking as she looks into my face—the tired, wizened face of an old lady.

The last time that I saw my grandmother Midori was at my father's funeral, three years ago. My grandmother was eighty-eight and in frail health. She sat in a wheelchair, staring straight ahead, and didn't say a word. I could only imagine how she felt, seeing her child die before her. Then I thought of Cate and how she would feel when I left, and my tears fell for both her and for Max. When my grandmother saw me, I saw a glint of surprise in her eyes, followed by recognition. Almost five years had passed since we'd last seen each other. She nodded her head and smiled kindly as if she understood. During that time, we had both become frail, old ladies watching the world pass us by.

When I turn away, Laura gently turns my face back to hers again. All the time, a smile never leaves her lips, and she doesn't register the slightest bit of surprise at what she sees. She's still so beautiful. Her perfect features have improved with age, gained depth and character; a sudden rush of embarrassment rises inside of me, and I have to look away again.

"I could never stay mad at you for long," I say, my voice high and dry.

I wish I could disappear so she can't see how much I've changed. I can only hope that in the dim light she'll see me gradually, like in one of my father's Polaroid snapshots, fading in slowly so it isn't such a shock.

Laura laughs. "Here, let me help you out."

"Please," I say. "My mother will." And before I can say anything else, Cate is there, carefully lifting me. Together they help me walk into the house.

"I've had an accident," I turn and confess into Laura's ear. "I've wet myself."

"I know," she whispers back to me. "Your mother warned me."

I swallow and don't know what to say. It's almost comical. After more than ten years, my wetting myself is the first thing we talk about.

"Did you ever think of getting some of those adult diapers?" she asks. "John's mother uses them when she goes out, just in case. They save her a lot of trouble. I'll pick some up for you tomorrow if you like," she says.

I laugh out loud at her answer. A few weeks ago, it was my greatest fear, losing control, regressing to wearing diapers. Now, here is Laura offering to get them for me.

"Do they come in designer colors?" I ask.

She laughs. "I'll find out."

I look back when I hear muffled voices, remembering there were other people in the car with Laura. The two figures cast hazy shadows standing by the car.

Laura turns and says to them, "Josie and Camille, come in and meet your godmother." Out of the misty fog, they step forward, and I can see that one girl is tall and gangly with wavy dark hair and the other, shorter and rounder with Laura's golden locks. I strain to get a better look at my goddaughters, then give up and concentrate on taking each careful step, one at a time.

I can feel my mother pressing closer, holding on to me tighter, her reassurance that everything is going to be all right.

JOSEPHINE

Strangers in the Night

Hana is so tiny, walking between my mom and hers. I've never seen a grown-up so small, except for midgets and dwarfs, but they were born that way. Camille and I are standing by the car freezing, when Mom finally remembers she has two daughters and tells us to come over. But we can barely see Hana as she's quickly escorted into the house.

Girls, wait in the living room," Mom tells us when we get inside. It's a big, old house, but it's warm and comfortable, with a huge fireplace and lots of pillows on the sofa. I have to pinch myself to believe that this morning we were in New York, and now we're in California.

Camille looks at me and says, "It smells strange in here," then sits down on the cream-colored sofa, takes out her Game Boy, and starts playing again.

"It's just the smoky smell from the fireplace," I tell her, though there's a tinge of something else I can't quite place. I walk over and look at all the photos on top of the piano. Most of them are family snapshots. None of them is recent, but I recognize a younger version of Cate standing next to an Asian man, who must be Hana's father. Another shows Hana as a little girl standing in front of a birthday cake with her parents and two older couples, one of them Japanese. I guess they must be Hana's grandparents. In the majority of photos, I see Hana at the same age that she is in Laura's picture back in New York, a young girl who looks much more like her father than her mother. It's good to know that we have something in common.

CATE

Floating

The last person I ever expected to see again was Laura, and not far behind—her daughters, Josephine and Camille. Their very presence feels like a breath of fresh air. The long, cold winter had left Hana and me both feeling languid and stagnant. Add to that Werner's more aggressive symptoms this week, and I felt Hana losing the fight that's always been in her. But like a saving grace, here is Laura, and I can see a flicker of light return to Hana's eyes.

When Laura called last week, I was the one who answered the phone.

"How is she?" Laura asked.

"As good as can be," I answered. That was just before Hana's ankles began to swell. I was trying to sound hopeful, but my words fell flat.

Laura sighed. "Do you think she'd mind if I brought the girls out to see her?"

"I don't know," I answered truthfully. The last thing I wanted was for Hana to feel any more self-conscious about the way she looked. At the same time, something inside of me screamed for Laura and the girls to come now, before it was too late.

"Just for a short visit."

"You'll have to ask Hana," I finally said, all the while thinking, Yes, come. Come now.

"I will." Then she added, "Again."

I smiled, knowing how stubborn Hana could be. "Is she still giving you a hard time?"

"She doesn't give an inch." Laura laughed.

"No, she doesn't." I shook my head. Then I added, "Thank you, Laura, for always being such a good friend to Hana. It has meant the world to her."

"I always thought it was the other way around." She laughed over the phone.

When they were growing up, I used to be afraid that Laura would abandon Hana for the captain of the football team or for a group of healthy, popular friends. I knew it was a natural part of life, but I still braced myself for it. From childhood they'd been like sisters. Then one day I overheard a conversation she and Hana were having. They were in high school at the time, and had become more secretive and possessive of what was happening in their worlds.

"What do you suppose dying feels like?" I heard Laura ask. Part of me wanted to rush right into Hana's room and shut her up, but I couldn't move. I stood at the doorway waiting for Hana to say something.

There was a long pause, and then she finally did. "I guess it's like closing your eyes and going to sleep."

"Are you ever afraid to go to sleep?" Laura asked.

"I'm not afraid of the sleep part," Hana said. "I just hate to leave my parents and you."

I couldn't listen anymore. I slowly backed away from her doorway and down the hall to the living room, unable to stop shaking. I hadn't realized that they had reached the level of intimacy that actually allowed them to speak about Hana's death. If it had been a question about sex, it would have been perfectly natural, but *death!* At first, I was angry with Laura. Max and I had steered away from the subject, treating Hana as much like a normal teenager as we could. But when I calmed down, I reminded myself that Hana's life would never be normal, and that she needed someone like Laura to relieve her burdens, to help her through it. In many ways, Max and I were always too close for her to confide in us.

But when Hana got off the phone with Laura, I knew her answer just by the look on her face. "She wants to come out with the girls," she said. A thin thread of hope. "But I said no." Quickly replaced by reality.

While I'm helping Hana get cleaned up and changed, Laura is in the kitchen, making us something simple for dinner.

"Laura certainly surprised us," I say, helping Hana lower herself slowly into the bathtub. Her body is so thin I can see her ribs protruding, the two small mounds of her breasts dimpling the water. The ulcers have left dark scars on her legs and feet, but the swelling around her ankles has gone down, and I breathe a sigh of relief. I remember how Max used to bathe her when she was a baby, her chubby limbs splashing in the warm water. He lowered her in gently as if she might break. Now I can feel how her body instantly relaxes when she's in the water.

Hana smiles. "She always did get what she wanted."

"Are you all right with them staying here?" I ask, having already made the offer to them.

Hana stirs the warm water. My right arm cradles her neck as if she were a baby again, only it's an old, kind face that looks up at me.

"Laura can stay in my old room and the girls can use the guest room," she finally says. There's a tinge of defeat in her voice, or is it just fatigue?

"It'll be fine," I say. "The girls can't help but love you. Laura loves you."

"Those girls would rather be home with their friends," Hana says. "The only reason they're here is because Laura wants them to be." Her hand slaps at the water. "Did you get a good look at them?" she asks. Her eyes look hopeful. I know she wants some clue as to who her goddaughters are, a slight edge when she comes face-to-face with them. But we had spirited Hana into the house so quickly, I realize now, that I hadn't really seen the girls at all.

I shake my head. "Laura looks good," I say instead.

"Laura has always looked good." Hana lies back in the water, my arm still supporting her neck. She says this matter-of-factly, without a trace of envy in her voice.

"Don't worry," I reassure her. I lean forward and turn on the faucet, splashing water into the tub again. Hana loves the feeling of floating.

While Hana rests, I drop her soiled clothing into the washer, then help Laura with dinner. The girls are in the living room watching television.

"Care for a glass of wine?" I ask. I realize it's the first time I've offered anyone a drink in a long time. "I think I still have a bottle somewhere."

"You've read my mind." Laura smiles.

I open the pantry and rummage through the contents, at last finding a bottle of 1996 Merlot. It was the year Max died. While I'm opening it, Laura tells me about their trip. "I decided last week, after Hana and I got off the phone, that we were coming to Daring, even for a weekend, whether Hana wanted me to or not. I want the girls to know Hana and see where I grew up." She pushes a strand of hair away from her face. "At first they thought I was crazy. But believe it or not, Cate, I haven't been very crazy in the last ten years."

I hand her a glass of wine, and she lifts her glass to me and takes a big swallow.

"We flew into San Francisco around noon, rented a car, and I drove straight up to Daring." She stops to pour the cooked spaghetti into a colander. "Anyway, it's a good way for them to see some of California."

I can hear the blare of the television, every once in a while punctuated by one of the girls' voices yelling out something at the game show contestant. "They must be exhausted with the time difference."

Laura laughs. "They never seem to be exhausted. I'm the only one exhausted."

"Here, let me do that."

"No, please sit," Laura says, "I'm having a great time. I rarely have time to cook back home. Mostly, it's takeout after a long day at the office."

"Who watches the girls?" I ask.

"We have a housekeeper," she says.

I look at Laura, and she catches my eye.

"Frannie's been with us since the girls were born. She treats them as her own." Laura divides the spaghetti onto five plates, pouring sauce over each small mountain. "The salad's in the refrigerator," she says, taking another sip of her wine. "I see Hana's kept every photo and drawing of the girls."

"She loves all their letters and pictures," I say.

There's a pause between us before Laura asks, "How is she, Cate, really?"

"You've seen for yourself," I answer, a bit abruptly. "She has her good days and bad days. Tonight she wasn't at her best and she's embarrassed about it."

Laura turns to face me. "It's now or never. I want them to have a sense of who Hana is. She's their godmother, and they deserve to know her."

And what about Hana? What does Hana deserve? I ask myself. I've selfishly wanted Laura and the girls to come, to see this precious child of mine before it's too late, but now I feel guilty. Just thinking of Hana having another accident this afternoon, and seeing her fragile body in the bathtub tonight, I feel suddenly afraid that this visit will be too much for her.

"It's just that she doesn't need to feel any worse about herself," I finally say. "For whatever time she has left, I want her to be comfortable."

"How will seeing her goddaughters again make her feel any worse?"

I sit down at the table, suddenly drained from the day. "It's how your girls will see her that really scares her."

"They know all about Werner." Laura fidgets with a napkin on the counter. I can see that she's exhausted, her nails bitten down to the quick.

"Knowing and seeing are two different things. Until now, they've only heard that their godmother has some kind of aging disease. They haven't really seen firsthand that she's your age but looks like your grandmother," I say.

Laura comes and sits beside me at the table. "I won't lie and tell you I wasn't shocked to see how much she's aged," she says thoughtfully. "But all she had to do was speak to me and I knew she was the same Hana I've always known. Give the girls a chance. They're wiser and stronger than you think," Laura says, reaching across the table and touching my hand.

But all I can think of is how everything has changed in just one day, how our life this morning began with Hana and me, just as it always did. And now there are five warm bodies in the house, filling it up and making it feel like a home again. "Thank you for coming," I say softly, placing my other hand on top of hers.

HANA

What I See

By the time Cate and Laura help me to the dinner table, the girls are already seated and waiting. I refuse to use the wheelchair and manage with their help to make my grand entrance on my own two feet. Which may have been the wrong thing to do, since the simplest motions seem to take forever. The girls glance up, then look away when they see me enter. It's nothing unusual, but there's something inside of me that wishes for more.

"Josie and Camille, this is your godmother, Hana," Laura introduces.

They both look up and say hello, almost simultaneously, as if rehearsed.

I smile. "Hello."

My voice is high and squeaky. I try to imagine how I must look and sound from their point of view. I'm small and withered looking, just a tiny husk of a person. Look at me, I want to say to them, though they quickly glance back down at their spaghetti.

"Hana last saw you both when you were still babies," Laura tells her daughters, though they must have heard the same line over and over.

"I can hardly recognize you," I say.

When we're all seated, Cate lights the candles on the table and turns off the overhead light. The room softens, and I immediately feel more comfortable. We all look much more relaxed in the flickering light. I barely touch my food, stealing quick glances at each of the girls, whose downcast eyes focus on their plates. Look at me.

This is what I see. Josephine is thirteen, long and lean like Laura, her face peppered with pimples, some of which she has picked, leaving small red scabs. She's serious looking, but maybe evasive, and wears big, baggy jeans and a tight long-sleeve T-shirt that rises to expose her navel. There's a kind of fiery curiosity about her that I can't quite pinpoint. Eleven-year-old Camille has Laura's coloring and is softer and rounder, with the last remnants of baby fat. She definitely seems the happier of the two. Still, Josie's eyes brings my gaze back to her, as if something uncertain and fragile is caught in their darkness. I take all of this in like one cool swallow of water and wonder what Cate is thinking as she watches them.

Cate and Laura keep up the conversation, until I clear my throat and say, "Who's ready for dessert?"

Camille looks up just long enough from her plate to smile and say, "I'd like some."

"Me, too," I say.

Cate looks over at me, and I can tell she doesn't have much in the way of a dessert. It has been off the menu for a very long time, and I've lost the taste for anything sweet or rich. Cate gets up and goes to the kitchen to rummage around the cabinets. In the end, she brings back only a new jar of strawberry jam and some stale oatmeal cookies, which she has warmed in the microwave.

"Tomorrow we go grocery shopping," she says when she returns to the dining room.

The warmed-up oatmeal cookie with gobs of jam on top doesn't taste that bad. When Camille asks for another, I look over to see Cate smiling at me. It's a tenuous beginning, but it's a beginning. After so many months of cold, it feels as if spring has finally arrived.

Later, when Laura is putting the girls to bed, Cate comes to my room to say good night. "You look tired," she says.

"Lots of excitement today," I answer.

"You feeling okay?" she asks. Neither of us mentions the accident.

I nod.

"Laura will be in to say good night in a few minutes."

I look up and smile. "It went pretty well, after all."

"Yes, it did. The dessert was a big hit." She laughs.

"Stale cookies and jam. What kind of mother are you?" I laugh, too.

"The creative kind," she answers.

Cate leans over and kisses me on the cheek, her warmth against my own coolness. No fever. No bed-wetting. No more bad days.

JOSEPHINE

Conversation

Hana is small and looks old and birdlike. She reminds me of a character in a George Lucas or Steven Spielberg movie—but one of the good, not evil creatures. It's hard to believe that she and Mom are the same age, or that they were once such good friends. But then I see how gentle she is with Hana, how she leans over and whispers in her ear, how she carefully pushes in her chair, and it's a different Laura Stevens I see. Not the one who's always working, rushing from one meeting to another, hardly stopping long enough to have a quiet conversation with anybody. This Laura Stevens is careful and kind, like when Camille and I are sick with a fever.

I was happy Cate lit candles and turned off the light during din-ner. The flickering candlelight dimmed the room and made everyone look softer and more relaxed. At first, I could hardly eat with Hana staring at us so much. Camille kept nudging me with her foot under the table, while I tried to concentrate on minding my own business. Still, even in the dim candlelight, or maybe because of it, I dared to glance over at Hana now and then. Once I looked, only to find her watching us. Her dark eyes seemed to pull me in. They made me want to keep looking at her and turn away at the same time.

Even Camille stayed quiet for a change, while Mom and Cate kept the conversation going, talking about people and places we'd never heard of. I wound up a forkful of spaghetti, sipped my water, and tried to appear interested. But my thoughts were all over the place. It's really hard to believe that Cate is Hana's mother. It looks the other way around because she's tall and looks like some older actress I've seen on television.

Then Hana's high, squeaky voice asked for dessert. And it wasn't until Cate brought in some oatmeal cookies, which weren't very good, that things lightened up.

When Mom comes upstairs to say good night, she tells us Hana wants to spend some time with us tomorrow. Mom sits down on the side of the double bed and sighs. I don't think she realizes how much she sighs since Dad left. It's as if she's slowly letting out something trapped inside of her.

Camille looks at her and speaks up first. "It felt kind of creepy at dinner, like Hana's trying to memorize us."

"I believe she is," Mom says. "She hasn't seen you since you were babies. She's just trying to catch up on all that's she's missed." Laura leans over and kisses us both on the forehead. "And tomorrow you'll get to know her better."

"What if I have nothing to say?" I ask.

Mom stands up from the bed. "Josie, when have you ever been at a loss for words?"

Camille laughs.

"Now go to sleep. It's late," she says.

Before she reaches the door, I can't help myself and blurt out, "Now I know why you moved to New York. If I had to live here in no-man's-land, I'd get as far away as I could, too."

Mom looks at me and shakes her head. She has had to put up with my snide comments a lot in the past few months. As much as I try, I can't seem to stop myself, like there's someone else inside of me. Afterward, I regret what I've said, but it's too late to take it back.

"You know, Josie"—she sighs again—"if you gave both Daring and Hana a chance, you might see things differently. I bet if you actually looked and listened hard enough to someone other than your disc player, you might actually learn a thing or two, which wouldn't be such a bad idea."

I can hear her disappointment in me, and all at once I feel the hot pressure of tears against my eyes. In the next moment, Mom closes the door and is gone.

"Nice going," Camille says, yawning.

"Who asked you?" I say.

She turns on her side away from me, and I know there's a smile on her face.

I have a hard time falling asleep. I lay in bed, listening to Camille's even breaths, wishing I could take back what I said.

HANA

Change

There's a light tap on my door, and I know it's Laura.

"Come in," I say, just as the door opens and she's standing in my room.

"Everything okay?" she asks, pushing her blond hair back and away from her face. She looks tired.

"Do you always do everything you're told not to?" I ask, trying to sound stern. "Didn't I tell you not to bring the girls? How in the world can you be a good lawyer when you break the rules all the time?" I'm sitting up in a blue nightgown, and I must look a hundred years old to her.

Laura laughs and sits down on the side of my bed. "Admit it," she says. "You're glad we're here."

"It's so good to see you," I say, reaching out and touching her arm. "The girls, too."

She smiles, and I'm reminded of the young Laura. "And to-morrow you'll get to know them better."

"I was hoping you'd leave while we were ahead."

Laura pauses. I imagine that's how she is in the courtroom, her timed pauses, using every beat for total effect.

"Hana, you have nothing to be afraid of. Those two girls are much tougher than you think. Do you really think you're going to make them quiver and hide?"

"Didn't you quiver a little, when you first saw me this evening?" I ask.

Laura takes her time answering again. Only this time her eyes travel down the titles of the books I have on my nightstand, from Wallace Stegner's *Angle of Repose* to Jane Austen's *Persuasion*, then she returns to me with an answer.

"I've been just as nervous at the idea of seeing you as you were about seeing me," she says. "I was afraid I wouldn't recognize you. Let me rephrase that, that I wouldn't *know* you anymore. That you wouldn't know me. Ten years is a long time. People change, and in more ways than one. But all it took was to talk to you again to realize that even though you've changed on the outside, you're still the same Hana on the inside. I see it in your eyes, in your smile. You can't fool me."

I don't know what to say. I turn my head, and my eyes drift away from hers so she can't see the tears filling them. How can she be so beautiful and so wise? I finally turn back to her and smile. "So what took you so long?" I ask.

Laura has kicked off her shoes and is lying on my bed next to me. "What's this button for?" she asks, pressing the blue one, which raises us forward into a sitting position. She quickly presses the red button and it stops. There's only the slightest scent of her perfume now, along with the faint remnants of wine. I can't recall the last time I had a warm body so close to me, except for my mother's.

"So how have *you* been?" I ask. Now that Laura is right next to me, I want to know everything.

She looks at me and then away again. "There's lots of time tomorrow for us to catch up."

"How's John?" I ask, realizing his name hasn't been mentioned once all evening, neither by his wife nor by his children. A tall, good-looking, self-absorbed guy is how I remember him from the funeral of Laura's parents. Josephine looks a lot like him. Laura had met him in New York, and he was the youngest son of some old money Philadelphia family. I imagined she'd gotten everything she always wanted. If I ever felt envious, it was not because of Laura but because of everything I'd never be able to have.

Laura swallows, shifts on the bed, and turns on her side to look me straight in the eye. "John's moved out. We've been separated for the past nine months. Looks like we're headed for the divorce courts."

"I'm so sorry" is all I can think to say. Since childhood, I've imagined nothing could go wrong in Laura's life, that, like some fairy princess, she only had to wish for something and it came true. Yet not only were her parents killed tragically but now her marriage is breaking up.

"It's okay," Laura says, lying back and closing her eyes for a moment. "It's been a long time coming. I'll explain more to you tomorrow. You better get some sleep. I better get some sleep," she says, opening her eyes again.

"Are the girls all right?"

"Most of the time they are," she answers, her voice low and tired. "And some of the time they aren't, especially Josie. She hasn't been doing very well in school lately, or everyday life, for that matter. She seems angry with everyone, especially me. But that's another story."

Laura slowly rolls away from my side and stands up, putting an end to my questions. I immediately miss the warmth and weight of her body next to mine. She smiles and leans over to kiss me on the cheek. "Don't be mad at me, Hana. I'm the one who needed to see you."

"I'm not mad," I say, thinking how much we sound like two kids. I want to tell Laura how happy I am she came, how I felt like giving up this afternoon after the second accident, how glad I am she didn't listen to me. I feel strangely alive just having her lie next to me, as if I'm a real person again, not someone who has become a mere shadow, someone simply waiting day after day to disappear completely.

"See you tomorrow then," Laura says, walking away from me toward the door.

"Yes, tomorrow," I whisper. A new mystery as to what the day will bring. Today has been like a dream I'm afraid I'll wake up from. A dream of what a normal life would be like, all the scents and colors of the park, followed by the voices and laughter of Laura and the girls. I wonder if it's too late to let myself hope a little. See what it might be like actually to get to know Josie and Camille.

I suddenly wish Laura were in a sleeping bag next to me again like when we were young, listening to music and talking into the night. Only this time I'd reach out and take her hand, close my trembling fingers around hers just before we drift off to sleep.

After Laura leaves, I pick up the recorder on the nightstand and play a short melody Howard once taught me. "It's basically just six notes repeated," he told me. "The simple power of music." It soothes and comforts. Afterward, I lean over and turn out the light. Under my blankets, I slowly rotate my left, then right ankle in small circles, as Dr. Truman showed me, the dull pain slowly easing. Upstairs, a door softly clicks shut. Then I listen in the darkness for the familiar sounds, knowing everything has changed.

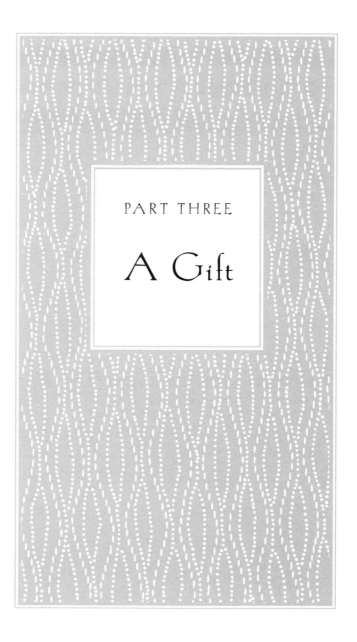

PART THREE

A Gift

CATE

One Fine Day

I wake up early this morning and push the curtain aside to see that the fog has lifted and the sky is bright and clear. Another day, already different from yesterday, I think to myself. For the first time in so many years, the house feels full and there's something sweetly satisfying about it, like quenching a thirst or feeding a hunger.

I dress and make my way downstairs, where I pause in front of Hana's door. I gently turn the doorknob and peer in, relieved to find her still asleep. Quietly I stand by her bed, studying the once sweet face, now creased and furrowed. She's thirty-eight, not even forty, I remind myself, and sorrow like a sharp pain moves through me. Her life will end when most are just entering their best years, when wisdom softens the hard edges of youth, when life can finally be enjoyed to the fullest.

But I should consider myself lucky. Unlike those who lose a

child suddenly in illness or in an accident, I've been given the gift of time together. I've had years to prepare myself for Hana's leaving, but still it feels like a brand-new hurt each time I look at her. I watch my daughter sleeping like a small child under the covers that rise and fall with each breath she takes. Her head lies lightly against the pillow, her lips parted as if in midsentence. I lean over, and my fingers barely touch her cheek. Its warmth immediately puts me at ease. Stay with me, I say silently to myself.

When Hana turned four, she began to come into our room every morning before dawn and crawl into bed between Max and me. No matter what we did, we couldn't break her of the habit. As time wore on, we began to stumble through each day from lack of sleep. Finally, I explained to Hana that we couldn't get back to sleep after she woke us up so early and that, even though it was hard, she had to sleep in her own bed. "It's not that we don't love you, but Daddy needs to sleep in order to go and teach." She looked at me with her dark eyes and nodded her head in understanding. The next morning we slept until the alarm clock rang, waking with Hana nowhere in sight. We both assumed she had slept through the night in her own bed. Only after we'd risen did we see Hana sleeping soundly on the floor at the foot of our bed. Her lips were parted in just the same way as now, and I remember bending over her small body and feeling the warmth of her cheek.

I close her door quietly, then go to the kitchen to start a pot of coffee before slipping out to the garden. I'll have enough time to water before the others wake and the new day begins. I put on my jacket and gloves, step quietly out into the sharp morning air, and take a deep breath of the rich, sweet fragrance of pine. It looks as if it'll be a beautiful, mild day.

In our front yard is a huge redwood tree that I've always admired. During the summer it shades us from the heat, and in winter its thick, full branches ward off the rain. I touch the solid trunk as if it's something spiritual, like a totem pole, and maybe it is, because I draw a sudden strength just standing by it. Long after I'm gone, it will still be standing here. I look down our quiet street to the green house that's now painted a salmon color where Laura's parents, Mary and Jack, had lived since Hana was a baby. Their deaths ten years ago were so sudden and unexpected that we were all in a state of shock. Now that hollow feeling of loss returns. Killed in a train accident on their way to New York to visit their grandchildren, they left Laura and her brother, Jake, suddenly without parents, without foundation. I can't imagine it being anything other than fate. Fate reaching out its hand, picking and choosing, deciding who will live and who will die. I kept hoping Jack and Mary never knew what hit them when the train derailed, that their last moments were happy ones as they sat in the dining car eating, drinking wine, and toasting the long-planned trip. Their eyes might have locked onto each other's at the sudden shrieking sound of the brakes, but they never knew that a car had been parked on the tracks by a young man who had just lost his girlfriend and was waiting for the 7:42 to end his misery. Sometimes I wish for the same, a quick and mindless death. By the time you realized what was happening, it would be over.

I unreel the hose and turn on the water. Laura came home with both little girls for the funeral. She had finished law school, gotten married, and had two babies within six years. Josie was barely three years old, and Camille was still a baby. Her husband, John, had come too. They were the perfect family standing there at the cemetery, and I remember that I couldn't help feeling jealous seeing them and knowing this was something Hana would never have. I still feel bad thinking about it now. Laura had just lost her

parents and I was grieving for Hana. I wanted to reach out to
Laura then, tell her that Hana and I would always be there for
her, but even in tragedy she seemed so self-assured that my mumbled sympathy sounded hollow as I gave her a hug.

I hear a rustling sound and look up to see Josie standing on the
front step. She has tied her long, wavy hair back into a ponytail
and looks like a typical teenager in blue jeans, T-shirt, and a red
sweater. Her dark, darting eyes survey the garden and come back
to rest on me.

"Good morning. You're up early," I say. "Did you sleep well?"

She shrugs. "It's already ten in New York," she says matter-of-
factly, arms crossed over her chest. There's something defiant in
her stance. "I don't need very much sleep."

"Are you hungry? Would you like some breakfast?"

"I don't usually eat much breakfast. Just orange juice." Josie
shoves her hands into the pockets of her jeans. The pale white
skin of her wrists gleams against the dark blue material.

I smile. "I think we can arrange that."

For the first time since we've met, I see a slight smile cross
her lips. "Where do you go to school?" I ask, hoping to break the
ice.

Josie takes a step toward me, but the glint in her eyes has
vanished. She touches a small patch of scabby pimples on the side
of her face. "Lincoln Academy," she answers. "It's private."

"Do you like it?"

She shrugs again. "It's okay."

"What's your favorite subject?" I feel like I'm playing twenty
questions. I've forgotten how hard it is to make conversation with
a teenager who isn't interested.

"Nothing, really."

I look up at her. "Come on, everyone likes something. I liked English."

"Yeah, English is okay, and history, I guess." She steps closer to me, pulling her sweater tighter against the chilly morning air.

"If you could be anywhere in the world right now"—I try another tactic—"where would you be?"

She looks down and kicks a pinecone away from the flagstone path. "Anywhere but here," she says, kicking again at air. She glances over quickly to see my reaction.

But I don't give her the satisfaction of reacting. I can hear the birds singing, and it's too lovely a day to have it ruined by this tall, skinny girl, even if she is Hana's goddaughter. What happened to the sweet-looking child in the photos on our refrigerator door? I think to myself.

"Yes, I guess New York's a lot more exciting," I finally say.

She shrugs, drops her eyes, and doesn't answer.

I continue watering, glancing over at my rosebushes. "Do you know, I have a rose with the same name as you," I say, wondering if she'll even care about such trivia, but I keep talking nonetheless. "The Josephine rose was named after Empress Josephine, the wife of Napoleon. They say she used to carry a rose with her everywhere she went to hide her bad teeth when she laughed."

"For real?" Josie's eyes come alive. She steps closer to look at the bushes.

I nod, delighted finally to have found something that interests her. "That's what the history books say."

"Do all roses have names?"

"Plenty of them do," I say. "For instance, some royalty or movie stars have strains of roses especially cultivated and named after them."

Josephine smiles, showing a row of green-colored braces. Lily, who keeps up with the latest high school fads, told me braces now come in all colors of the rainbow.

"That's so cool," she says. "So what color is the Josephine rose?"

I'm amazed by her enthusiasm. Who would believe this sullen girl would actually be interested in roses? "It's pink," I tell her. "A beautiful, pale pink."

"I wish I could see one," she says, sounding like a little girl again.

"Some wishes do come true," I say. "I'll send you a photo when they bloom."

"Really?"

"Tell you what, if you finish watering this Josephine rosebush for me, not only will I send you her photo in a few weeks but I'll go in and start breakfast right now." I point out the bush, and hand her the hose with instructions not to overwater my newly planted bulbs.

"Cate?" she calls out.

I turn around. "Yes."

"Is Cate your full name, or is it short for something else?"

I smile. "Caterina, with a C. My family's Italian. Why?"

"Just curious," Josephine says. "I like names." She smiles and turns back to her watering.

For a moment, I watch Josie's quick, graceful movements as she bends over and carefully waters the rosebushes. She sweeps her ponytail over her shoulder and out of the way, and as I watch the long, thin limbs of a healthy, growing child, I can't help but feel a touch of envy.

HANA

The Light of Day

I wake up to the high-pitched trills of the birds singing in the trees this morning. It's the first time in months that I've slept so well, and for a split second, still groggy with sleep, I feel young again. The aroma of pancakes wafting in from the kitchen stirs a sudden, sharp memory in me, like Proust's beloved madeleines. I can hear Howard laughing at the comparison. "Pancakes aren't half as romantic as madeleines," he'd say. Nevertheless, they strike the very same chord of childhood, of some comfort that lingers lightly in the air.

When I was a little girl, Max always came to wake me up on Saturday mornings, letting Cate sleep in. Then he piggybacked me downstairs to the kitchen and made pancakes for breakfast. I remember the strong aroma of coffee, the sweet, thick maple syrup that left my fingers sticky. The same warm, wonderful scent drifted up to their bedroom and eventually brought my mother downstairs. While my parents usually sat in the kitchen and read the paper together, I watched cartoons in the living room. Even now, when I think back to those precious Saturday mornings, when each of us had Max and his pancakes for a little while to ourselves, I can't help but smile.

I get up slowly. For the first time in a week, the swelling in my ankles has gone down enough so that I can stand and dress myself. It gives me hope that it'll be a good day. From my closet I pull out a pale blue shirt, with a pair of matching slacks that are now too loose around the waist. Somewhere, I know I still have a belt. How funny it is to think that my once most prized possessions—my black patent leather shoes, the much too expensive green silk blouse, my collection of hand-painted scarves—mean so little to me now. They sit in the closet, abandoned. Most days around the house, I wear a sweatshirt and loose cotton-knit pants, all bought in children's sizes. The last time we were in a department store, the saleswoman smiled at us and asked Cate, "For your grandkids?"

I watched my mother's face stay calm as she looked at me and said, "For my daughter."

The saleswoman looked from Cate to me in a moment of confusion, then reclaimed her smile. "Yes, well, thank you and enjoy."

It's been a long time since I've worried about what I was going to wear and how I might look in the latest fashions. But last night the thought filled my mind with indecision.

I change and sit down for a moment to catch my breath. From the kitchen I hear the low murmur of voices. Our house is usually so quiet, with just the two of us, that it frightens me now to think of facing Laura and the girls in the light of day.

I close my eyes and recall the little girl I saw at the drugstore a few weeks ago, one of the few times I'd ventured out lately with

Cate. The little girl couldn't take her eyes off me. While most people glanced my way only to look quickly away, the girl stood rooted in place, watching as we walked slowly into the store. She couldn't have been more than three or four years old, but she didn't appear afraid, simply curious. What do you see? I wanted to ask as I gazed back, her youth and beauty so tender at that age. She rubbed her eyes and smiled, then looked at me again from between her fingers. She was playing peekaboo. When I peeked back at her from behind my hands, she giggled sweetly. She saw not some wizened old troll that might have invaded her nightmares but someone she wasn't afraid of.

"Got it," Cate said then, reaching up to the top shelf for her eyedrops. "Need anything else?"

"Not a thing." I cleared my throat.

"What are you smiling about?" she asked.

I pointed toward the little girl down the aisle.

"She's beautiful," Cate said.

Just then the girl's redheaded mother turned and glanced at my mother, then looked past me as if I wasn't there. *A tiny old woman. A whisper of a person.*

"You aren't that much younger than I am," I said, just loud enough for her to hear, my voice calm and even. "And I could have a daughter the same age as yours."

The words lingered in the air. I don't know what possessed me to say them out loud. I sensed my mother standing right behind me.

The woman glanced back at me again. *Crazy old woman.* "Come along," she said, reaching for her daughter's hand.

The little girl stood her ground.

"Now!" The mother's sharp tone and quick tug set the child moving. But as she was being pulled down the aisle, the little girl turned around for one last time and waved.

And I waved back. It was such a simple exchange, yet that afternoon in the drugstore is a moment I'll always treasure.

I wish it could be as simple with Laura's daughters. I want them to see past Werner to who I really am. But Josie and Camille are older, with minds of their own. I'm a stranger to them. My feeling of exhilaration just minutes ago is gone, replaced by a sinking in my stomach. What if they don't see me as that little girl did but turn their backs on me like her mother? I push away the thought, stand up and straighten my shirt, then walk slowly to the door, each careful step taking me forward.

JOSEPHINE

The Josephine Rose

When I come in from watering the garden, Cate has pancakes and a glass of orange juice waiting for me on the kitchen table. "I have to get something," I say, smiling at her. I run upstairs to find Camille still in bed, her head buried under the covers, as I dig through my bag for the name book. When I return to the kitchen, Cate is sitting at the table drinking a cup of coffee. I'm just about to look up the meaning of her name when the front doorbell rings, startling both of us.

"Be right back," Cate says. "Eat your pancakes before they get cold," she instructs with a smile.

I lean forward in my chair and watch her walk down the hall. It's strangely quiet here, no horns honking or sirens blaring down the street like in New York. Silence is a sound that takes some getting used to. I look around the big, comfortable kitchen, with a blue-and-white-tiled island in the middle and pots and pans hanging from an iron frame suspended from the ceiling. Small pots of flowers line the windowsill looking out to the backyard. It's the kind of kitchen you see on television, with a happily married mother and father, their precocious children, and the family dog. It doesn't seem like real life.

On the refrigerator door are postcards and drawings that we've sent to Hana over the years. I get up and look at them—from shaky alphabets to wobbly cursive—some dictated to my mom when we were too young to write. Baby photos and recent ones stare me in the face. The history of Camille's life and mine hangs on blue, green, and red magnets in front of me.

I glance down the hallway. Cate is talking to a tall, gray-haired man at the door, their voices a soothing murmur so they don't wake up anyone. Mom and Camille haven't come downstairs yet, and the door to Hana's room is still closed. I walk back to the refrigerator and, one after the other take down all the cards we've written to Hana, then return to the table and begin reading them.

Dear Hana,

I am seven. We went swimming today and I drank pool water. Mommy says it won't hurt me but my stomach feels funny. Mommy says you like to swim. Maybe one day you can come and swim with me.

Love, Josie

Dear Hana,

Camille and I went skiing this weekend. We're not very good but I like the feeling of flying down the hill as if I'm out of control, then pushing the tips of my skis together and slowing down. It took Camille forever to get down the hill and then she didn't want to go back up again. You'll have to come with us one day.

Love, Josephine (Age 11)

I sip my orange juice and bite into the stack of pancakes Cate has made for me as I read. Each card brings back a memory of the time and place—all the holidays and family vacations. I swallow and feel suddenly sad. Not just for me, seeing all our happy family holidays, but for Hana. Almost all of the notes tell her to come and visit. Both Camille and I had figured out it was an easy way to end our notes quickly. *You'll have to come and see. I'll show you when you come to visit. Can't wait to see you.* Thinking back, I can't remember if I ever really meant for Hana to come.

I drink down my orange juice, then stick each card and photo back on the refrigerator door just as they were. I step back and look at the collage of notes, drawings, and pictures. Only now do I realize that Hana understands so much more about us than we do about her. The few things I've learned about Hana come quickly to mind. I remember from all the cards she has sent us that her handwriting is small and uniform, as if it took hours to get it all perfectly lined up. I also know that Hana means "flower," and that she's like a small and fragile bloom. Then, for the first time, I feel that spark of curiosity about why Mom wanted us to visit Daring and meet Hana. *Change does come in all shapes and sizes,* I think to myself again.

What I've learned so far is that there's a rose named after Empress Josephine. I think of the soft, silky petals against her lips, the sweet scent beneath her nose as she held it in front of her mouth when she laughed. It's a story I already love. How a flower shielded her from the world. I pick up my name book on the table and turn the pages slowly, only to be pleasantly surprised when I find Caterina and, next to it, the one-word meaning: *pure.*

CATE

Comfort Food

I didn't expect Miles to drop by so early this morning. I open the front door to find him waiting on the step, his pale blue eyes still tinged with sleep, gripping his black medical bag. He's kind enough to stop by the house to check on Hana's leg ulcers and swollen feet. Sometimes I don't know what we would do without him. It's another one of those reliable comforts in life, like Lily's macaroons that she dribbles chocolate on top of and brings over two or three times a year, just before she's ready to go on another diet. "Just the thing you need," she says, "before going off to battle."

"I'm sorry," Miles apologizes. "I know it's early, but I won't be able to stop by later in the afternoon."

"It's fine," I say, opening the door wider.

He smiles. "I thought I'd come to the wrong house at first," he says, gesturing at Laura's rental car parked in our driveway. "Visitors, at this early hour?"

"Hana's old friend Laura Stevens, who used to live down the street. She's visiting with her daughters," I explain. Just saying it makes me feel as if it's something that happens all the time.

Miles steps inside. "Mary and Jack's daughter," he says. "It's been quite a while since she's been back."

"Over ten years."

"Maybe this isn't a good time to check up on Hana. I just wanted to see if the swelling has gone down." He takes a step back.

"The swelling went down some yesterday," I say. "She started to get up and around a bit last night." I can't bring myself to tell Miles about Hana's wetting herself again at the park yesterday. For just today, I want things light and hopeful. "Have you had breakfast?" I ask.

"Coffee," Miles answers.

"Then join us. We're having pancakes, with lots of butter and syrup," I tease.

"Just the way I like them," he says.

I usher Miles into the living room, where we sit and I update him on Hana's ulcers and our unexpected outing to the park. I hear doors opening and closing upstairs, footsteps on the stairs and down the hall to the kitchen. "Let's go have breakfast," I say to Miles.

The chorus of voices startles me at first, as if I've stumbled into someone else's kitchen. Hana is sitting at the table between Josephine and Camille, while Laura is at the stove flipping pancakes. I smile to see that Hana has dressed herself, and she catches my eye and smiles back—her pale, tired face lighting up—letting me know that everything is fine. And then, right in front of me, a medley of life—the voices and laughter of the girls, the clinking of forks against plates, the gurgling of the coffeemaker, as we all sit down and eat pancakes like one big, happy family.

Before I know it, the girls are in the living room watching cartoons and Laura stands up and announces that she and Hana are off to visit some of their old haunts. "I'll have Hana back in a little while," she says.

It all seems so astoundingly ordinary that I'm the one who's tongue-tied. But what if, I want to say, though the words catch in my throat.

"It'll be good for you two to get some air," Miles says. "It's a beautiful day. Let me help you to the car," he tells Hana.

"We can take the wheelchair," Laura adds.

"No wheelchair," Hana says emphatically. "I'll be fine." She slowly stands, balancing herself against the table. Her eyes catch mine again and she says softly, "I'm fine, really," to reassure me. Only then does she reach out and take hold of Laura's arm.

After Hana and Laura leave, I'm alone with Miles in the kitchen. I feel a small stab of panic. The girls are watching cartoons, their short spurts of laughter and the fast-paced music seeping in from the living room. We are sitting at the kitchen table like normal adults having a conversation when it strikes me that we're talking not about Hana or Werner but about our favorite old movies, like *Some Like It Hot* and *The Great Escape*. Miles grins, then takes another bite of pancake. I've never really noticed his smile before, a bit crooked in that boyish sort of way.

In the next moment, a great sadness washes over me, as I think of Max and me sitting at the kitchen table on weekend mornings, eating pancakes and reading the paper. Bits of conversation would bubble up now and then, but there was no need for talk. We felt that comfort of being together, of knowing that nothing more needed to be said. I can hear the rustling of the newspaper and Max clearing his throat. I miss those times, and they come flooding back to me as I sit here with Miles.

"Are you all right?" he asks. He sets down his coffee cup.

"Oh yes," I say, standing up. "More pancakes?"

Miles pats his stomach. "Since I'm the doctor, I'd better listen to my own advice."

"You're as slim as the day I met you," I tell him.

Max had introduced me to Miles after they'd started playing tennis together. He brought Miles home to the small one-bedroom house we rented when we first arrived in Daring. I remember how the vase Max's mother had given us as a wedding present had intrigued Miles so that he reached out to examine it and it tipped toward the edge of the mantel. I already imagined it shattering on the hearth, all our good fortune gone, when with lightning reflexes he reached out and caught it. He was quick and agile—the signs of a good tennis player.

Miles laughs. "I have to work at it," he says, "not like you. You're naturally fit."

I turn toward the stove, blushing to think that he has actually paid attention to my body. But then he's a doctor, and doctors notice such things. "More coffee?" I reach for the pot.

He drinks down the last bit in his mug. "No, I'd better get going. I've got patients to see at the clinic." He stands up and puts on his jacket.

"So when do you rest?" I ask.

"I don't," he says. He looks over at me and smiles. "You know, there's the Annual Daring Health Clinic fund-raising dinner next Saturday night, maybe you'd be interested in going with me?"

I pour myself another cup of coffee, my heart suddenly beating faster. Get a grip, I say to myself. You've known Miles Truman forever. He's like your brother. There's nothing wrong with going to a fund-raiser with your brother. Miles was the first friend here the evening Max died. I called an ambulance and then Miles, who arrived only slightly behind the shrieking siren. But I didn't need a doctor to tell me that Max was gone. Long after Hana was asleep, after Lily and other friends had left, Miles stayed on. I knew that I needed him to stay. I wanted someone there who knew Max well—so that somehow, between our shared history of him—Max would still be there with me for a while longer.

Now I look up at Miles, with his graying hair and calm patience, and feel such gratitude for all he's done for us over the years.

"If Hana continues to feel better," I say.

"Of course." He smiles. "I'll come by and see how she's doing in a couple of days."

I lean forward against a chair. A burst of music comes from the television. "Thank you, Miles," I say, trying to keep everything light, even as Hana's words come back to me. *Dad will understand.*

"Tell her to stay off her feet if she can. No dancing for another week."

I laugh. "I'll tell her."

After Miles leaves, the kitchen feels strangely empty. Sunlight streams through the window, setting everything aglow. I walk around the table picking up dishes and cups, taking them to the sink, and rinsing them to put in the dishwasher. Everyday chores that I do without thinking, only this morning I hold on to the mug Miles drank from for just a little bit longer.

HANA

Bishop's Orchard

When we first step out the door, I lose my balance, but Laura's arms go around me before I can have another accident—one that could have severe consequences, my bones snapping like brittle twigs. From that moment on, she doesn't let go. I lean into her embrace like an elderly grandmother, and we walk slowly to the car.

"What will people think?" I laugh.

"That the girls are back together again," she says. She helps me into the passenger seat, the polished, new car smell making me dizzy.

The last time I was in a car driven by Laura, it was a very different story. I was still living and studying in Berkeley, and Laura was driving us to the library when I offhandedly glanced out the window and saw my reflection in the glass, highlighted by the revealing sunlight. And in that moment, I detected the first signs of Werner on my face. It wasn't just the glint of gray in my hair but how the skin on my face had taken on an almost transparent pallor. My eyesight was also giving me trouble, but in the bright light I could see the fine lines that had formed around the thickened edges of my eyes, along with the darkening pockets below. Werner had been a shadow hovering over me for so long. They were all the overt signs that Dr. Truman had told me about, yet even so, I felt physically ill when I actually realized I was growing old. Like in some silly sci-fi movie, I felt as if I was changing right before my eyes.

"Please take me home," I mumbled to Laura, feeling nauseated.

"What's wrong?" she asked, glancing wide-eyed in my direction.

"I want to go home," I said louder, growing more anxious with each breath.

Poor Laura didn't know what was happening. She wanted to take me to the hospital, thinking I was in great pain. Which I suppose I was. I buried my face in my hands and just began to cry.

"Hana, are you okay?" she asked over and over, reaching across and stroking my arm.

"I just want to go home," I insisted.

Laura turned the car around and drove me back to the apartment, never realizing that what I wanted was to return home to Daring.

Let's go to Bishop's Orchard," Laura says now when she gets into the car beside me. "Remember?" she asks.

I nod.

How could I forget? When Laura and I were sixteen, we dreamed of moving away from Daring to a big city where no one would know us. We'd live in skyscrapers and shop at quaint boutiques. Having lived all our lives in a small town, we wanted adventure and anonymity. Our favorite place was Bishop's Orchard, where we sat hidden among the pear trees under a tree we named Big Betsy. There, we told each other our deepest, darkest secrets, studied fashion magazines, and discussed whom we wanted to marry and what we'd wear at our weddings. I forgot about being sick during those afternoons, when it seemed too far away to be really true.

What we liked about the orchard was the way Mr. Bishop, an amateur orchardist, had gone crazy grafting different species of pear trees together. "You've got to admit, he really had some imagination," Laura said. Planted on a southern slope to protect the early bloom from frost, the trees in Mr. Bishop's orchard were as different as faces in a crowd. Some tall European varieties loomed two stories high, while others, grafted onto dwarf understock, seemed small and friendly. What they had in common was that each tree had been grafted with cuttings from several varieties. When their branches leafed out, they merged as one. Like me, they were of mixed origins. This mixture always turned the orchard into a crazy quilt of blossoms in the spring and a symphony of flavors during harvesttime, which stretched from July through October. First came juicy Flordahomes and Moonglow pears, followed by the small, spicy Seckels. My favorites were the later Max-Reds (for their flavor and color, as much as their name), then the Anjous and Comice. But best of all were the big round Asian pears, which didn't need to ripen in cold storage like the others but could be eaten out of hand, crisp and golden, in the waning days of August, while Laura and I lay on our backs in sun-drenched silence.

Under the tree we called Big Betsy, we looked up one day to

see the wide expanse of blue overhead, dotted with clouds that seemed to carry us along. Laura had closed her eyes, and I knew she was dreaming of all the places she would someday go. Places I might never get to see. I felt a bitterness rise inside me, but I quickly swallowed it back down. Sometimes, I thought, you saw too much in the daylight. It was beautiful, but I preferred the night sky. Heaven's blackboard, my grandfather Henry used to say, lit by the moon and the stars.

Laura turns down Pine Street, then makes a right on Spruce, slowing down here and there to point something out. We pass by our old elementary school, the library, the corner drugstore. All our old haunts. "What happened to that huge oak tree?" She slows down and points to the park across the street.

"They had to take it down several years ago. Some kind of disease had gotten to it," I explain.

She makes a clicking sound with her tongue and steps on the gas. "I don't remember so many houses," she says to herself.

I wonder if Laura is looking for the Daring of her youth, somehow frozen in time. She seems disappointed that it isn't the same small town she couldn't wait to leave.

"So, are you going to tell me about John?" I ask. My right hand begins to tremble, and I press it against my thigh.

Laura turns to me for a moment, then looks back at the road. "I don't really know what happened to us. In the beginning of our marriage, we couldn't stand to be away from each other. But in the past few years, there were days we barely exchanged more than ten words."

"When did he leave?" I can't believe anyone would want to leave Laura. "All our phone conversations and you never said a word. Are you all right? Are the girls?"

"Almost nine months ago," she answers. "The girls aren't happy about it, and while John can be a jerk, he's a decent father." She wets her lips with her tongue. "Sometimes I think my life's falling apart. Josephine seems to hate me since John left, and Camille keeps waiting for her daddy to come home."

I let Laura's words sink in. Her eyes brim with tears, and I reach over to touch her arm. "I'm sorry," I say softly. "It'll get better."

She glances over. "It's not how I thought my life would turn out. Remember when I wanted to rule the world? Instead, I can't even manage my own little one."

I take a closer look at Laura. She looks wonderful in a pair of jeans and a pale blue sweater, but for the first time, I can see that she has aged too, in the tiny lines spreading from the corners of her eyes when she squints against the sunlight.

"I think you've managed just fine. You have two lovely daughters and a job you're great at."

"And a failed marriage," Laura adds.

I lean toward her. "Just because a marriage ends, it doesn't mean you've failed."

"You think so?"

"I know so."

We drive in silence for a few minutes, and I suddenly feel as if all of life has passed me by. While the lives of most people took twists and turns, mine simply followed a two-lane road that led right back to Daring.

"So what will you do now?" I ask.

"I'm here with you," Laura says, watching the road. "Daring is where I want to be right now. And when we return to New York, life will go on."

Yes, it does go on, I want to tell her. Seeing Laura again reminds me that there was one little twist in my life, that long ago glimmer of hope that I'd found my prince. It was after I left Daring with Laura to go off to college at Berkeley. His name was Mark, and I remember how the hard, quick sound of his name clicked off my tongue a few times before I actually had a chance to say it to his face. He was the best friend of Laura's then boyfriend Charlie, during our junior year. The first time Mark came to our Berkeley apartment I was running out the door to an evening class. He held the door open for me as I walked out right under his arm. I remember looking up and seeing his long hair and the dark stubble of beard along his chin. When Laura introduced us, she said he was majoring in English and was devoted to Coleridge.

When Mark started coming around the apartment more, I found myself going to the library less and studying in my room, lured out of it by the low hum of voices and the Jefferson Starship blaring from the living room. I began to notice small things about him—his quickness and humor in conversation, the closeness and understanding between us, how he reminded me of a nineteenth-century poet with his beard and long hair. He must have felt the same way as we talked and laughed late into the night, comparing the writings of Coleridge and Blake. I began to miss him when he wasn't around and wanting to be with him when he was. They were feelings I'd never felt before, and they frightened me as much as they brought me happiness. Was this love? Was this the same longing my parents felt that had carried them across so many barriers? For the first time, I dared to allow myself the possibility of a normal life.

On our first real date, Mark took me out for pizza and beer. Afterward we walked the three blocks back to my apartment. It was the end of fall term, nearing the holidays, and the night was dark and cold. There was a damp, wet smell of concrete in the air. I breathed it in and felt slightly light-headed from the beer as the sharp wind stung my cheeks. We were in the middle of a conversation when Mark suddenly stopped walking and leaned over to kiss me. His hands rested on my shoulders as if I were a small child he was kissing good night. What I remember is his face suddenly in front of mine, his warm breath soothing my cheeks as his lips parted and pressed against mine. Afterward, we kept walking and he took my hand in his, leading me in the opposite direction, back to his apartment.

His room was small and cramped with books and clothes strewn everywhere. It smelled closed and musty. There was a desk and chair to one side and a mattress on the floor. I made him turn off the lights, nervous and afraid that he would see my body— my flat breasts and too thin legs—and not want to be with me. I wanted him to love me. And he did. I felt his arms around me, heard him whisper "Hana," before kissing me, touching me, and then laying his body so gently on top of mine.

Can a fairy tale have an unhappy ending? I wonder. Then I remember the little girl with the red shoes who couldn't stop dancing until her feet were cut off, and the little match girl who struck every match she had and still died in the cold. My fairy tale isn't quite so dramatic. After our night together, I told Mark about Werner. At first, he acted as if it didn't matter. But then he stopped coming by the apartment. He didn't call to ask me out and dropped the one class we had together. Kissing Mark hadn't turned him into my prince after all. He had thought better of it and headed for the hills. Laura never forgave him, while I grieved in silence, a knot lodged at the base of my heart, making it hard to breathe. Even after so many years, I try not to recall that time and place, but as if it's an old wound that leaves phantom pains, I sometimes still feel that whisper of love.

Then a couple of years ago my mother and I drove down to San Francisco for some tests. We had just walked out of the hospital into a beautiful, bright day, and I had slipped on my sunglasses and hat. "My robber's disguise," I told Cate. "Any banks close by?" She was laughing there beside me, saying something about our getting lunch, when, on that busy street, I looked up to see a slightly older, short-haired, clean-shaven Mark walking toward us with a well-dressed woman. He held her arm just above the elbow in that intimate way, firm and possessive, as they walked right past us. He glanced quickly at me and then away again. In that instant I saw the same dark, intense eyes of our youth, while all he saw was a small old woman, now a complete stranger.

I always wanted to tell Laura, but I simply couldn't.

Laura turns down Poplar Street and slows down. It takes us a moment to realize that there's no more Bishop's Orchard. Both of us turn to check the street sign again, then look back at where the once beautiful orchard was. In its place are rows and rows of identical houses, all single- and double-story Craftsman-style, where our grafted pear trees once were.

"Damn!" Laura says. "Nothing stays the same, not even here in Daring."

First Trigger, now Big Betsy, I think to myself. All the foundations of my childhood gone. I swallow, and a slight tremor that's nothing but sadness moves through me.

JOSEPHINE

Photographs

While Camille watches television, I take another look at all the photos on top of the piano. In the daylight they seem different, brighter and more alive. I can see traces of Hana in the cute and healthy kid in the snapshots, especially in her dark eyes. I stare at the pictures for so long, I feel as if I almost know each and every one of the faces smiling back at me.

"What are you doing?" Camille suddenly asks.

"Looking at photos of Cate and Hana and their family," I answer, glancing at her sitting on the sofa. "Here's another one of Mom, too."

Camille comes over to my side and follows my gaze. "Hana's so young," she says softly.

"Yeah," I answer, as if I'd known her back then, still lively and full of mischief. I turn back to the photos and study the faces.

"It must be awful," Camille says.

I stare at a snapshot of Hana and Mom on their bikes, so happy and carefree together. I can't imagine what it must have been like for Hana, finding out that her life would never be like everyone else's. Mom said Hana was about the age I am now when she first found out about the disease. What about her dreams? Did she ever have a boyfriend? What would it be like to have the whole world pass you by in so short a time?

Camille steps back and says casually, "I mean, how creepy to be so old when you're really young."

"No kidding," I say, irritated, really wanting to say, Can you think of a more stupid statement? But I hold it in. I know enough not to embarrass Mom with one of our fights when Cate and Dr. Truman are in the kitchen. "Just imagine if it happened to you," I say instead.

But when I turn around, Camille is already back on the sofa watching a cartoon, the high-pitched voices and quick-paced music echoing through the room.

CATE

Salvation

I don't know what I expect, but ever since Miles left over an hour ago, I've been scouring the kitchen, anxiously waiting for Hana to return. It's the first time in years that she and I have been apart for more than a few minutes, and it feels as if part of *me* is missing. I can't help but think that this is how it'll be when Hana is really gone. I'll always be waiting. I'll have a garden blooming with flowers, the cleanest kitchen in Daring, but no Hana.

It was Lily who first broached the subject of letting go, as she put it, when we were right here in the kitchen last week. It sounded like a topic for an afternoon talk show.

"It's the one who's left behind that has it the hardest," she said to me; she's never been one to mince words. She pressed the cake crumbs on the table with her fingertips and deposited them back onto the plate.

"I know," I said, trying to keep my voice steady. I offered her another piece of cake, wondering how we'd gotten on this subject.

She looked at me and shook her head. This was serious business. Lily never turned down a piece of cake.

"After Max died—" she said.

"Max was unexpected," I cut in. "Hana's different."

Lily watched me for a moment, then said gently, "No matter how long she has, Hana's leaving will be a shock, too."

"What should I do then?" I asked, my voice a dry whisper. I looked slowly around the kitchen. Everything was the same as it always was. I knew Lily was right. Without saying a word, I laid my head on the kitchen table like a small child who just wanted to go to sleep.

I heard Lily's chair scrape back, then felt her hand on the back of my head, lightly stroking my hair.

I drop my sponge in the sink and watch water swirling down the drain. All the years I've prepared myself for Hana's death and I'm still surprised at the emptiness that looms ahead of me. The thought fills me with such longing that a sharp, strangled scream rises from my throat. I cover my mouth and steady myself against the counter, wondering if the girls have heard. But other than the chatter coming from the television, all's quiet. And just then, the phone rings and my heart leaps.

"Hi, it's me," Lily says. "What's up?"

I sigh with relief. "I'm here screaming in my kitchen," I answer.

"In ecstasy?" She laughs.

"In agony," I answer.

Thirty minutes later, when Hana returns from her drive with Laura, I can see by her expression that she's happy and feeling good. When she was a little girl and something upset her, Hana became very quiet and her lips pinched tightly together in misery.

248

Now, all I see is a serene smile, her eyes bright and alert.

I help Laura to settle Hana into a kitchen chair. "You two look like you had a good time," I say.

"Not bad. We took a drive down memory lane," Hana says.

I look over at Laura, who frowns and nods. "Only all the memories are gone. How were the girls?" she asks.

"I hardly knew they were here," I answer.

"Then I'd better check on them." She laughs. "All that silence makes me nervous."

"Laura?" I ask, before she leaves the kitchen. "Would you mind going grocery shopping with me in a little while?"

"I'd love to," she says. "Maybe the girls can stay here with Hana." She looks over at Hana, who smiles but doesn't say a word.

"Yes, they could," I finally say.

As Hana sits at the kitchen table, I bring her a glass of water. "Hungry?" I ask.

She shakes her head.

"Where did you go?" I ask.

"Bishop's Orchard," she answers. "Or where the orchard used to be."

"New houses?"

Hana nods.

Daring has grown each year. What used to be a small, sleepy backwater town is now a desirable place to live and raise a family. "Everything's changing. Laura must have been shocked," I add.

"She used to hate Daring." Hana laughs. "Now she wants her charming small town back."

"Those were the days."

"You know," Hana says, her dark eyes looking up at me, "I'm glad Laura came, even though I told her not to. It's easier than I thought it would be to remember that I wasn't always this way, that I was young once, too."

I want nothing more than to take Hana in my arms and hold her, but I simply pat her arm instead.

"Will you be all right here with the girls?" I ask.

She looks at me, not in fear but in contemplation. "I was thinking." She stops and takes a breath. "It might be nice to get to know them one at a time. That way I can see what they're really like. Do you think that would be all right?"

I smile. "I think that would be just fine," I say. "Who would you like to spend time with first?"

"Josephine," Hana answers, taking a sip of her water.

I'm not surprised she chose Josie, the one who needs her most, because it's a different Hana I'm seeing this morning, one who's up to a new challenge, ready to step back into the world again. "They're both lucky girls to have you as their godmother," I say.

Hana clutches the water glass in a thin hand marked with age spots. Coffin rust a friend once called them. She looks pale but happy in the stark morning light. "That remains to be seen." She laughs.

I smile back. I know how lucky they are.

HANA

Night and Day

Josephine and Camille are like night and day. That much I can see just by watching them. While Josie is closed and quiet like the night, Camille is open and vibrant as day. Camille is a fuller, less complicated child—it shows on her face and in the way she moves. I can see that life will be easier for her in some ways. But she lacks the intensity, the intuitiveness of her mother and older sister. Still, they are both smart and eager girls, and I can see traits of Laura in each of them—in Josie's penetrating gaze and in Camille's smile and fine blond hair.

It's a warm afternoon, and after Cate and Laura have left with Camille to go grocery shopping, I suggest to Josephine that we sit on the back deck. "It's a beautiful day," I say. "Let's enjoy it."

She nods shyly. "Okay," she says, her eyes never meeting mine.

I walk slowly, pausing against furniture and doorways, while Josie, carrying two glasses of lemonade, turns around and waits for me. What I expect is someone angry and disagreeable. What I don't expect is that she's so courteous and polite. It all feels like a scene moving in slow motion, and I'm winded by the time we sit down at the table under the umbrella. I take a deep breath and resist the urge to cough, to appear even more fragile in Josie's eyes. We both stare at the trees and mountains in the background as I search for something clever to say to break the ice. Yet the silence isn't uncomfortable, just more reflective, as if every word we say now somehow counts.

And then, out of nowhere, the memory comes to me. "Do you know," I say, "five birds once died right here on this deck. They committed suicide by flying into the window." I lift my hand and point to the large plate-glass window.

"Why?" she asks, her dark eyes wide and alert.

"They were drunk," I answer.

She laughs. "For real?"

"I wouldn't lie to you," I say, with a smile. "The birds ate the berries that had fermented on a bush in our yard, became drunk, and crashed into the window." I repeat the words Cate had told me so many years ago. "We buried them over there, under those bushes."

And then another memory I keep to myself. Max once told me that when he was a boy at Heart Mountain he wished he was a bird so he could fly over the barbed-wire fence to freedom. I remember I spent all evening trying to figure out what kind of bird my father would be. A hawk or a falcon, something defiant, I thought in those days. But now I see him as a bluebird or a red-breasted robin, something proud and beautiful.

"It's pretty here," Josie says, sipping from her lemonade. "I didn't know what to expect."

I smile at her honesty. "I expect it's the opposite of life in New York," I say.

Josie glances at me then and finally lets her gaze rest on my face—my pasty white skin, the wrinkles, the thin wisps of hair—but she doesn't look away this time. Her foot taps nervously against the deck. "Have you ever been to New York?" she asks.

"I'm afraid not," I say sadly. "I've always wanted to go."

"Not even when you were young?" she asks.

I shake my head. "But I've been to Boston to visit my grandparents."

"Are they the ones in the photos on the piano?" She looks down at her long, thin fingers, which wrap around her glass. Josie doesn't miss a thing.

"That's right." I smile. "There's a photo with all of my grandparents in it. It was taken on my third birthday."

"I saw it," Josie says, with that definite way that teenagers have.

"Tell me about New York," I say.

Josie looks at me for a moment, and I think she's going to shut down, tired of humoring an old lady. But instead it's as if I've flipped a switch, and she lights up and begins to talk. "It's crowded and noisy and filled with people from all over the world. On the corner where we live, there's a grocery store that sells everything, from light fixtures and school supplies to salads and pocket bread filled with grilled lamb and onions. I like all the sights and sounds of a big city, and the way people see and don't see each other."

Josie sparkles with intelligence and animation. It's been a long time since I've felt such youthful energy. "It sounds wonderful," I say.

"Maybe you can come visit some—" she says, stopping in

midsentence, as if she's said something she shouldn't have. "I'm sorry," she says.

"For what?" I ask.

"For asking you to come visit when, most likely, you can't." She looks at me and then away again.

"Maybe I'll surprise you one day," I say, quickly picking up the conversation.

Josie nods but has lost her enthusiasm. "What was my mother like when she was young?" she suddenly asks.

I smile at the question. "She was popular and lively and as beautiful as she still is now," I answer without thinking.

Josie watches me, then asks, "Were you ever jealous of her?"

Her question catches me off guard, and it takes me a moment to answer. I try to think back to a time when I was jealous of Laura, but only silly, adolescent scenes come to me. None of it matters anymore, though I can see how much it means to Josie to know more about Laura. "Every girl in Daring was jealous of your mother," I say, "including me."

"Me, too," she says softly. "Sometimes." Her eyes glance up at mine. "Not really jealous, just envious, maybe."

I wish Josie knew just how much I can understand what she feels. And for a brief moment, I too feel envious, for even now Laura's upstaging me. "You have nothing to be envious about," I tell her, "as smart and pretty as you are."

She smiles shyly. "Did she have many boyfriends?"

"She went steady with a boy named Greg in high school, and another named Charlie in college," I answer. "Your mom could have had as many boyfriends as she wanted."

"How about you?" Josie asks.

"Things were much more complicated for me," I say, sipping from my lemonade. It tastes both sweet and sour. "I wasn't exactly what you'd call stunning. How about *you*?"

"Me, either." Josie drops her eyes and blushes. "Boys don't much like me."

I watch the tall, thin, awkward young girl hunch over the table and wish I could reassure her that her journey is just beginning. "There'll be plenty of time for boys in your life. No need to rush things," I say.

Smiling, Josie looks at me, then pulls the rubber band off her ponytail. With a quick shake of her head, she sweeps her long hair back and lets it fall to her shoulders.

"So tell me what your mother's like now."

At first Josie stays quiet, licking her lips. I sit back in the chair, my back stiff and aching. I can't tell exactly where the ache is coming from as I shift uncomfortably.

"Sometimes I wonder why she ever had us," she says. "All she does is work. She says it's to provide for us, but I think it makes her feel better thinking it does."

Josie's voice is high and raw as the words pour out of her in one hurried breath. I lean forward to touch her hand and she doesn't pull away and her gaze doesn't leave me. She appears younger and sadder to me. "She loves you both a lot. There are no two people in the world who have made her prouder."

"But she doesn't love my dad anymore."

I swallow, thinking of the right words to say. "Sometimes married people grow apart. It doesn't change what she feels about you and Camille."

Josie taps her fingers on the glass tabletop, draws little circles with her fingertips. "Everything's changing," she says.

"Change is part of life, but what doesn't change is how much parents love their children." I say this with such fervor that Josie looks up at me, and I remember something I once heard my father say. "Don't count backwards," I tell her. "Count forwards now."

After a long pause, she asks, "Can I ask you another question?"

"Anything," I say.

"What's it like to grow old so fast?"

I look up at Josephine and take my time answering. I watch a blue jay fluttering from one privet bush to the next. It's such a simple question, but for a moment it still surprises me, like something vinegary and tart on my tongue. "It's no fun at all," I say lightly at first, then, after a pause, I tell the truth. "I've had to learn to let go."

Josie looks at me, serious and determined. "How?" she asks.

"It's hard," I say. "But I let go of all of the meanness and spite first. No use carrying around useless baggage. Then I let go of the things I love, like swimming in the ocean, eating pizza and burgers, and buying new clothes to wear. Now I'm dealing with the hardest part, letting go of all the people I love."

Josie looks up at a squirrel running along the ledge of the house, then lets her gaze meet mine. "It must be impossible," she says, her voice rising then falling again.

At that very moment, I know I love this girl, this goddaughter of mine. "Well, you do get to keep some of the most important things," I say. "Like listening to music, reading a good book, talking with friends like you. That's what you learn from life, Josie. It's never long enough, no matter how many years you have. And it's always a gift, so don't waste it." I stop then, not wanting to preach too much.

But rather than scoff, Josie watches my every move, hangs on every word. She nods. There's the faraway sound of a motor running, a power saw or a lawn mower.

"You know, you don't look *that* old," Josie suddenly says. "Camille was afraid of you at first."

"But you weren't?"

She hesitates for a moment. "It seemed kind of creepy at first, that you were young and old at the same time. Like in some movie."

I laugh out loud. I like Josie for her honesty. She says what she thinks, which is one more trait of Laura's that she's inherited. "You remind me a lot of your mother," I say.

Josie smiles widely. "No one ever seems to think so."

"They will, as you grow older," I say. "You're perceptive, the same way she is."

Josie pauses in thought. "I guess that's how I can see that you're still young inside," she says.

"How can you see that?"

"Your eyes," she answers. "When I look into them I see someone young."

I lean closer to Josephine and wish I could hug her, press my warmth against hers, but the fear of frightening her stops me. "Thank you," I whisper instead, as if we're sharing an intimate secret.

JOSEPHINE

Games

When Camille and I were young, we used to play a game called switch-it, which was completely made up by me, so the rules could change at my whim. It would drive Camille crazy when she did everything right but was still wrong. "That's why it's called switch-it," I said. Now, when I think back to those times, I feel bad. Camille was a sweet six-year-old, and I couldn't help feeling jealous that she so easily captured my parents' attention. There were lots of other things I did to torment her. But talking with Hana reminds me now that Camille is my sister, my only sister.

What are you thinking about?" Hana asks.

"Nothing," I say, as if I've been caught doing something wrong. I still feel terrible about telling Hana to visit us in New York. When will I get it? I ask myself. Only this time, I really meant for her to come.

"You're not under investigation." She laughs, then sits back in her chair with a wince.

"Are you all right?" I ask. "Do you need anything?"

Hana smiles. "Everything I need is right here, right now," she says.

And then I relax and sit back in my chair. "Do you think any drunken birds will come crashing into your window this year?" I ask.

Hana shakes her head. "I cut down that berry bush a long time ago. But if you give me a hand, I'll show you where we buried the birds."

In the next moment, I'm beside Hana, helping her out of her chair. She seems so light and fragile, like she'll break if you pull too hard. So I carefully offer my arm and she holds on and leans against me, which feels warm and comfortable.

"This way," she says, as we slowly walk across the grass. She stops for a moment and so do I, looking up at the mountains. "They're something," she says softly. "Have you ever heard of Heart Mountain?"

I shake my head.

"It was an internment camp."

"Like Manzanar?" I ask.

Hana smiles. "Exactly like that, only in Wyoming. It's where they sent my father and his family when he was a boy."

I nod. Heart Mountain, I think to myself, could there be a more ironic name?

"There, at Heart Mountain, the mountains frightened him. He felt they were always watching him. I've always felt the opposite, that they were somehow protecting me."

Then we continue on to the far side of the yard, where a mass of thick green shrubbery has grown. "Right here," Hana says. "This is where we buried them."

"Under that?" I ask, wondering how anything could be buried beneath such dense covering.

Hana laughs. "The year after we buried the birds, that privet bush began to grow, and it hasn't stopped since. We call it our miracle memorial. Every spring the most beautiful white blossoms bloom."

We stand there, with Hana holding on to my arm as we gaze at the shrubbery, and I try to imagine the five small birds from which the plant took root and began to grow. It amazes me how something so beautiful can bloom from something terrible.

CATE

Satisfaction

The house is quiet when we return from grocery shopping. I walk in first, all ears, not knowing what I expect to hear. It seems ages since I last saw Hana. I've felt afloat all morning, sailing down the supermarket aisles without her to anchor me. Once, when Laura and Camille had disappeared down another aisle, I felt completely alone among rows and rows of food items that blurred past me. Again I thought, this is how it will be when Hana's gone. And then out of nowhere came blond, blue-eyed Camille, who waved from the end of the aisle and said to me with a smile, "We're over here," and for the moment I felt saved.

But I don't hear a sound as I hurry through the house and onto the back deck. From there I can see that Hana and Josie are out on the grass, looking at the bushes where we buried the birds so many years ago. My tiny Hana, standing next to Josie, holding tightly on to her arm for balance. In one glance I can see that everything is fine. I quietly turn around and go back into the house.

"Things seem to have gone well here," I say to Laura as she and I put the groceries away. Camille goes out to set up a game of Scrabble on the deck.

"It's going to be okay," Laura says, just as pleased as I am. She hands me a bag of cookies. "I wasn't wrong to bring the girls, then?"

I put the cookies down on the counter and give Laura a hug, holding her tight. Her body slowly relaxes in my grip, and I feel her hugging me back. "No, you weren't," I whisper into her ear. "Thank you, Laura. You can bring them back any time you like."

When we finally pull apart, Laura asks, "How long does she have?"

"A year of mobility, more or less, barring no major complications. And then, we'll see."

Laura sighs. "With all the technology and discoveries they make every day, why can't they do something?" Her voice is anguished like a child's as she echoes the words that I've said or thought over and over since Werner entered our lives.

"No one has the answer to that question," I say, unimaginably calm after all the years of hoping.

When Hana was still young I thought that, by some act of God, a miracle drug would be developed and Werner would suddenly reverse itself. Like Sleeping Beauty, Hana would wake up young and beautiful. But as the years went by and the opposite effect developed, I lost hope, letting it go like ashes in the wind. Now I see that hope comes in many forms. Hana's body won't be saved, but her spirit has been.

"We're not too late, then," Laura says, almost to herself. "I thought we might be too late when I first saw her."

I stare out the window to see Hana flanked by Josie and Camille as they play Scrabble at the table on the deck. This is happiness, I think to myself as their laughter rings out.

"No," I tell her. "You're just in time."

HANA

Full Circle

While Cate and Laura make lunch, I play Scrabble with the girls. "International Scrabble," I announce, "in any language you want. Just like your mother and I used to play."

"You're kidding!" Josie says, mixing the facedown wooden tiles and rolling her eyes at me.

"That's not fair," Camille adds.

Josie laughs. "I think it's great."

"You would," Camille snaps back.

"It gives us lots more choices," Josie says, picking from the mixed tiles and passing the box over for Camille and me to do the same.

I watch the ordinary movements of my goddaughters with great satisfaction.

———

After lunch Cate leans forward and taps her spoon against her water glass. I'm always amazed at how conversations stop at that sharp, dinging sound. If only wars and disagreements could be ended so easily. All heads turn her way. She clears her throat as if she's been waiting all through lunch to make her announcement. I haven't seen her so happy in a very long time.

"We're going for a drive," she announces.

"Where?" Camille pipes up.

Laura and Josie look up expectantly. I glance at Cate with the same question in mind. It surprises me how fast we have all settled into each other.

Then Cate clears her throat once more and says, "We're going to Falcon Beach."

In an instant, my childhood days at Falcon Beach return to me. And, like Camille, I want to sing it out. *We're going to Falcon Beach!*

My love of water comes from Max, from his joy in watching the ocean and swimming through it. He taught me to swim when I was just a little girl, and I too became addicted. "Yes, that's it, Hana!" Max said proudly, when he saw that, even at three, I wasn't afraid as I pushed my body through the water. Even now, when I dream of jumping into the ocean and swimming against the strong pull of the waves, floating, losing myself in the comfort of the water's embrace, I feel alive and well again, and I know my father would understand.

I was twelve the last time we came to Falcon Beach. I had spent lots of time in doctors' offices that summer, and I can still feel the cold, round head of the stethoscope pressing against my back. My asthma was worse, and I hadn't grown an inch all year. "Take a deep breath," I hear Dr. Truman saying, his voice low and serious. I coughed, because I had taken the breath too quickly, and he said, "Good, Hana," but it wasn't good. I caught a chill at the beach that day and ran a fever for a week.

Afterward, I couldn't bear the thought of returning to Falcon Beach. I saw myself in the mirror and refused to put on my bathing suit anymore. I looked ridiculous. Some of my friends had already begun to menstruate and develop breasts, while I was still small and skinny, trapped in a child's body. The summer I turned thirteen, I chose to go alone to visit my grandparents in Los Angeles instead.

Cate and Max must have felt the same. After that summer we just stopped going to Falcon Beach, as if the waves and sunlight were somehow to blame. But I knew it was for the opposite reason—Falcon Beach would always be a reminder of all our good times, and it was too hard to return when things became difficult.

I go to my room to rest for a short time while Cate, Laura, and the girls get ready for the beach. Just as I close my eyes and let my mind wander, there's a light tap on my door. Thinking it could only be my mother, I'm surprised to see it's Laura who enters.

"I hope I'm not disturbing you," she whispers, closing the door gently behind her. "I'm sorry, but I needed—" She has changed into cotton slacks and a T-shirt.

"Come here," I say softly. I move over and pat the bed beside me. Laura carefully lies down next to me. Our last slumber party. Finally we have this unexpected moment to talk, to catch up on all the years in between, the silences we couldn't speak about on the phone. Yet we don't say a word—simply lie silent, side by side, comforted.

JOSEPHINE

Truce

W e didn't bring our swimming suits," Camille tells me when we're back in our room trying to decide what we should pack for the beach.

"Shorts and a T-shirt should work," I say. "It's probably too cold to swim anyway."

Camille smiles and nods, turns her canvas bag over so that all her clothes fall onto the bed. "Why do you think Cate wants to go to the beach all of a sudden?" she asks.

"There's not much else to do around here, or haven't you noticed?" I ask too sharply, then add in a softer tone, "Maybe she's just being nice because she knows we like to swim."

Camille seems to take everything I say in stride. "How does she know we like to swim?" she asks.

I unzip my bag and shrug. "From all the letters and cards we've written to Hana."

Camille accepts this explanation and drops a pair of shorts and a T-shirt into her bag. "Ready," she says. And then, turning back to me, she asks, "What was it like with Hana this morning?"

"Fine," I answer.

"Did you feel strange being with her?"

I look her in the eye and say, "No, why should I?"

Camille shakes her head. "I just wondered."

I smile at her and say reassuringly, "She was nice. It was actually real easy to talk to her."

"Do you think I'll have anything to talk to her about?" Camille asks.

I can hear a slight wavering in her voice, like when she was a little girl and frightened of strangers or of anything unfamiliar. And, for the first time in months, I don't feel the urge to snap back at her. "I think you'll have lots to talk about. You'll like her. I do. Really." It feels good giving out big-sisterly advice.

"Do you think Hana will be okay going to the beach?" Camille asks.

"Sure, why not? There's no reason why she should just sit around the house all day. She's walking again, so she must be feeling better," I add.

"She looks so breakable," Camille says.

I throw a blue sweater into my bag and point to her white one on the bed. Without a word, Camille puts the sweater into her bag.

"You'd be surprised just how strong she is," I say, as if I'm some kind of expert after one conversation with Hana.

Camille nods. "Yeah, I bet she's really strong on the inside."

I smile, realizing that Camille does understand. And it's enough to make me lean over and kiss my sister on her smooth, unblemished cheek.

CATE

The Edge of the World

With Laura's help, Hana has changed into an old Hawaiian shirt with pineapples on it, cotton pants, and tennis shoes. Together, they're like young girls again. I couldn't stop laughing when they emerged from her room. We drive to Falcon Beach in two cars. That way, I tell the others, there'll be room in case Hana needs to elevate her feet, or rest in the backseat. But the real reason is that I need to make this drive back to Falcon Beach with Hana alone. Josie and Camille ride with Laura in the car behind us.

What started out as an unusual day has become a real adventure. We're actually running away for the afternoon. I feel wonderfully free as I drive—past the park, past the strip malls and the new outlet stores, and onto the Coastal Highway, heading south toward Falcon Beach. When I drive past the park without stopping, I glance over to see Hana simply smiling at me in perfect agreement. It's as if we know each other's thoughts, the kind of intuition gained by living together for so long. "Let's get out of here." She laughs, rolling down the window and letting in a cool wind to upset the stale air.

I click on the radio, the low hum of voices keeping steady company. It's a beautifully clear day, with no fog in sight. As we drive along the coast, I feel as if we've come to the edge of the world. Jagged cliffs fall away below the ribbon of road, and there's nothing but ocean as far as the eye can see. I take each turn slowly, one perilous curve after another wrapped around the rugged mountains. Every so often, I check my rearview mirror to make sure Laura is right behind us. The stretch of highway farther north is called the Lost Coast, yet I feel as if I've found something coming back here. The screeching seagulls overhead welcome us back. After twenty-five years I'm just thankful that Hana is still here with me.

"Are Laura and the girls behind us?" Hana asks. She turns in her seat.

"Yes, they are," I answer. I wouldn't lose them for the world, I think to myself. I reach over and grasp her hand, which feels soft and bony, like a kitten's ribs.

Hana smiles and settles back into her seat.

I roll down the window and breathe in the salty, kelp-scented air, then turn down the radio to hear the waves break against the rocky shores below. Driving past the smaller Pelican Beach, I'm tempted to stop. But I know that it isn't much farther to Falcon Beach. Less than fifteen minutes down the road, as I slow down and round a sharp curve, I see three large boulders leading to the entrance to Falcon Beach. The Three Stooges Max used to call them. Moe, Larry, and Curly. And right away it's as if I'm that young woman again, who was so in love that just the thought of going to Falcon Beach brought a sense of freedom and adventure. I'm transported back to the many nights I sat here with Max in the Thunderbird, the memory so sharp I can almost hear "Love Me Tender" playing on the radio, smell his sweet cologne, and feel his warmth beside me. Max, who had driven across the country to find himself, only to find me instead. Max, I want to whisper, who dreamed of water as a young boy at Heart Mountain, Max, whom I still reach for in the dark of night.

I swallow the lump in my throat that comes from wishing he were right here with us and turn into the dirt and gravel parking lot overlooking Falcon Beach. I park near the lookout point where the rocky dirt path leads down to the beach. There's only one other white car parked at the far end of the lot. And just behind us Laura's car pulls into the parking lot, crunching gravel as it settles into the space next to us. I turn off the engine and take a moment to gaze down at the blue-gray mirror of water gleaming in the afternoon sunlight.

HANA

Bettina Troy

I slip on my baseball cap and sunglasses, then lean forward and stare out at the ocean, where a fishing boat rocks in the far distance. "We're here again," I say softly to Cate, thinking how it doesn't really seem like a lifetime ago. What felt like endless slow motion just last week has turned into a flurry of quick scene changes since Laura and the girls arrived. My mind flickers with memories that pop up as clearly as if they had happened only yesterday.

Bettina Troy. Her name was Bettina Troy. I remember my father telling me the story when we saw her at the Maritime Museum when I was fourteen, and how the story infuriated me. A life wasted. I didn't know then how Werner would one day waste mine.

"Who is she?" I had asked, staring wide-eyed at the eight-foot-tall carved wooden torso of a woman—a young woman with long, curly blond hair that fell delicately onto the open collar of her faded blue dress.

"She was a figurehead perched on the bow of a ship," Max told me.

I gazed at her faded features, battered from years of salt water and rough seas; her pale blue eyes with their sad, faraway look. I scrutinized each scar and chip that marred the once beautiful face in its glass case. I imagined what it would be like to run my fingers over each crack and crevice, touching each small wound.

There was a tragic story attached to the figurehead. "Her name was Bettina Troy," Max explained, "the only daughter of Captain John Troy. After Captain Troy's wife and second child died in childbirth, Bettina was all he had left. When he was away at sea, on his ship, the *Passage*, his sister, Ada, took care of Bettina. They lived happily with this arrangement, the captain's daughter growing more beautiful with each passing year. All she ever wanted was to follow her father to sea, but he flatly refused, since it was no place for a respectable young lady in those days." Max walked around the display case and continued.

"Before Captain Troy knew it, Bettina had grown into a beautiful young woman, with every eligible bachelor near and far wanting her for his wife. As fate would have it, she fell for a ne'er-do-well named Robert Harcourt, who left her when he learned she was pregnant with his child." Max looked over at me. "It's an old story, but back then Bettina didn't have many choices. She either disgraced her father's good name or she killed herself. She chose the latter. When Captain Troy returned from another long voyage, his beloved daughter was dead. She had hung herself from the big oak tree in the backyard. The first thing Captain Troy did was cut down the old oak; the second thing was to have his daughter's likeness carved from it. From that time on, Bettina Troy became the eyes on the *Passage* and always accompanied her father out to sea."

Max stopped and looked thoughtfully at me.

I remember glaring at the solemn face of Bettina Troy, angry with her for ending her life even though she'd found a way to go to sea after all. "I wouldn't ever kill myself like she did," I said adamantly.

Max leaned over, hugged me tightly, and said, "No, no you wouldn't."

Just before he died, Max had talked about driving out to the coast again. "It's been too long," I remember him saying. "If Hana's feeling better, we can drive out this summer." He died three days later. I wonder if Cate remembers.

"You all right?" Cate asks, watching me. A familiar look of concern shows in her eyes, the lines that crease her forehead.

"I'm fine," I answer. "It's been so long since we've been back here." I turn and smile at her to put her at ease.

"Yes," Cate simply says.

"So what's it like, coming back to your old haunt?" I ask.

"Like I want to laugh and cry at the same time," she says, her hands gripping the steering wheel.

I know just how she feels.

Car doors open and slam as Josie and Camille run over to the lookout point and glance down at the beach below before Laura has even gotten her seat belt off. As a child I couldn't wait, like Josie and Camille, to get out of the hot, stuffy car. I roll down the window all the way, letting in the cool ocean breeze, the thundering sound of the surf, and the strong, eager voices of Josephine and Camille. In the distance I can hear music, a radio playing from some far off picnickers, the high shrill of laughter. It's curious, how my hearing remains intact even as the rest of my body fails.

Camille waves at us to join them and Laura at the lookout, but for a moment I watch the three of them laughing and jostling each other and pointing down to the beach. The bright sunlight makes me dizzy. I take a deep breath and let it out slowly, then another and another until I've regained my balance.

There's a slight chill in the air as Cate opens my door and leans in toward me, but her arm is warm as she helps me out of the car to join the fun.

JOSEPHINE

Sand Castles

When Camille and I were four and six, my parents took us to the beach on Long Island for the first time. We were armed with buckets and shovels, a plastic blow-up walrus, blue and red plastic lifesavers. It was Mom's idea, since she'd grown up near the ocean. My dad was more suspicious. He believed in swimming pools with concrete boundaries. Such a large body of water didn't seem in the natural scheme of things.

"If humans were meant to swim, we'd have been born with gills," he remarked.

My mother brushed his cheek with the palm of her hand. "That's what makes it exciting: we don't have gills, but we do it anyway."

He looked at her unconvinced, but he spent hours with us building a sand castle, molding turrets and a deep moat that he had us fill with buckets full of seawater. In my mind, it's still the most beautiful castle I've ever seen.

Camille cried when we had to leave, wanting to take the castle home with us. But Dad picked her up and said to her, "We have to leave it, Sweet Pea. Sand castles have to stay at the beach. There are lots of things in life that we can't take with us, no matter how much we want to."

Camille looked puzzled. "Then why did we spend so much time making it?" she asked, which I thought was a perfectly good question.

"For the sheer pleasure of making it," he said. "We can take *that* with us." He nuzzled his face into Camille's neck, and Mom gave me a quick wink.

It's only now that I understand what he meant.

Let's take a picture," Mom says, returning to the car to retrieve her camera.

I watch Hana and Cate, but neither of them makes a move or says anything. All the photos I've seen of Hana were taken when she was very young. None of them shows her recently.

When Laura walks back with her camera, I quickly say, "Maybe we can take one later." Unlike Empress Josephine, Hana doesn't have any roses here to protect her from the world.

"A snapshot right here would be nice," Mom says, not listening to a word I'm saying. Maybe she can't imagine that Hana might not want her picture taken. "Girls, stand on either side of Hana and Cate," she instructs.

I take my place by Hana as Camille stands on the other side of Cate. I wish I could protect Hana from an image she may not want to see. "I'm sorry," I whisper to her. "She gets like this."

Hana smiles. "It's all right. It'll remind me you were here," she says.

"Okay, everyone, smile," Laura says, taking a step back.

Then, just before the camera clicks, Hana takes my hand in hers.

CATE

Seascape

While Laura and the girls get the blankets from the car, I wrap my arms around Hana and feel her lightness against me as we stand at the lookout. She leans her head back, and I cradle her gently. The rush of the waves hums through our bodies, and for the longest time there's no need for any words. I hold her tighter, and we watch hypnotized as the waves rush in, then recede, leaving a white, milky foam behind. The air is cool and salty, and I leave Hana for a moment braced against the railing while I return to the car for our jackets. Walking away from her, I glance back once to make sure she's all right. For an instant I imagine again the beautiful Hana in my dreams, but there instead stands a Hana so small and frail against the endless sky and ocean she looks like a child in a painting or a photograph. The child Max and I wished for and received.

———

Hana reaches for her jacket; her face is flushed pink from the sharp salt air. When she lifts her sunglasses, I can see by the gleam in her eyes that she's happy.

"I could stay here forever," she says, holding on to the rail.

I only wish we could. Forever would mean that Hana would still have countless years ahead of her. And, for just a moment, I too am ecstatic with the thought. "You'd miss Daring," I tease.

"I'd miss the sea more. It's in my blood."

I smile, hearing her voice the words Max spoke when we were here so many years ago. And in that moment I can feel him watching over us.

"I believe it is," I say.

HANA

Stopping Time

I love watching the ocean, the rough, demanding waves that pound the shore, carving out the magnificent mountainsides that dominate the coastline. The waves roar forward, then recede, leaving behind a white, frothy streak on the sand. Seagulls squawk and fly overhead. But it's a different world beneath the surface, a calm I've never considered before. I try to imagine what it must feel like hundreds of feet under the water, in the slow, relentless currents of the deep, wrapping itself around me like a blanket. In a world so dark and cold and quiet that all time stops.

JOSEPHINE

Soon Enough

Josie, come help Hana down the path," Mom calls. I turn around and see Hana moving slowly toward the beach path between Mom and Cate. When I reach them, it's Cate who steps aside. Camille is already halfway down the path, waving and yelling for us to follow.

"Aren't you coming?" I ask Cate.

"I'll be right there," she says. "Just need a minute by myself."

Hana turns and watches Cate for a moment before her gaze returns to me. "Care to help an old lady cross the street?" she asks.

"Glad to," I say, taking her arm.

Mom nods and smiles at me, and I feel something warm move through my body.

"Mom says we can come back and visit again this summer," I say, tentatively.

"That's the plan," Mom chimes in. Her arm is wrapped around Hana possessively.

Hana looks up at Laura and then at me. "Don't I get a say in this?"

"No!" Mom and I say simultaneously.

Hana laughs, high and squeaky.

We move slowly and carefully down the path to the beach. There's no hurry, I say to myself. I like this pace, the sheer pleasure of knowing we'll get there soon enough.

CATE

A Gift

From the ridge above Falcon Beach, I watch a seagull circle over-head, turn, and swoop down low in a perfect arc against the sand. In the next moment, the gull is up in the air again, clutching something tightly in its beak as it circles once more and flies out toward the sea. I watch until my eyes water, until the gull becomes a dark speck and I blink to find it has disappeared into the im-mense blue sky.

I can see Hana in the distance, her wisps of white hair blowing in the wind. Laura's arm is protectively around her as they walk slowly down the beach, flanked by Josie and Camille, who run in circles around them, chasing each other. They remind me of a small band of gypsies. I smile at the sight of my daughter so surrounded by life—by the love of people whose lives she's touched. Hana won't be forgotten—she's the child Max and I loved and adored, the friend Laura has never abandoned, the godmother of two fine young girls who will always remember her. Each day Hana has been with me is a gift.

I'm not going far, not anytime soon," Hana said to me when she was fifteen years old. Her words came out of nowhere, most likely because she saw me sitting in the kitchen, staring off into space, my eyes red and moist.

"That's good." I looked up and smiled, my hands folding and unfolding a piece of Kleenex. She'd had three bouts of flu that winter and was just beginning to get some color back in her cheeks, but she still looked pale and gaunt as she hesitated at the back door. "And even when I'm gone, I'll still be here," she said.

I was astounded that Hana would be consoling me. "I know," I whispered.

She waved and in the next moment was out the door to meet up with Laura and her friends. I closed my eyes and tried to imagine Hana still before me, her spirit lingering, but all I felt was a cool breeze that made me shiver in the empty kitchen.

Now, as I watch Hana down on the beach, I'm reminded of that young girl, who even then tried to comfort me. With my hand I shield my eyes from the afternoon sun, and just then Hana turns around and looks for me. She lifts her arm and waves. From the distance, in that moment I can't tell if she's waving hello or goodbye. I wave back, then call out Hana, once, twice, three times, but her name is lost in the roar of the waves and carried out to sea. HelloGoodbye. Only then do I make my way down the sandy path to her.

HANA

Starlight, Starbright

My grandfather Henry died when I was twenty-eight. He was eighty-two and extremely frail the last time I saw him. We had flown down to Pasadena, and I remember how happy he was to see the three of us. He had shrunk a great deal and walked slowly with a cane. He looked at me and smiled, even though my face had aged and my hair had started to gray. I knew he still saw me as that young girl who used to sit beside him outside his greenhouses watching the night sky.

"Shall we meet tonight under the stars?" he asked me when we arrived.

"Yes," I answered, thrilled that we would have the chance to talk together again beside the greenhouses.

But after dinner my ojī-san sat down in his chair and fell asleep, even as all our voices buzzed around him. I waited a little while for him to wake up, but before the sun had set I knew we would never again watch the stars together.

After dark, I walked alone out to the greenhouses, where hazy yellow lights glowed through the glass. The smell of damp earth and blooming flowers filled my head, along with the soft sounds of crickets. If we couldn't meet under the stars as planned, then I would still be there for the both of us. I pulled out two wooden chairs, just as he had done so many years ago, and sat down in the smaller one, gazing up at the night sky. The stars glistened, and I could feel my ojī-san right there with me, hear his voice telling me again, *No need to be afraid, ever.*

When the time comes, I'll tell Cate the same thing. But when I look up and watch her walking down the path to the beach toward us—so tall and straight—I can see that it's something she already knows. Something she has learned over time.

JOSEPHINE

God shall add . . .

My name is Josephine, which means *God shall add*, and for the first time, my name makes sense to me—Hana and Cate have been added to my life. After less than two days with them, the life I knew back in New York seems flat and ordinary. I try to remember everything, Hana's eyes, Cate's *Josephine* rose, the roar of the ocean, the sea-salt smell of the cool air, the damp spray against my face. I'll take it all back home with me. I'll never forget.